The Deadly Special

My diner!

My heart started pounding. I'm not the greatest in an emergency. My brain just sits there in my head like a lump of dough that won't rise.

Max and Clyde ran toward me, and I rushed to meet them. The snowflakes hit my face and eyes and melted on my contact lenses.

"Trixie." Max breathed heavily, and puffs of steam hung between us. "The kitchen."

"Oh no! Fire! Is anyone hurt?" I immediately thought of Juanita. I knew that she was single, and, oh merciful heavens, I didn't know anything else about her or how to contact her loved ones. I didn't even know her last name. "Juanita?"

Clyde grabbed a chunk of my sleeve and pulled me down the path to the diner. "No! She's okay. Everyone's okay. Well, not everyone."

Either my brain wasn't computing or Clyde was speaking Swahili. "Huh?"

"It's Marvin P. Cogswell the Third," Max said.

The name sounded vaguely familiar.

"Huh?" I repeated.

"Marvin P. Cogswell the Third," they said in unison.

Oh yeah, that helped . . . so much.

"The health inspector!" Max added. "It looks like he had a heart attack."

Do or Diner

A Comfort Food Mystery

CHRISTINE WENGER

AN OBSIDIAN BOOK

OBSIDIAN
Published by the Penguin Group
Penguin Group (USA) Inc., 375 Hudson Street,
New York, New York 10014, USA

USA | Canada | UK | Ireland | Australia | New Zealand | India | South Africa | China

Penguin Books Ltd., Registered Offices: 80 Strand, London WC2R 0RL, England
For more information about the Penguin Group visit penguin.com.

First published by Obsidian, an imprint of New American Library,
a division of Penguin Group (USA) Inc.

First Printing, August 2013

ISBN: 978-0-451-41508-0

Printed in the United States of America
10 9 8 7 6 5 4 3 2 1

ALWAYS LEARNING   PEARSON

There are so many people that I'd like to thank, but this book reached publication due to the brilliance of my agent, the very special and delightful Michelle Grajkowski of 3 Seas Literary Agency, who believed in me. And to Jesse Feldman, editor, Penguin Group, who said YES! This one's for you, ladies! Thank you so very much!
Chris

Chapter 1

*W*hat on earth did I do?

A thrill of excitement shot through me as I stood in front of the Silver Bullet Diner. It was still hard to think of it as *my* diner, but the wad of keys in my pocket assured me that it was.

It was mid-March in upstate New York, Sandy Harbor to be exact, and the snow was falling in big fat flakes, adding to the six-foot banks around the parking lot. Still, the bright red neon of the diner's name and the blue neon proclaiming AIR-CONDITIONED and OPEN 24 HOURS shone through the snow and lit the way for patrons arriving for lunch.

It was my diner now.

Maybe it wasn't excitement that I felt, but more like anxiety. In diner lingo, maybe I had bitten off more than I could chew. Or maybe I was having buyer's remorse.

Probably all of the above!

As I surveyed my new kingdom on the frozen shore of Lake Ontario, I mentally listed all the things with which I needed to familiarize myself.

A huge gingerbread Victorian house located to the left of the diner and closer to the water had been recently vacated by my aunt Stella. It was also now mine. It had almost disappeared in the heavy snow, with its pristine white paint and dark green shutters. It had a major wraparound porch that I planned to use in the summer. I'd sit in a forest green Adirondack chair and watch the waves of Lake Ontario lap at the shore.

I looked over at the twelve little white cottages that dotted the lakefront. It looked like the big Victorian had a litter.

They were called—*care to guess?*—the Sandy Harbor Guest Cottages.

My mind flashed back to the two weeks every summer that my family rented here. We always rented Cottage Number Six, on the front row of the first chain of cottages. My sister, my brother, and I would stay in the water from sunrise until sunset. Mom and Dad had to drag us out of the water, slather us with sunscreen, feed us, and listen to our pleas to go back in.

Now all twelve cottages belonged to me, and I'd be renting them out to the next generation of fishermen and families who'd enjoy them.

The Silver Bullet was the centerpiece of my little kingdom. Smiling, I saw that the parking lot was filled with cars that were frosted with a couple inches of snow. Customers entered the diner in groups, laughing and talking and looking forward to a good meal. They left the same way they came, but now sated by delicious comfort food and finishing their conversations before brushing the snow off their cars.

The scent of baking bread drifted on the crisp

winter air and mixed with other cooking scents. My mouth was watering just thinking of what I was going to order later.

Slogging through the snow to the side of the diner, I savored every aspect of its outside appearance: the curved lines, the metallic diamond-shaped edging around the windows, and the porchlike entranceway. The Silver Bullet looked like it had just been towed into place, not like it had been there since 1950.

I looked for the cement cornerstone, which I'd always thought was so romantic, but it was buried under several feet of snow. I knew what it said by heart: STELLA AND MORRIS "PORKY" MATKOWSKI, MARRIED 1950, TOGETHER FOREVER IN OUR LOVE.

They were together until Uncle Porky died a month ago.

I sighed, thinking about the two of them. Porky and Stella always finished each other's sentences and walked hand in hand. But now Stella was alone, just like I was alone, but I hoped to change that as soon as I met more people in the community. I remembered Sandy Harbor as being a friendly place, and that was just what I needed—friends.

Actually, Aunt Stella wasn't alone right now. A gaggle of her friends came for Porky's funeral and stayed at the house. They helped her through the first month of losing her husband, and now she was en route to a senior community in Boca with them. They planned on living like the *Golden Girls* characters, but first they were going on a cruise around the world.

Because she was busy entertaining her friends, packing to leave, and searching for her missing passport, Aunt Stella didn't have much time to show me the entire operation.

"The same people have been working here forever. They know what to do," she'd told me several times.

I pointed my boots toward a slushy path that led to my new house. Maybe I should unpack and get settled, but I was eager to get more acquainted with everyone and everything.

I took a deep breath and let it out. All this was so overwhelming. Mostly because I, Beatrix Matkowski (formerly known as Beatrix Burnham), was starting over at age thirtysomething.

I was freshly divorced from Deputy Doug Burnham after ten years of marital nonbliss. And, after ten years of trying to start a family and failing at it, Deputy Doug proved that it wasn't his fault by getting Wendy, his twenty-one-year-old girlfriend, pregnant with twins.

The day after I found out about Doug and Wendy, I was downsized from my job as a City of Philadelphia tourist information specialist, a position that meant I sat at a walk-in tourist information site and dispensed heaps of tourist information.

How things had changed in a few months!

They say that bad things always come in threes: Uncle Porky died before my divorce and the downsizing.

After the cemetery, where we left Uncle Porky's ashes in the Matkowski family crypt, everyone came back to the diner for food and remembering. My mother, who had rolled into town with my father in their motor home, cried and laughed with relatives and friends who she hadn't seen in years. My father told humorous tales of Uncle Porky, his older brother.

My mom, Aunt Stella, and Aunt Beatrix all got a little tipsy and giggly, and they fell asleep in one of the back booths of the diner.

When my mom sobered up, she decided that since Stella was going around the world, she and my dad should go to Key West and take Aunt Beatrix with them. I didn't get the parallel, but early the next morning they all took off, except for Aunt Beatrix, who was taking Amtrak back to NYC because she'd been to Key West "fifty years ago, and it's probably the same."

It was over the Wednesday special at the diner, ironically a Philly steak sandwich and a small chef salad, that Aunt Stella discussed selling me "the point." "The point" is local talk for the Silver Bullet, the cottages, and her Victorian house—everything that Stella and Porky owned.

"I'll make you an offer that you can't refuse," she'd said. "And we'll figure out a payment plan." She wrote down some dates and dollar amounts in columns on the back of a paper place mat that advertised local businesses.

Aunt Stella was far too generous. She was practically just handing me the whole pierogi. Almost.

So I went back home to think about it, and then my life fell apart with Doug.

Then the pieces fell together again.

Doug, acting very civilly, offered to buy out my share of the house, furniture, and whatever. Apparently Wendy liked my faux–Williamsburg colonial and the school district, and she had just come into a trust fund. She wanted Deputy Doug, my house, and its entire contents enough to buy me off handsomely, on the condition that I leave town.

I shook hands with my husband of ten years and took a last look at my beautiful house just outside Philadelphia. I had a pang of regret at leaving all the lovely antiques that we'd accumulated throughout our marriage.

But I wasn't going to be an antique! I was going to start over—clean slate, fresh, new, reborn.

I stuffed my personal belongings into my boring gray Ford Focus and drove from Philly to Sandy Harbor in one day.

Suddenly, I had a nice chunk of money for a down payment—Wendy's "kiss-off" check—that was burning a hole in my Walmart purse.

Aunt Stella told me that the mayor of Sandy Harbor had made a purchase offer on "the point" but she'd turned him down. He wasn't family, she'd said, and besides, "He owns half of Sandy Harbor already."

She'd also turned down another restaurateur who wanted to add another restaurant to his empire because he wasn't family either.

Aunt Stella emphatically stated that the figures on the place mat were only a guideline . . . that I was her niece, and she knew that I'd take good care of what she and Uncle Porky had built.

I'd told her that I absolutely would take care of everything and keep our family memories safe, from the smallest black-and-white picture of Porky hanging on the wall to the huge collection of recipes from family and friends.

But the diner had me worried. As the flickering red neon sign on the top of the diner said, it was open twenty-four hours and had been since 1950. The Silver Bullet was an icon in these parts.

Aunt Stella shook off my concern with a wave of her hand, telling me not to worry.

Yeah, right, I had thought as I'd pushed a check for partial payment over to her and she'd dropped the keys into my hand.

Aunt Stella had patted my cheek and said that Uncle Porky would've been very happy. They hadn't had children of their own, and they had often wondered what they'd do with their property.

Owning my own diner was heaven-sent. I just loved to cook. It had been my salvation on those lonely nights when Deputy Doug wasn't home. I made comfort food, and heaven knew that I needed comfort. As a matter of fact, I comforted the whole neighborhood with stews, pierogi, mac and cheese, pot roasts, chili, and hip-enlarging desserts.

Perfect diner food.

I decided to savor my first trip to the Silver Bullet as its owner and save it for last on my list of places to visit and observe.

Or maybe I was procrastinating. I could cook; I knew that. I grew up in the Silver Bullet kitchen and waitressed there when I was in college, but I didn't know if I could handle the business aspect of it all. I'd learn, however. My first step would probably be ordering food and supplies and how to do payroll.

I headed to the bait shop on the other side of the boat launch. It didn't belong to me, but there was someone there that I needed to visit. It'd been a long time since I'd seen Mr. Farnsworth.

Opening the front door of the bait shop, I walked in. Smiling down at me from a high ladder was Mr. Farnsworth. He hadn't changed a bit since I was a kid . . . well, maybe a bit. His hair was as white as the snow falling outside, and I noticed a few more lines to his face, but he was as slim and as friendly as ever.

"If it isn't little Trixie Matkowski!" He slowly climbed down the ladder and pulled me into a bear hug against his red flannel shirt. "Stella told me that she sold to you. Wanted to keep it in the family, she said."

"Well, Mr. Farnsworth, I'm not so little anymore, but, yes, I'm the new owner."

He dropped his hands and stepped away. "You're the spitting image of your aunt Beatrix. She's a looker, that gal."

Aunt Beatrix is my dad's older sister and like my fairy godmother. I could never predict when she'd surface from her penthouse on Fifth Avenue in New York City and appear, but she always seemed to know when I needed her the most.

So, Aunt Beatrix (and don't call her Trixie!) should be arriving any time now.

I walked over to look at the cement tubs that usually contained minnows and the like. They were empty, and the familiar gurgling of the water pumps was absent.

Way back when, my sister, brother, and I, along with a bunch of friends, would hit the bait shop at least once a day to watch the bait swim around.

It was almost better than TV.

"Mr. Farnsworth, are you getting ready for trout season? Getting worms?" I expected a big fishing season when the lake defrosted. The more fishermen, the more business I'd have.

"Sure. I've ordered worms for those who use natural bait, but I've also ordered poppers, spoons, plugs, and jigs. And for the fancy fishermen types, I've ordered buzzes, blades, cranks, tubes, and vibrators."

Vibrators?

"Is there anything I can do to help?"

"Not a thing, Trixie. I'll be fully loaded and ready for trout season."

"Good. Thanks, Mr. Farnsworth. I'll help you stock the shelves if you'd like."

He shook his head and grinned. "No way. It's my favorite part of my job."

I half expected him to hand me a lollipop and send me on my way, as he'd done when I was a kid. Mr. Farnsworth always had an ample supply of them. Then I noticed a fishbowl on the counter by the register. It was full of colorful lollipops.

As if he'd read my mind, he walked to the bowl, pulled out a grape one—my favorite—and handed it to me with a slight bow.

It had been years since I'd had a grape lollipop. I tore open the plastic wrapper and popped it into my mouth.

I pulled out the lollipop. "You remembered?" I asked, stunned.

He shrugged his thin shoulders. "Of course."

I heard a thumping noise from the side of the shop. From what I could recall, the stairs led to a storage area above. The noise got closer, then stopped.

Then at the bottom of the steps, by a display of army green waders, was a . . . cowboy?

He tweaked the brim of his hat to me. "Howdy, ma'am."

This guy seemed like a bona fide, real cowboy. Museum quality. Now, he was something you didn't see every day in little old Sandy Harbor.

His black cowboy hat and boots made him seem about six foot four. He had on a pair of dark denim jeans that he was born to wear. A crisp-looking white shirt was tucked in, and a brown leather belt with silver conchos surrounded his waist. A belt buckle the size of one of the Silver Bullet's platters sat on his flat stomach. His boots were spit shined— maybe snakeskin—and he wore a brown suede bomber jacket.

I managed to pull the grape sucker from my mouth.

"Hi."

I noticed that his sky blue eyes traveled down the length of my body, taking in my red, puffy knee-length parka, my shin-high hiking boots, and the purple scarf draped around my head and neck like a mummy. I wondered if he noticed how my purple mittens and purple scarf matched my grape sucker.

Mr. Farnsworth walked to the cowboy's side. "Trixie, this is Mr. Tyler Brisco. He's all the way from Houston, Texas, and he's renting the apartment above my shop. Ty, Trixie is the new owner of the Silver Bullet."

The cowboy held out his hand. "I guess that makes you my neighbor, Mrs. Matkowski."

His voice was low and gravelly and incredibly sexy with a hint of a drawl, not that I'd noticed. I moved my grape sucker to my left hand and held out my right.

We shook hands, my purple-mittened hand in his. I hoped that it wasn't sticky.

"Just call me Trixie. And I'm not a Mrs. anymore. Just Trixie. Trixie Matkowski. I took my maiden name back after my divorce." Why on earth did I find it necessary to tell everyone about my divorce? I changed the subject. "I didn't know that there was an apartment up there."

Mr. Farnsworth nodded enthusiastically. "Yeah, your uncle Porky helped me renovate it a while back."

I couldn't take my eyes off the Texas cowboy. "How long have you lived in Sandy Harbor, Mr. Brisco?"

"Call me Ty." With his drawl, those three simple words lasted forever. His smile was warm and infectious. "I moved in just after the first of the year."

His voice was so mesmerizing, I'd listen to him read the Silver Bullet's dinner menu. I jerked back to reality, and my reality was to concentrate on my new business ventures, not a Texas cowboy.

"So we're both new to Sandy Harbor. What brings you here, Ty?"

I told myself that I was just making conversation, that I really didn't care what he was doing here.

"I'd had enough of big-city crime," he said. "You know, I'm just going over for lunch at the Silver Bullet. Join me and we'll talk?"

His eyes twinkled, and I wondered if he knew how sexy he actually was. Of course he did. A guy as good-looking as Ty had women stacked up like cordwood.

I wasn't going to be one of them. No, thanks.

But I was headed over to the diner anyway, wasn't I?

"Uh . . . I'd love to join you, but I'm a bit busy right now," I finally answered.

Mr. Farnsworth butted in. "Trixie, go and keep Ty company. There's nothing that can't wait. We take things a little slow here in Sandy Harbor."

Oh great. I was trapped into having lunch with the cowboy.

I pulled out my notebook and a pen from the

recesses of my coat. I'd take the opportunity to jot down some ideas I had for making the diner my own.

"What do you say, Trixie?" the cowboy drawled again, and my knees turned to mashed potatoes. My two-syllable name took on a life of its own.

Reluctantly I nodded. At another point in my life, maybe fifty years from now, I wouldn't mind spending time with the cowboy. He might be interesting to get to know, but right now, all I could think of was that he was a man, and I was in a world of hurt, courtesy of Deputy Doug.

"I eat all my meals at the Silver Bullet." Ty patted his flat stomach. "I think I've gained sixty pounds since I moved here."

Yeah, right, cowboy.

I pulled out a crumpled tissue from the pocket of my coat and wrapped it around what was left of my sucker. I probably had purple teeth and tongue, but I didn't care.

We went outside, walked around the boat launch between the diner and the bait shop, and cut through the launch's empty parking lot to the back door of my diner.

"Let's cut through the kitchen this time, Ty. I want to check on the cook."

"Juanita?"

The man even knew the name of the morning cook. "You do come here often, don't you?"

I smiled and waved to Juanita, whom I'd met briefly when she came to the Victorian to say good-bye to Aunt Stella.

"Everything okay?" I asked.

Juanita gave me a quick nod, and we hurried to the front of the diner to get out of her way.

I just loved the kitchen. Everything was aluminum or chrome and just shone. The smell of bacon frying permeated the air as did bread taking a ride on the toaster. Aunt Stella always called the revolving toaster a Ferris wheel for bread. I could just picture Uncle Porky at the cast-iron stove, working several orders at a time.

A good crowd was already gathered at the diner, but there were at least two booths available.

"Over there?" I pointed to the booth toward the back.

"Lead the way, darlin'."

"I'm not your darlin'," I mumbled. Doug used to call me darling. It rang hollow even then.

"Pardon me?"

"I said, 'I love this diner.'"

A hush fell over the patrons, forks stopped moving, and it seemed like every pair of eyes looked in my direction. Several customers—mostly women— smiled and waved.

Happy to be recognized after all these years, I did the same back.

Then I realized they weren't greeting me. It was all for Ty Brisco.

Glancing back at him, I saw that he was waving and tweaking his hat. The women were swooning. Good grief.

I shed my bulky coat and hung it from a post on the side of the red vinyl booth. Good riddance to it, for a while anyway. I unraveled the scarf from my head and neck and patted down my hair. It was loaded with static electricity. Adjusting my brightly striped sweater, I slid into the booth.

Ty slid in across from me, took his hat off, and deposited it on a hook by my coat.

He had hat hair, but I had to admit that it looked good—like he'd just walked out of the shower and hadn't had a chance to tame it yet. Brown with some reddish highlights that the fluorescent lights of the diner were picking up, it was longer on top than on the sides.

As I settled in, I looked around the diner. The white and black checkered floor needed some repair, but it could wait. I loved the mirror behind the counter. It made the place look bigger. What I loved the best was the revolving pastry fridge. As a kid, I could watch the cakes and pies going by for hours at a time, trying to decide what I'd like for dinner.

The chatter inside the diner signified that everyone was having a good time. A waitress walked around with two pots of coffee—regular and decaf—and I could smell more coffee brewing. A waitress I hadn't met yet appeared with two menus and two glasses of ice water.

"Good afternoon. I'm Nancy. Welcome to the Silver Bullet Diner, the place for good food since 1950." She addressed the entire speech to Ty and didn't even glance in my direction.

"Hi, Nancy." I held out a hand to her. "I'm Trixie Matkowski."

"Oh!" She moved her order book over her mouth to hide a gasp. "You're the new owner?"

"Yes, but don't let me make you nervous." I set my un-shaken hand down on the table.

"You won't." Nancy shook her head, and then tilted it toward Ty. "The daily special for you, Ty?"

"What is the special?"

"Monte Cristo sandwich. Ours is a ham, chicken, and cheese sandwich that's dipped in egg and fried like French toast."

He handed her the menu. "Sounds perfect. And a cup of coffee."

She broke into a big grin. "Hot and black and thick enough to float a horseshoe."

He nodded. "You've got it, Nancy, darlin'."

She giggled and turned to leave, but when I loudly cleared my throat, she realized her mistake.

"I'll have the same thing—the Monte Cristo special and coffee. Only I'll take my coffee with cream."

"Got it." Nancy scribbled on the pad, then grinned stupidly at Ty.

What was wrong with some women?

Although I could appreciate a studly looking man, I wasn't in the market for a relationship. Ty was simply one of my neighbors, and I was going to be nice and treat him as such.

I crossed my arms and leaned forward on the table. "So how did you land in Sandy Harbor, Ty?"

"I used to come here when I was a boy. Salmon fishing. My grandfather, father, and I. We always rented Cottage Number Four for a week, and we always had a fabulous time—just us men. I felt so important, taking a week off from school."

He had a brilliant smile, darn it.

He continued. "So when things got to me in Houston, I decided to move to the place that I've thought about the most throughout the years. Here."

Looking out the window at the boat launch, I could imagine the three Houston cowboys rolling out their boat to go fishing.

Nancy set his coffee down carefully, and she was rewarded with a wink of a blue eye. My coffee slopped onto the saucer as she sped away.

"Can you believe that your aunt Stella remembered me after twenty years?" he asked me.

When he smiled, his whiter-than-white teeth gleamed, and the laugh lines at the corners of his eyes deepened, but I wasn't noticing.

I nodded. "There weren't many people she forgot."

His cell phone went off, and he slid it from a clip on the waistband of his belt. Making a face when he studied the number, he then looked up at me.

"Sorry, Trixie, I have to take this."

"Go ahead."

He mostly grunted and made some garbled comments. Suddenly, he stood, grabbed his hat, and put it on. He reached into the pocket of his jeans, pulled out a wad of bills, and peeled off several.

He smiled. "We'll have to try this again sometime. I gotta go. Duty calls."

I was curious. "What duty is calling you?"

"The Sandy Harbor sheriff's department."

My throat tightened. "Please tell me you're a criminal and not a cop," I ordered.

He raised an eyebrow. "I'm a deputy sheriff."

"You've got to be kidding!" The words tumbled out before I could bite them back. I had a flashback to Deputy Doug and could hear the crackle of his official radio.

Ty raised a perfect brown eyebrow. "Kidding?"

"Nothing. Really. Nothing. Um . . . lunch is on me."

I didn't want him to think of this as a date or something like that. Also, I owned the place, so lunch was on the house. I pushed his money toward him, but he shook his head. I left his money as a tip for Nancy.

He tweaked his hat, pivoted on his boots, and walked away.

Yes, he was definitely born to wear jeans. Not that I cared. Not now, especially not now.

The Monte Cristo specials appeared. As I dug into my meal, a visibly disappointed Nancy packed Ty's into a white foam container.

Finally alone, I made some notes in my notebook: "get estimates for floor, fancier garnishes on plates other than lettuce leaf and tomato, lightbulb out behind counter, offer chicken or turkey on Monte Cristo." Leaning back into the worn red vinyl seat cushion, I looked out the window.

Then a bloodcurdling scream came from the kitchen.

Chapter 2

I leaped up from the booth, hurried up the aisle, and pushed the silver double doors that opened to the kitchen.

Scanning the room, I didn't see anything out of order—well, other than Juanita standing on the top rung of a step stool. She brandished a bread knife in her hand like a medieval knight with a sword.

"Juanita? What? Are you all right?"

"M-mouse."

I took several deep breaths and hoped that my heart would stop pounding in my ears and slide back into my chest where it belonged.

Max and Clyde, the handymen whom I'd met earlier, were chuckling by the back door. Juanita pointed the knife at them and swore in crystal-clear English.

I glanced uneasily at the pass-through window to the front of the diner, hoping that Juanita's swearing couldn't be heard over the clinking of the silverware and the murmur of voices in conversation.

"He was this big," Max said, holding his palms apart widely.

"Bigger," Clyde teased.

Then a string of Spanish phrases, probably not G-rated, hung in the air next to her English cursing, just like the instructions that came in every do-it-yourself project.

I held out a hand to take the knife from her. She bent down and carefully gave it to me. Then she stood, crossed her arms, and shook her head. "Where is the mouse?"

"Godzilla is in the Dumpster," Max said.

Juanita pinched her lips into a tight, white line, yet her eyes twinkled at their joking. "Please get to work," she said. "Adios."

"I second that, gentlemen," I said. "There's a lot of work to do around here to get ready for spring. So, please get to it. Or clear more snow."

Like a pair of children who'd just been chastised, they hung their heads and left the kitchen. But Clyde gave Juanita a sideways glance, and his expression told me that they weren't a bit sorry for teasing her.

I held out my hand to Juanita, this time to help her down. She took it and backed off the step stool as regally as a queen.

"I don't like mice," she said.

"I don't like mice either—not where I eat, anyway."

She smoothed her pristine white apron, shaking her head. "Max and Clyde—they smoke. They smoke too much. And they open and close the back door all day long. They come in. They go out. And the mouse, it come in."

"Have you ever had a mouse in here before?"

"No. No mouse. Never." Juanita scooped up the knife again and began slicing a loaf of Italian bread.

I wondered for a moment if there really had been an actual mouse or if Max and Clyde were just playing a joke on Juanita and she'd fallen for it.

What was this? Fourth grade?

"I'll speak to them," I said, with more authority than I felt.

"Never mind. I quit." Juanita shrugged.

Something drained out of me—my sanity.

"Juanita, I need you." As much as I wanted to roll up my sleeves and start my life as a short-order cook at my own diner, I was just too tired for a baptism of fire. I wanted to gently glide into the kitchen and observe, study, learn, eat.

And stall, just a little longer until I got my bearings.

I put a hand on her shoulder. "I promise to talk to them and tell them that their teasing isn't welcome, but don't let them drive you away. Aunt Stella told me that you've been here a long time."

"Seven years." She smiled, standing taller. "Ever since I moved to Sandy Harbor."

"And you like it here?"

She nodded.

"And how many times have you threatened to quit because of Clyde and Max?" I guessed that their pranks had been ongoing.

"More times than I can count."

"Aah." I was right. "Are you going to let them drive you out of a job that you like?"

"No." She pulled one of the orders from a metal

clothespin, studied it, and pulled a sub roll from a plastic bag. She pointed it at me. "You talk to them. Now, out of my kitchen."

I was just about to tell her that this was my kitchen, but I would quit while I was ahead.

Then it hit me. What was I going to tell the customers out front? I mulled that over for a while. If they found out that the Silver Bullet had a mouse—or mice—running around the kitchen, my new diner might become a ghost town.

I took a deep breath and pushed on the swinging metal doors. When I walked out in the front dining area, every pair of eyes met mine, staring and waiting.

I was confident that I could lie. After all, I learned from the best: my ex.

"Um . . . Juanita was listening to the radio—the weather report," I announced. "She heard that we might have six more inches of snow. I guess she just fell apart."

The patrons nodded, made comments in agreement, and went back to their meals. They could identify with Juanita. Like everyone in the Northeast, they all felt like screaming at Mother Nature. Enough snow already. Everyone—and I was no exception—wanted spring.

Spring brought the fishermen. Summer brought the families, the boaters, the tourists, and more fishermen. Fall brought the salmon and more fishermen. Winter brought the snowmobilers, cross-country skiers, and townspeople who had cabin fever.

And everyone would be hungry and would need to be fed. I hoped that the Silver Bullet would be hopping.

I needed to be ready.

And then there was that balloon payment to Aunt Stella due on Labor Day. I didn't want to touch what was left of Wendy's "get out of Philly" money to pay Aunt Stella. I wanted the Silver Bullet Diner and the Sandy Harbor Guest Cottages to make a profit as a result of my own hard work and creativity—just to show myself that I could do it.

I slid back into the booth and took a bite of my cold Monte Cristo. To her credit, Nancy appeared again and volunteered to heat it up for me. I thankfully handed her the plate.

I went back to my notes, but I couldn't concentrate and found myself staring outside instead. Max was running the snowblower, clearing a path from the diner to the parking lot where the snow had drifted. Clyde was using a shovel on the stairs and sprinkling some kind of deicer on the steps to melt the snow. I remembered that salt wasn't used around here due to environmental issues.

Looking left, I noticed a food-delivery truck backing in alongside the kitchen next to the ice-covered boat launch, and I hoped that it wouldn't get stuck in a drift. I wondered who took inventory and ordered supplies. Probably me. I made another note on my pad to ask someone.

As I looked over all my notes, I wondered yet again if I was in way over my head.

If only Aunt Stella could have stayed longer to

show me the ropes instead of booking a world cruise so soon, but Greece, Rome, and the Vatican drew her like a magnet, like a plate of pierogi and fried onions drew me.

Nancy, the waitress, returned with my sandwich and a brown paper grocery bag. She set both down in front of me. The bag immediately tipped over, and several envelopes slid out and hit the floor. Nancy scrambled to pick them up and return them to the overflowing bag.

"Mail," she said. "Stella didn't have time to look at it all, so Juanita said to give it to you."

"Thanks."

I eyed the bag but decided to eat my sandwich while it was still warm. When I'd finished, I picked up a handful of mail from the bag. The envelopes were mostly addressed to Stella Matkowski. They looked like bills. And they looked old. Some had SECOND NOTICE or LAST NOTICE stamped on the front.

My Monte Cristo sandwich sat like a cinder block in my stomach. I had to take care of the mail, and quickly. I decided that I needed to get settled into Aunt Stella's office—now *my* office—in the main house. There was a laptop sitting on a big rolltop desk, and with any luck, she might have a spreadsheet set up or some kind of program that she used.

Gathering everything, I stuffed myself into my coat, pulled on my gloves, swaddled my scarf around my head and walked to the front of the diner.

I picked up a menu by the cash register. On it

was a scribbled note that the evening special was pork and scalloped potatoes. Yum. Pork and scalloped potatoes had been my mother's specialty for years. That was, until Mom decided to hand over her overstuffed cookbook—filled with favorite recipes from the Matkowski family, Aunt Stella's Timinski ancestors, and my mother's Bugnacki family—to me.

Then pork and scalloped potatoes became my specialty. It was a dish that was always served at most of our family gatherings. It was hearty and easy to keep hot for latecomers or anyone who might drop in. I didn't exactly know who started the tradition, but when I thought of family getting together, I thought of pork and scalloped potatoes served in a big turkey roaster.

It seemed like the Silver Bullet Diner could do better than a note scribbled in black felt marker and paper-clipped to the menu. Maybe a handout with the whole week's specials would be better. Or a nice whiteboard. Or one of those funky neon blackboards. I could even search Web sites for cute ideas to make the diner even homier.

And I had some ideas for specials and new menu items that I couldn't wait to introduce. The menu hadn't changed in more than thirty years. Maybe it was time to put my mother's cookbook to use.

Or maybe I shouldn't mess with a sure thing.

Before I left, I tipped Nancy and noticed Tyler Brisco's uneaten meal nicely boxed in a white foam carton with his name on it. Should I leave it for him in his apartment over the bait shop? He probably would be hungry when he came back from whatever crisis he was handling in Sandy Harbor.

A crisis in Sandy Harbor? The biggest problem that ever happened here, according to Aunt Stella, was tangled fishing lines. And once, when a fisherman was casting on the bridge, his line got caught on the antenna of a passing car and the pole was yanked from his hands. He called the Sandy Harbor sheriff's department to stop the car. After all, he had a top-of-the-line Henderson Fishblaster Plus rod, and he wanted it back.

I decided to let Nancy handle Ty's dinner. She seemed to have the hots for him.

As I walked outside, the blast of cold air made me gasp. Flakes drifted around me, and I nodded to Max and Clyde, who were still clearing the parking lot. I'd promised Juanita that I'd talk to them about their pranks. I would, but not now, not while they were busy working.

I shuffled along with my grocery bag full of mail and tried not to slide on the hard-packed snow of the parking lot and fall on my face. Luckily, someone had cleared a path to the main house, but the steps weren't shoveled. I gripped the metal banister with a mittened hand and pulled myself up each snow-and-ice-crusted step.

Once inside, I stepped out of my boots, put them on a rubber mat, and unwrapped myself, glad to be free of my parka and the rest of my winter gear.

Heading for the kitchen to make some tea, I

stood for a moment in the doorway and surveyed the huge country kitchen with its long counters and walk-in pantry. Thick oak cabinets lined each wall, and the stove, fridge, and microwave were all commercial-sized. What I loved the most was the "nook" where a round oak table stood, surrounded by floor-to-ceiling windows. I could see the diner from the nook.

It was a perfect place to invite friends over for dinner, if only I had friends here.

Aunt Stella had updated the kitchen, yet the room seemed to maintain the original ambience. I put on the kettle, then sat at one of the oak chairs around the thick oak table and watched the snow fall. Fat, fluffy flakes drifted to earth, piling up on every surface and drifting into places where people had to walk.

Watching it was peaceful and calming, taking my mind off the numerous tasks I had waiting, not the least of which were unpacking my Focus and picking out a permanent bedroom.

I watched as a mother and her son, who were eating pie at the counter when I was at the Silver Bullet, walked down the stairs of the diner. I held my breath at the unsteady balance of the mother on the sidewalk.

I didn't want my customers to fall, and I was glad that Max and Clyde were clearing the snow.

Insurance! I'd never thought about insurance.

I pulled out my notebook and made an entry to check on it, although there was probably a bill for it in the bag in front of me.

The kettle whistled, and I plodded to the stove in my socks. I made my Earl Grey tea, added some sugar for pep, and grabbed the grocery bag of mail. I made my way to the rolltop desk in a large sitting room off the kitchen and started sorting the mail: handle immediately, handle now, handle at once.

A letter from the Health Department, Bureau of Restaurant Inspections, caught my eye. Reluctantly, I opened it.

Scanning the letter, I gleaned that the kitchen of the Silver Bullet had some problems as noted by the inspector on his previous visit. I read and re-read the problems, trying to comprehend what it all meant.

The diner had some violations, none of which seemed critical: a dirty floor near the back door and the storage area, a broken thermometer at the steam table, the Dumpster lid left open, and employees were observed eating in the prep area.

It was signed by Inspector Marvin P. Cogswell III.

The dirty floor by the back door and storage area was likely due to Clyde and Max walking in and out of the kitchen and tracking in snow and mud on their boots.

They were probably the ones eating in there, too, and the ones who'd left the Dumpster lid open. The broken thermometer was easy to fix. Everything was easy to fix.

Then I noticed that the inspector had scheduled a return inspection for . . . today! Later this afternoon! If the diner didn't pass, it could be closed down.

I decided that I should personally concentrate on making sure that everything was in order for the inspector.

I had to go back to the diner.

I took a sip of the hot tea and dressed again in my boots and winter survival gear. Clinging to the railing to make my way down the front stairs, I plowed through the snowdrifts with the health inspection letter stuffed in the pocket of my coat.

Pausing, I heard the wail of an ambulance. Then it got closer and closer still. Red lights flashed against the snow like a strobe light in a disco. Soon I could see an ambulance, a fire truck, and a couple of sheriff's department cars hurrying as fast as they could down the road leading to the diner.

My diner!

My heart started pounding in my chest. I'm not the greatest in an emergency. My brain just sits there in my head like a lump of dough that won't rise.

Max and Clyde ran toward me, and I rushed to meet them. The snowflakes hit my face and eyes and melted on my contact lenses.

"Trixie." Max breathed heavily, and puffs of steam hung between us. "The kitchen."

"Oh no! Fire! Is anyone hurt?" I immediately thought of Juanita. I knew that she was single, and, oh merciful heavens, I didn't know anything else about her or how to contact her loved ones. I didn't even know her last name. "Juanita?"

Clyde grabbed a chunk of my sleeve and pulled me down the path to the diner. "No! She's okay. Everyone's okay. Well, not everyone is okay."

Either my brain wasn't computing or Clyde was speaking Swahili. "Huh?"

"Marvin Cogswell," Max said. "He's not okay."

The name sounded vaguely familiar.

"Who? What happened?" My heart started to pound. This wasn't good.

"Marvin P. Cogswell the Third," they said in unison.

I stood frozen to the snow, wondering why my brain was frozen, too.

"The health inspector!" Max added. "It looks like he had a heart attack."

The letter. The health inspector. Oh no!

In the parking lot, the procession of emergency vehicles stopped, and a dozen people hustled up the front steps. Nancy held the door open for them, and they disappeared into the silver building.

Clyde half pulled me up the diner stairs.

"He's a goner," Max mumbled.

"Goner?" Did anyone actually say goner anymore?

"Dead," Max blurted.

Now *that* penetrated my brain.

Nancy, the waitress, nodded solemnly to me. I nodded back. "Where?"

"Kitchen," she said.

I glanced around the dining room. The patrons were craning their necks to watch the action. Some were on their cell phones, no doubt passing along the news.

A tall, thin deputy with rosy cheeks stood in front of the double doors that led to the kitchen, blocking my way. He had twinkly blue eyes, but they weren't as blue as Ty's, and he reeked of my grandfather's favorite aftershave, Old Spice.

He looked down at me and suddenly seemed formidable.

"I-I'm the owner. Trixie Matkowski."

He finally smiled. "Nice to meet you. I'm Vern McCoy. I'm a fan of the Bullet's meat loaf. Matter of fact, you'll always find the entire Sandy Harbor sheriff's department—all three of us—here on Tuesday night for the meat loaf special."

I pulled off the wet mitten on my right hand and we shook. As soon as I could function, I'd have to make a note to keep the Tuesday meat loaf special for the entire Sandy Harbor sheriff's department—all three of them.

Deputy McCoy opened the door for me. "Don't touch anything."

I wondered why he'd said that. It was probably just a cop thing.

The kitchen was packed with official-looking people. Juanita was crying, not very quietly, by the back door of the kitchen away from the circle that had gathered around the prep table. My former lunch date, Ty Brisco, standing a head taller than the others, had an arm around her.

An EMT shook her head, then bent over to take something out of a bright orange duffel bag. I had a clear view of a man in a camel-colored dress coat sitting on the top rung of the kitchen's step stool in front of the stainless steel prep table.

It was the same step stool that Juanita had stood on earlier to escape the (probably) imaginary mouse.

The man was slumped over with his face in what looked like a plate of the dinner special— pork and scalloped potatoes. He still had a fork in his hand.

But he wasn't moving. It was then I realized the EMT was zipping up her bag, not looking for something in it.

Poor Marvin P. Cogswell the Third, health inspector, was obviously dead.

I guessed that Juanita had given him a plate of the evening's special, and I hoped that he'd enjoyed his last meal.

The pork and scalloped potatoes was originally my great-grandmother's recipe, and my family's favorite dish. Uncle Porky adapted the recipe to make large quantities for the diner.

Deputy Ty Brisco was writing furiously in his notebook. Juanita was crying and dabbing at her eyes and nose with a wadded-up tissue.

"We'll talk again later, Juanita," Ty said. "At the sheriff's office." Ty hugged her tight to his side, and she wailed louder.

Juanita met my gaze and sniffed. She rushed over to where I was standing and stomped her foot. "I quit. *No más.* No more!"

"Juanita, this isn't your fault, and—" A man

having a heart attack next to her was far worse than a phantom mouse.

She stomped her other foot. "No! I quit. I can't take it anymore!"

"Go home and rest," I suggested softly, taking her arm and escorting her out the double doors. Deputy McCoy nodded to us, and I nodded back. "Try to forget all this and rest."

I quickly escorted her out the front door of the diner and down the stairs to her car. I hugged her, and she clung to me like a cat on a curtain. "Do you want me to drive you home?"

She shook her head. "They are going to need you here. I'll be okay."

"Drive carefully, Juanita." With a nod and a sniff, off she went.

I needed to do damage control at the diner. The customers were waiting to hear something. I entered the diner once again and went straight through the double doors to the kitchen.

I asked Ty if I could tell my patrons that the health inspector had suffered a heart attack. He hesitated, then shook his head.

"No. Not until his emergency contact identifies the body." He consulted his notebook. "A girlfriend by the name of Roberta Cummings. She's meeting the body at Manning's Happy Repose Funeral Home. Apparently, Hal Manning is both the county coroner and the local funeral director."

"Small town," we both said in unison.

"Mr. Cogswell has no living relatives that we know of," Ty added.

"So what should I tell them? That it's a suspected heart attack?" I asked.

"Tell them that the cause of death is being investigated by the Sandy Harbor sheriff's department. Don't mention the pork and scalloped potatoes, though, and it's no longer today's daily special. I'm confiscating all of it."

I raised an eyebrow. "But why? What on earth does that have to do with his heart attack?"

"We're still investigating," he said, seeming very coplike and cagey.

The *rip* of the zipper on the body bag echoed through the din of the kitchen. I scooted out front. I didn't want to see poor Mr. Cogswell being slipped and zipped into it. No, thanks.

Once in the dining room, I raised my hands for silence and waited. When everyone was quiet, I said, "It appears that someone has passed on, but that's all I can say until his family members have been notified."

I turned to go back in, but then I remembered that there was no special available, and no cook, and I didn't know how long everyone would be in my kitchen. I had this sick feeling in my stomach, knowing that I had to close the place, probably for the first time ever. But what could I do? "And the kitchen is closed for the evening. But pastries and beverages are on me. The waitresses will serve you."

I nodded to Nancy and to a waitress whom I didn't know, and they both sprang into action.

"Help yourself, Deputy McCoy," I said.

"I will," he replied as he opened the doors for me.

I made the same announcement to those milling around the kitchen, and gradually they moved from the kitchen to the front of the diner, mumbling their thanks. Ty and the third member of the Sandy Harbor sheriff's department remained. I read his gold nameplate: RUTLEDGE. I didn't know his first name yet.

"Lou, hand me the evidence tape," Ty said.

Okay, so his first name was Lou. Lou Rutledge. He was a Santa Claus clone, with twinkling brown eyes and a face that was friendly and bright. He had white hair and a white beard, and his stomach hung over his belt. Probably anyone who'd been naughty would admit his guilt to Deputy Rutledge.

Ty dropped Mr. Cogswell's fork into a plastic bag, sealed it with evidence tape, and initialed the tape where the bag met the seal.

Then he did the same with his pork and scalloped potatoes. In went the plate, too.

"Ty, what are you doing?" I asked.

"Covering all bases, darlin'. That's all." He smiled at me; then the smile left his face. "By the way, where were you when Mr. Cogswell was here?"

My face heated up and my stomach lurched. "Why are you asking me that, Deputy Brisco?"

"Just answer the question," he said curtly.

What on earth . . . ?

"This sounds like *CSI: Sandy Harbor*," I joked.

A corner of his mouth turned up into a half smile. "So where were you?"

I took a deep breath and let it out. "At Aunt Stella's house. I mean . . . at my house. I was going over some bills that Nancy had given me. And then I came back to meet Mr. Cogswell."

"So you knew he was here?" Deputy Rutledge asked.

"No. I didn't. I was just coming back to fix things up for his inspection."

"Then you knew he was coming?" Ty asked.

"Yes. I found a letter from him in the mail, saying that the Silver Bullet had to fix some problems from his latest inspection—minor things—and that he would be returning today in the afternoon."

"Did that make you mad, Miss Matkowski?" Deputy Rutledge asked.

"No. It made me worried."

"Anyone see you at your house?" Ty asked.

"Well, Clyde and Max saw me leave the house to return to the diner."

"But they never saw you actually inside?"

"I guess not," I said. "But they saw me walking down the porch stairs." Merciful heavens, what was going on here?

"Can I have the letter?" Ty asked.

I pulled it out of my pocket and handed it to him. He read it with Deputy Rutledge looking over his shoulder as I stood there, breathing hard.

"I'm going to keep this," Ty said. "Okay with you, Miz Matkowski?"

He used to call me Trixie. Now he was all business.

"I have nothing to hide. Keep the letter." I watched as he bagged the letter, too. "Do I need a lawyer, Deputy Brisco?"

"Do you think you do, Miz Matkowski?"

I shrugged. "Didn't Mr. Cogswell have a heart attack?"

I'd thought Ty Brisco was cute when I first met him. What was I thinking? He was a cop, just like my ex, and I had to remind myself that I wasn't interested.

"I don't know for sure if he had a heart attack or what happened here," he said. "We'll have to wait for the autopsy reports to be sure, or maybe Mr. Manning will have a preliminary finding. Then he'll send samples to the New York State Police lab. Then we'll know for sure."

"What are you looking for, Deputy Brisco?" I asked.

Several seconds ticked by.

"C'mon, Ty, this is my restaurant. I think I have a vested interest in what happened here. Please, tell me what you think."

Several more seconds ticked by, and I could tell that he was debating whether to tell me.

"Poison," I guessed.

He raised an eyebrow.

"That's why you're taking his food and the daily special. You suspect that the health inspector was poisoned. And you suspect . . . me?" I held my breath.

He shrugged. "I don't know yet for sure. I'm just—"

"Covering all bases. Yes, I know." I was more sarcastic than I should have been.

Then something caught my eye. "Wait just a minute, Deputy Brisco." I inspected the dozen or so huge evidence bags lying on the butcher-block counter of the steam table, filled to the brim with the daily special.

"Can I have a closer look at that bag? The one with the plate in it?" I pointed. "Mr. Cogswell's meal?"

"Why?" Ty said.

"Because I see mushrooms." I pointed at the contents of the bag.

"So?"

"There aren't any mushrooms in the special that Juanita made. The mushrooms are only in Mr. Cogswell's meal."

"Interesting," Ty said.

I relaxed a bit. "No self-respecting Timinski, Bugnacki, or Matkowski would ever be caught dead putting mushrooms in their pork and scalloped potatoes! So, you see, Deputy Brisco, I couldn't have poisoned Mr. Cogswell!"

Chapter 3

*T*y laughed, and I felt somewhat better, but it didn't clear the frosty cloud of suspicion hanging over my head.

"You do have a motive for wanting him out of the way. You failed his inspection." Ty's accusation didn't sound better with a Texas tone. "And you said you read the letter and were on your way over here."

"To clean, not to kill, for heaven's sake."

"I hear you." He nodded, but then his blue eyes bore through me like a laser. "Did you make the pork and scalloped potatoes?"

I shook my head. "Juanita made it. According to Silver Bullet custom, the day cook makes the specials." I felt like I was casting suspicion on Juanita, so I quickly added, "But Juanita didn't poison anyone."

"I can't rule her out yet, or you either. I can't rule anyone out yet. I will do a thorough investigation, I promise you that."

I swallowed hard. Here I was, the owner of a diner that didn't have a morning cook, and I was now under suspicion of killing the health inspector.

This wasn't going to be good for business.

Deputy Lou Rutledge looked amused by the entire exchange.

I wasn't.

"I think we're done here, Ty," Deputy Rutledge said, after three hours of snooping, bagging, labeling, and dusting for prints. "Let's grab a cup of coffee and a doughnut, courtesy of Miz Matkowski, and then pay Hal Manning a call at the Happy Repose. We can interview Cogswell's girlfriend there."

I wanted to rescind my offer of free coffee and doughnuts for Ty Brisco. He dared to suspect me? Well, he could just pay for his own.

Deputy Rutledge pushed open the doors and left. Deputy Brisco continued to stare at me, and suddenly I felt guilty, even though I totally was not.

Guilt came naturally to me, especially when I skipped church, cheated on my diet, or let dust accumulate without prompt annihilation.

"Are you done in here?" I asked him. "Since Juanita might have just quit on me, I need to get my bearings and open the kitchen. After all, the sign says that we're open twenty-four hours a day. Using your baseball cliché, I need to step up to the plate and cover all bases."

"Just one more thing. Show me where you keep your mushrooms."

I looked at the palms of my hand, as if I'd written the location of my supplies there. "I assume they're in the walk-in cooler, if we have fresh ones, which I doubt. Canned mushrooms would be in the stockroom. But from what I remember, Uncle Porky would never let a mushroom cross the threshold of this diner. He hated them, and, therefore, everyone else had to hate them."

Ty followed me to the back of the kitchen. I climbed the one cement step, yanked on the metal handle, and flipped on the industrial light switch. We walked in.

"I don't see any mushrooms," I said. "And we just had a delivery today, but I'm almost positive we didn't order any mushrooms. I can check the invoice, if I can find it."

"No mushrooms?" Ty asked, checking the shelves. "There were mushrooms in Cogswell's pork and scalloped potatoes. You pointed them out yourself." Shining a flashlight at the shelves, he lifted the lids of the boxes and peered in.

"Ty, if I were the person who poisoned Mr. Cogswell, would I keep a supply of mushrooms around, poison or edible?"

"I've seen criminals do some pretty dumb things."

"I'm not that . . . dumb."

His chin jerked downward, and a grin teased the corners of his mouth.

"Oh, you know what I mean!"

He chuckled.

This was a puzzle.

His radio went off, and he listened to a garbled message. I couldn't make out a word, but all law enforcement and emergency people could understand radio talk.

"I'm supposed to call Hal Manning," he translated.

"Who?" That name sounded familiar, but my brain was shutting down.

"The coroner-slash-funeral director."

"Oh yeah."

We escaped the cooler and walked into the stockroom. No canned mushrooms.

We returned to the kitchen, and Ty pulled his cell phone from his jacket pocket and punched in some numbers.

"Hal, this is Ty Brisco."

All I heard was "Yes . . . No . . . Oh . . . Is that right . . . ? You don't say" as I stared at the spot where Mr. Marvin P. Cogswell the Third had had his last meal.

There would be no Marvin P. Cogswell the Fourth.

I was itching to move the step stool, but I didn't dare. I wanted to disinfect the spot on the steam table where the plate of pork and scalloped potatoes with the allegedly tainted mushrooms had sat.

"This is now a crime scene," Deputy Brisco said.

I jumped at the sound of his voice, and then slowly his statement penetrated my doughy brain.

"I think you figured that out already," I said sadly. "But, please believe me, Deputy Brisco—I had nothing to do with Mr. Cogswell's death. I would never, ever do such a thing."

He raised a perfect black eyebrow. "Not even for a failed inspection?"

I raised two blond eyebrows that needed to be plucked. "Hell no!"

Heat washed over me like a blast from the pizza oven. I shed my parka and tossed it on the step stool recently vacated by the man I was accused of poisoning. I quickly picked up my coat and held it.

I was thankful there was a late-night cook due to arrive any moment now, fingers crossed.

Just then, Nancy stuck her head through the pass-through window. "Bob, the cook, called. He won't be in tonight or probably the rest of the week. Something about the flu."

I felt my head getting spacey, even more doughy. "Fabulous. Just fabulous. What else can go wrong?"

I saw myself being handcuffed by Deputy Brisco and taken to the Sandy Harbor sheriff's department, wherever it was.

"Who's going to take care of the diner?" I heard myself saying to myself. "It's supposed to be open twenty-four hours. . . . The neon sign on top of the diner says so. . . . I have to cook. I can't go to jail. Can't go. Aunt Stella and Uncle Porky. Their diner. No, my diner. No mushrooms in the pork and scalloped po—"

It was so hard to hold up my head. I felt myself about to faint. I knew the signs, since I'd fainted once before—when I caught Deputy Doug cheating on me with Wendy on the floor of our bedroom. At least he hadn't used our bed.

My knees wouldn't lock. I was going to slump onto the wet and grimy cement floor—a floor that should be cleaner, according to the report filed by the late Mr. Marvin P. Cogswell the Third.

But strong arms circled me, holding me up. "C'mon now, Trixie, don't faint on me. Wake up, darlin'. Breathe."

I heard Deputy Brisco's voice in the distance, and I tried to get my knees to work. I could smell spice and leather. It was coming from . . . him. The cowboy from Houston. No, the Sandy Harbor cop.

"Mmm . . . ," I said, thinking how nice it felt being held by a man again. It had been a long time.

Then I remembered that he was the one who was accusing me of poisoning the health inspector.

I took several deep breaths, found my knees, and pushed myself away. "If you're going to arrest me, do it now and get it over with."

He smiled in that charming way he had, but I wasn't charmed.

"I'm not going to arrest you—not yet anyway." He had the audacity to grin. "I have to investigate further, talk to the coroner, wait for the tests to come back. I'm just trying to sort things out, and—"

"Cover all bases."

"Yeah."

He touched my arm. "If you didn't do it, don't worry. Right?"

I wanted to kick his tight butt right out of the diner.

"I have to go. Will you be okay?" he asked.

Will I be okay? He insinuates that I'm his primary suspect, and then he has the cheek to ask that?

"I'm going to cook . . . and bake." I had decided. That was what would take my mind off Mr. Cogswell's death. Besides, what else could I do? I had no help.

I saw Ty out of the diner, making sure he walked down the stairs and away from me. Then I noticed that the diner had a decent-sized crowd, but the revolving pastry carousel, that I'd loved to watch as a kid, was out of pastries, pies, and cakes. Nancy was making coffee. The other waitress—what was her name?—was refilling cups.

"Nancy, the kitchen is open. We have people that need to be fed, and I'm cooking. Let's rock. Oh, and pull all the daily-specials slips off the menu. There's no pork and scalloped potatoes remaining."

What a waste of good food.

"Okay, Miz Matkowski."

"Call me Trixie."

Call me pooped. Call me overwhelmed. Call me a suspect!

I did my best thinking while I worked. I wasn't going to be suspected of something I didn't do. I had to figure this out.

Mushrooms.

The first thing I was going to do was to check the invoices for mushroom orders—just as soon as I could find them. Aunt Stella must have kept them somewhere.

And the next thing I needed was another cook, maybe two. I couldn't do this for twenty-four hours.

Juanita. I had to ask her if she knew that there were mushrooms in the Wednesday special. Then I'd beg her to come in and take the morning shift. If she really intended to quit, I needed to find a replacement. Maybe I needed to hire even more help, especially if I went to jail. The Silver Bullet was a Matkowski legend. It had to go on.

Even if I couldn't.

"Two cows, and make them cry." Nancy stuck an order onto one of the metal clothespins on the revolving rack above the steam table in front of me.

"Two cowboys on a raft," said Chelsea, the other waitress that I'd just met, doing the same thing with her order.

I wiped my hands on a crisp new towel. "Ladies, you need to translate from Dinerese until I get used to it."

They laughed. "We had our own language with Porky and Stella." A gold bead pierced into Chelsea's tongue had me mesmerized. Every now and then, I could hear a slightly slippery *S*.

"Two cows are hamburgers. 'Make them cry' means to add onions."

"Got it."

Chelsea giggled. "'Two cowboys on a raft' means two western omelets on toast. Oh, and I'll need a wrecked hen and an order of done dough with axle grease. That's scrambled eggs with dark toast and butter."

"Wouldn't it be easier just to say that?" I asked.

Chelsea wet her lips, and the gold ball glinted in the fluorescent lights overhead. "Yeah, but it's not as much fun."

"True," I conceded. "By the way, would either of you know of anyone who'd like a cooking job here?"

Nancy snapped her fingers. "Cindy Sherlock. She just lost her job over at the Dollar-O-Rama for dipping into the cash register."

"Um . . . I don't think so," I said, cracking two eggs into a bowl for the wrecked hen.

"But she was putting money in, not taking it out," Nancy said, wide-eyed. "Her little brother, Jason, didn't have enough money to buy his mother a pair of salt and pepper shakers for her birthday." She turned to Chelsea and added, "They looked like sunfish."

"And you know this . . . how?" I asked.

"I was behind Jason in line. He was counting out his pennies and was short about fifty cents. Cindy took a dollar bill out of her own pocket, exchanged it for four quarters, and slipped two of them onto Jason's stack of money so the kid couldn't see. I guess that Mr. Haberton only saw Cindy taking money out of the till and slipping it into her pocket or something. Then he started yelling at her and said that she was fired."

I put bread into the toaster and put the setting on dark. Then I took out two hamburgers from the fridge nearby and tossed them onto the grill.

Nancy shook her head. "Cindy and I both tried to tell Mr. Haberton that he was wrong, but then

Jason started crying, and then Cindy got upset. She tossed her smock on the counter and walked out with Jason."

"And Cindy helps her mother with the bills. There are nine kids in the family, counting her," Chelsea added. "Her father died a couple of years ago—boating accident on the lake."

I decided to hire Cindy immediately; she needed a job. Then another question occurred to me: "Can she cook?"

They both shrugged, but then Nancy snapped her fingers. "She must be able to. There are nine kids in the family, and Cindy's the oldest."

That didn't mean that she could cook, but the sweet girl obviously needed a job. We'd both learn at the same time and take Dinerese 101 together.

"Can someone call her? Tell her to come to the diner. I'd like to meet her."

Chelsea whipped out her cell phone from the pocket of her apron. "I'll do it."

She punched in some numbers as I slathered axle grease on the toast and then flipped the burgers. They smelled divine. I had added a touch of Worcestershire sauce to the mix along with some bread crumbs, eggs, and my special herb mix.

"She can drive down now, but she has to bring her brothers and sisters. She's babysitting," Chelsea said, holding her cell toward me like the Statue of Liberty holding her torch.

"You can bring them all, Cindy," I said, talking to the air toward the cell. "My treat, if they're hungry."

"Hear that?" Chelsea asked the cell, then turned to me. "They'll be right here."

"Tell her not to rush. The roads must be slick."

Chelsea returned the phone to her ear. "Hear that?" she asked, then lowered her voice. "Yeah, Trixie's okay. She's nothing like Mr. Haberton."

I smiled as I turned to look for the hamburger rolls, wondering if I was supposed to toast them. I decided to toast anyway. I added sweet pickles to the plate, dill pickles that Aunt Stella had put up, a tomato and some lettuce to the side, and topped it off with a couple of carrot curls around a radish rose that hadn't had enough time to "bloom" yet in a bowl of ice water. As soon as I had time, I'd make more.

"Hey, Trixie, it's cute, how you arranged the veggies," Nancy said.

"Thanks. The radish roses are my favorites. My mother showed me how to do them when I was just a kid." If I had more time to prep, I could really dazzle her, but I didn't have that time. I was lucky if I knew where the axle grease was stored. I hurried to prepare the western omelet.

They both picked up their orders and left. I just had enough time to catch my breath before Chelsea tacked up another order, this time a large one.

"Four lead pipes with rounded cows, two pigs between two sheets, four grass clippings in the alley, and two groundhogs."

I held up my hand to Chelsea. I was getting a headache. "Chelsea, stop!"

"Sorry. Make that four spaghetti and meatballs,

two ham sandwiches, four side salads and two hot dogs," she said. All I could hear was the number of times I heard her slur an *S*.

"Oh, and Cindy Sherlock is out front. This order is for her brothers and sisters."

"That was fast. Please ask her to come back to the kitchen. She can help me prepare this order." This would give me an opportunity to try her out.

Cindy was a sweet, somewhat shy girl about twenty years old. She was tall—about five foot ten—and reed thin and pale, with a huge smile. She offered her hand to me, and her handshake was firm. Her fingernails were chewed down to the quick, and her bright cherry-red hair was thin and shaggy.

She had no piercings or tattoos that I could see. I was still old-fashioned in that regard and hated that look, especially on women, but neither would have prevented me from hiring her. I immediately liked the girl.

"I can't be too long, Mrs. Matkowski, or my brothers and sisters will tear your diner apart."

"Chelsea and I will watch 'em," Nancy said. "Take your time, Cin."

Cindy nodded her appreciation and turned to me with an uneasy smile.

"Can you cook?" I asked.

"Sorta. Kinda. I cook for my family. I mean, I can learn how to do this. And I really need this job."

"Okay, help me do your order, and we'll talk."

Cindy was a quick study. She'd do fine in time.

I remembered being glued to Aunt Stella's side as she instructed me how to fry eggs just the way the customer ordered. And right by the big shiny steam table, I remembered Uncle Porky teaching me how to make spaghetti sauce, the Matkowski way. Basically, you tossed in every veggie and chunk of meat within a five-mile radius and let it simmer on the stove for a month.

After Nancy and Chelsea carried the order out to her family, I motioned for Cindy to take a seat on the kitchen stool.

Yes, that kitchen stool.

I planned on tossing it in the Dumpster soon because it would always remind me of the poor health inspector.

"Can you work days or nights?"

"Any. All. Both. I just have to arrange things with my mother."

"And there's this whole language you'll have to learn. Dinerese."

She laughed, uneasily. "I took French in high school."

Oh good, she had a sense of humor. I liked that.

"I don't think that'll help you much." I smiled at her. "I'm sure there's paperwork for you to fill out, but I'll have to find it first. Do you think that you can train with Juanita for a couple of days?" I crossed my fingers, hoping that I could convince Juanita not to quit. "I'll be training with you, too."

"You mean I'm hired?"

"Anyone who can manage eight kids can certainly manage this kitchen," I said.

She took my hand and pumped away. "I really appreciate this, Mrs. Matkowski. I'll be the best cook you ever had."

"Great! And call me Trixie." And call me optimistic for hoping that I could talk Juanita into returning.

"Okay . . . Trixie." She fished around in her little purse. "I'd like to pay you for the meals, and—"

"Absolutely not. It's on me. I dragged you here when you were babysitting."

I could swear there were tears in her eyes. She took a step forward and raised her arms like she was going to hug me, but then she dropped them and stepped back. "I am so happy to be working for you."

She looked more relieved than happy, but if she wanted to stand on her feet and cook for a good seven hours at a stretch, I figured that Mr. Haberton must have been a real beast, and she really needed the money.

She seemed so young and overwhelmed. I could relate, well, at least to the overwhelmed part. I couldn't help myself, so I pulled her into a bear hug. With a happy sigh, she hugged me back.

I had an urge to feed her, to put some meat on those protruding bones.

"You didn't get anything to eat, Cindy. How about a—a—" I looked at the steam table. "How about a rounded cow on done dough with . . . um . . . red sauce?"

"A meatball sub with spaghetti sauce?" she asked.

I looked at her, astonished. I'd made the right decision; she was already fluent in Dinerese.

Just as Cindy walked out the double doors with her meal, in walked Nancy and Chelsea with several more orders. Before they could say a word, I held up a finger in warning.

"Okay, okay. English," Nancy said, and proceeded to read each order and stick it to the metal clothespins. Chelsea did the same.

I used to wonder why waitresses in a short-order restaurant read the orders. Now I knew that it was for the cook to get her bearings. I began to pull out dishes and place them on the steam table and pull things out of the fridge.

I was finding my rhythm, which was good. It was just like cooking for my ex, times fifty.

"Trixie, I just want to give you a heads-up. All the pastries and pies are gone," Nancy said, "and we're low on ground coffee."

"Would you check to see if there's anything in the walk-in cooler that we can use? Or maybe the freezer?" I'd forgotten the huge freezer on the other side of the storage room.

"I already did," Nancy said. "You gave away a lot of freebies. It was like a feeding frenzy."

"Do you know where we get the pastries from?"

"Sunshine Food Supply." Chelsea stuck out her tongue, and the gold ball piercing made a long appearance. She didn't seem impressed with the quality of our dessert menu. "I know where you can get delicious, freshly baked stuff-pies, turn-overs, brownies, and just everything. You name it, she can bake it."

Chelsea was an avalanche of information. "Okay. What's her name?"

"Mrs. Stolfus. Right, Chelsea?" Nancy asked. "The Amish lady?"

"Yup."

"Mrs. Stolfus just moved to Sandy Harbor with several other Amish families. She's totally the best baker." Nancy nodded. "She sells her goodies at Chuck's Gas and Grab on Route 3."

I flipped over a steak and quickly sliced some onions to fry. "Okay. Give Mrs. Stolfus a call, will you, Chelsea?" I asked.

Chelsea and Nancy both laughed.

"What?" I slapped some American cheese on the burgers that I had been frying.

"She's Amish!"

"Oh. No phone." I put some buns in the toaster that reminded me of a Ferris wheel, ladled some chicken soup into a bowl, and quickly made an antipasto. "Do you know where she lives?"

"I'll draw you a map," Chelsea said.

I'd take a ride over to Mrs. Stolfus's just as soon as I could.

Suddenly my back and feet started aching. I was never going to make it.

We still needed yet another cook. Maybe Stella and Porky could do twelve-hour shifts, or Stella and Juanita, but this thirty-something-year-old woman could not. As good as Cindy seemed to be, she still needed some time to get the hang of things. Me, too!

"Mrs. Stolfus lives on Route 173A in a huge white farmhouse with green shutters. There's a green shed out front that says 'Handmade Baskets' on it," Chelsea said, then must have noticed the blank look on my face. "I'll draw you that map."

"Thanks." I prayed that she made hand pies.

Nancy walked back in with a load of dirty dishes on a cart. "The snowplow drivers are coming in. They'll be mad that there isn't any pork and scalloped potatoes tonight. And nothing sweet is left either."

I took a quick inventory of the fridge. "Tell them that they can have steak and fries for the same price. And sweet corn is the veggie." I shut the door. "Do we have any ice cream?"

"Yes," Nancy said.

"And ice cream is free tonight for plow drivers."

"Free?" Chelsea asked.

"Yes, free." I was giving away a lot of things tonight. Why not ice cream, in the middle of a blizzard, to snowplow drivers?

I wiped my face with a paper towel. If I wasn't so hot from being in the kitchen, I'd shiver at the thought of eating ice cream with snow falling.

Ty Brisco took that moment to walk into my kitchen. Chelsea and Nancy greeted him profusely, ogled him behind his back, and then reluctantly left the kitchen.

I wasn't as welcoming.

"I see you're busy," he said. I surreptitiously studied him. He looked around; then he stared at me. "You seem tired."

"I am." I pulled off the next order, but a chunk of the paper stayed on the clothespin. I pulled that off and pieced it together. Four orders of the steak special: two rare and two well-done. I hid my face in the fridge as I unwrapped four New York strip steaks. "Did you come to arrest me, Deputy Brisco?"

"You know, I liked it better when we were just Ty and Trixie."

I slapped the steaks on the grill a little too hard. One skidded across the hard surface, plunked into the deep fryer, and started sizzling. I quickly bailed it out. "That was before you accused me of being a murderer. Which I'm not. I've never even had a parking ticket before."

"I know."

I knew how he knew. "You ran a background check on me, didn't you?"

"Yes. And on Juanita Holgado."

Holgado was Juanita's last name. Now I knew, but it didn't make me feel any better to know that Juanita was a suspect, too.

"I just got back from the Happy Repose Funeral Home. Hal Manning, the coroner, definitely thinks that Cogswell was poisoned, Trixie. Hal doesn't know what kind of poison yet, but the mushrooms are a good bet. The New York State Police lab will be testing them."

I braced myself with my hands on the steam table before I fell over.

Ty tapped his fingers on the steam table, and I wanted to slap them with my spatula.

"Mushrooms were on the plate that Juanita served him. You saw them yourself. I'm sure that the state police will find traces on his fork, too."

"But there aren't any mushrooms here. You and I looked," I said. "None. And there weren't any mushrooms in the four big pans of the special that Juanita had cooked earlier. The pans that you confiscated."

"I didn't see any there either. And we checked the garbage, too."

I hadn't thought of the garbage.

"So, they were just in Mr. Cogswell's meal," I said, sorting things out in my mind. Yeah, this was a puzzle, and my head felt like someone was hitting it with a hammer.

"Juanita. What did Juanita say?" I pinched the bridge of my nose. Some magazine article I'd once read said that doing that would help with headaches.

"She doesn't have a clue as to how they got there. She said she scooped out the special from the big pan in the steam table to serve Cogswell. Juanita had been serving the special all night. We checked on all the other patrons who ordered it. Only Mr. Cogswell had a reaction, a fatal one."

"I don't know how the mushrooms got there either, Deputy Brisco, but this is my diner now, and I'm sure as hell going to find out who poisoned Mr. Cogswell."

"No, you're not, Trixie. That's my job."

Chapter 4

I'm sure as hell going to find out who poisoned Mr. Cogswell.

That was sure a bold statement coming from me. I didn't know where to start, but when the word got out that my food was responsible for killing the health inspector, the Silver Bullet wouldn't be worth scrap metal.

"Leave this to the professionals," Deputy Brisco said. "I was a detective in Houston for the major crimes unit. I can handle this with some help from the state police lab. Stay out of it, Trixie."

We were on a first-name basis again, I guess.

"Look, Ty, I don't like being a murder suspect."

Really, this wasn't all about me. It was about "the vic," as they say on TV. His poor family. "What about Mr. Cogswell's girlfriend. Did she take it hard?"

"Surprisingly, no."

"No?"

"She was as cold as the ice on the lake."

"Maybe she'll have a meltdown later—when it sinks in," I suggested.

"Maybe," Ty said, pacing the kitchen. He paused, then turned to me. "Look, Trixie, I'll try to keep this as quiet as possible, but you know that Sandy Harbor—"

"Is a small town."

"If you can think of anything that would help in the investigation, please let me know." He was just about to push the double doors that led to the restaurant when he turned back to me. "And I'll handle it."

I didn't respond. Why lie? I was still going to do some investigating on my own. Minor stuff. I'd stay out of his way.

He left the room and immediately returned. "Would you put on the steak special for me? Rare."

"Aren't you afraid that I'm going to poison you?"

"I don't eat mushrooms," he said. With a dazzling, white-toothed smile he was gone.

But not really gone. He took a seat at the counter right in the middle of the pass-through window. I had a perfect view of him, and he had a perfect view of me.

I picked out a nice T-bone for him, sank some of my hand-cut fries into the fryer, and pulled out a plate from the top of the stack. Because I was feeling extra generous, I decided to make garlic bread for him. I sliced a couple pieces of Italian bread, spread some axle grease on them, sprinkled on some freshly minced garlic, parsley, and some grated cheese, and slipped them into the pizza oven to toast.

It was getting quiet in the diner. The snowplow drivers had left, and Deputy Brisco was the only customer left. I wanted to grab a cup of coffee and sink into a booth, but I'd never get up if I did. Besides, I didn't want to talk to Ty Brisco anymore.

I pushed a rack of dishes through the industrial dishwasher and turned it on. Nancy or Chelsea could have done that, but they were busy vying for the attention of the cowboy cop.

Good for them. I, however, had never learned the fine art of flirting with the opposite sex. I thought about my history with Deputy Doug and concluded that he'd needed me—needed me to help him pass high school, then four years of state university, then to help him get through the police academy.

Then he needed me to make babies. When that didn't happen, he moved on.

As the steam of the dishwasher blasted my face and wilted my hair even more, I felt a pang in my heart.

I'd experienced it before. It was the pang of loss. Not the loss of Doug or the loss of my marriage, but the loss of never having had children.

I would have been a great mother. I love kids, love the cute things that they say, the cute things that they do. When they get older and turn out good, they are a joy to be around. Then they gift you with grandchildren to spoil.

I'd thought of adopting, but I must have known my marriage to Doug wasn't going to last. I'd just known.

It wasn't that I couldn't conceive; I just hadn't. But Doug sure was a straight shooter with his girl-friend, Wendy. Then again, at age twenty-one, she was quite a bit younger than I and obviously more fertile.

Ty held up his coffee mug, and Nancy just about flew over to refill it.

"You little ladies take such good care of me," he drawled.

"Oh, for heaven's sake," I said under my breath. I told myself that he was a novelty in the northern tundra; that was why everyone seemed to gravi-tate toward him.

I, however, was immune to his charms. I was a suspect, and I'd better figure out something soon—anything.

As I waited for his steak to cook, I played with garnishes. I made some pepper shavings by grat-ing a pepper with a cheese grater, cut some carrot curls, added some cherry tomatoes, and arranged it all on a bed of kale.

Finally, his order was completed, and I rang the bell for one of the waitresses to pick it up. Appar-ently, Nancy won the toss.

I cleaned up the area, fussing too much. When I looked up, Ty gave me a "thumbs-up" sign as he chewed on the steak that I'd made him. He sported a big grin as he cut off another piece of meat. I just loved cooking for people who appreciated it.

Now what?

I knew what I would do. I'd bake. I'd bake something to keep our customers satisfied until I could get some goodies from Mrs. Stolfus. I thought of the snow outside and decided to make my mother's snowball cookies. How appropriate, considering the snowstorm raging outside.

Mom had made them every year at Christmas until she "retired from cooking and baking" and hit the road in the motor home.

I knew the recipe by heart—butter, flour, egg, extract and morsels like chocolate, peanut butter, or minis—but I got out pen and paper and increased it ten times to have enough for the diner.

I don't know how I managed to stay upright, rolling and baking thousands of little balls, until Juanita—thankfully—arrived in the morning. Cindy Sherlock arrived soon after. It turned out that Juanita knew Cindy and her family from church.

Small town.

I helped Cindy into a pristine white apron, then excused myself and, yawning, stumbled to the back door. I hadn't noticed that the door had been unlocked all night, most likely since the EMTs carried Mr. Cogswell out, and that anyone could have walked in.

I tamped down my paranoia. Probably no one locked their doors in Sandy Harbor, New York.

Small town.

I asked Juanita to shake the snowballs in powdered sugar when they cooled, and I bundled up in preparation for the walk back to my house. Maybe I'd stop at my car, fetch a couple more boxes, and bring them inside. I quickly dismissed that ambitious idea. I was pooped.

As I climbed the stairs to my house, all I could think of was the squeaky brass bed in the guest room. I wanted to snuggle under the down comforter and sleep for two days.

A horn beeped, shocking me out of my dream of blissful rest, and a man bounded out of a blue SUV. He came toward me climbing over the snowbank that surrounded the parking lot. He wore bright yellow boots that came up to his knees, and he was agile in spite of his heavy frame. He was carrying something.

As he got closer, I saw that he was carrying a bouquet of spring flowers.

He had a thick black moustache that looked like a snowbrush. It was wet with snowflakes in various stages of melting. Melting snow dripped down his chin, and he wiped it with the sleeve of his navy blue peacoat.

"I'm Rick Tingsley, the mayor of Sandy Harbor. I also own the restaurant in town, the Crossroads. I heard that you bought the Silver Bullet and the cottages from Stella—the whole point. On behalf of the town, I want to welcome you to Sandy Harbor."

He gave me the flowers and extended his hand. He had on gloves that were cut off at the knuckles, so some of his fingers showed.

We shook. "I'm Trixie Matkowski. Stella's my aunt. Porky was my uncle. I bought the diner and cottages from my aunt."

"Yes, I know. I tried to buy the point from Stella. Hey! You'd better get those flowers in water," he said. "And get them out of the cold."

"Yes. Yes, I should. They're beautiful. Thank you."

Turning to go up the stairs that led to the front door, I heard him loudly clearing his throat. Pausing, I remembered my manners.

"Would you like to come in, Mr. Mayor? I'll put on a pot of coffee." In my mind, I was begging him to say no. "I'm sorry, but I don't have any sweets to go with it." Maybe that would deter him from accepting.

"That would be nice. I'd love a cup."

Darn it.

As I pulled the wad of metal keys from my pocket and searched for the right key to open the door, he stood right behind me. He was so close that I felt his cold breath on my right ear. Ick.

"The flowers are just beautiful," I said, and meant it. "It must have been difficult to find spring flowers in little Sandy Harbor."

"Nah. Chuck's Gas and Grab had 'em."

He didn't step out of his boots once we were inside, and I was just about to tell him to do so, but he was already his way into the kitchen, dripping snow and ice-melt granules in his wake.

I hadn't moved from the living room. I just stood there, stunned at his boldness.

"I'll make this short and sweet." His hands were splayed on my counter, and he leaned like it was a podium and he was making a speech.

Slowly walking into the kitchen, I waited.

"I want to buy the point," he announced. "The whole enchilada."

"Pardon me?" I'd heard him, but I just wanted to see if he'd say enchilada again.

"I want to buy the point. The whole enchilada. The diner, the cottages, the bait shop, this house. All of it."

Ha! He'd said it again, and he even broke it down for me.

"That's nice of you, Mayor Tingsley, but I haven't even unpacked yet. I haven't even had a chance to get my bearings."

"You don't have to. I'll pay you two million, right now, if you sign this." He pulled a packet of papers out of an inside pocket and spread them on the counter.

Wow. That was a lot of money, and I could go anywhere or do anything I wanted with that kind of dough, but this was home now, and I loved it here. Besides, Aunt Stella trusted me with what she and Uncle Porky built, and I had my own memories of growing up here. I couldn't do it for any amount of money.

"No," I said. "This is my home, my business. I'm here to stay."

He yanked the papers from the table and shoved them into the pocket of his parka. "You'll be sorry you didn't accept my offer." He checked his watch. "I'm running late. I'm going to skip your offer of coffee. I'll be back. Rick Tingsley doesn't give up."

"Uh, Mayor Tingsley, what do you mean that I'll be sorry?"

"I heard what happened here. Marv Cogswell, the health inspector, died in your kitchen. Do you think that you'll have any business after word gets out that he was poisoned at your diner?"

"I'll walk you out," I said, heading for the door. I was half past cranky and couldn't tolerate the less-than-honorable Mayor Tingsley anymore.

We said our good-byes, and he reiterated that he'd be back. I'd be ready.

I shut the door behind him and locked it. I was exhausted, but I wanted to mop up his mess from the living room and the kitchen. It looked like an army had marched through my house, not just one mayor.

Forget it. I just had to sleep.

I had a death grip on the banister as I trudged up the stairs to the second floor. Every bone in my body screamed in pain. If I had had any muscles, they'd have screamed, too.

I was almost to the top step when the doorbell rang.

I looked longingly at the door to my room, visible down the long hall.

The doorbell rang again, and I turned around. It was easier going down the stairs, but not by much.

I answered the door. The entire Sandy Harbor sheriff's department stood on my porch. Ty Brisco stood between Vern and Lou with his hands in his pockets, looking refreshed and put together.

"Good morning," I said to everyone, raking my hair out of my eyes. I wanted to tell them that I didn't usually look like this, but I'd just spent fourteen hours cooking and the mayor had left me with a hideous headache.

I noticed Ty shifting from boot to boot. He met my gaze, stood a little straighter, and magically transformed into J. Edgar Hoover, minus the dress.

Ty held up a piece of legal-looking paper. "I have a court order to search your house."

"You've got to be kidding."

"Sorry, Trixie."

"But—"

"Sorry."

He had the sense to look sheepish. Good.

"Come on in. I have nothing to hide," I said, holding the door as everyone filed in.

They all put white booties on their feet. Vern and Lou carried duffel bags, and they spread out over my house like killer bees.

I noticed Ty looking at me. I was still standing by the door, still swaying on my numb feet and perversely wishing that I'd had a chance to really clean the place. Who wishes she had cleaned up for men who think she's a murderer?

This was so ridiculous. Why were they wasting time on me? They should be looking for the real killer.

Ty stood in front of me. "I am truly sorry, Trixie."

"What should I do, Deputy Brisco? Make coffee? I wish I had some doughnuts or something to serve. I should have brought some snowballs home from the diner." I couldn't help being sarcastic. I wanted them out of my house, and I wanted to get some sleep.

"This shouldn't take long. Just sit down and relax and try not to worry." He pointed to a reclining chair. If I sat there, I'd go to sleep immediately.

Oh, who cares? I sat down in the chair, yanked on the footrest handle, and sank into blue plaid heaven. I reached for a knitted afghan that Aunt Stella had left and shook it out over myself. Yum.

The next thing that I heard was Ty's low voice with the Texas twang, "Trixie, we're leaving now."

"Okay," I mumbled, raising the afghan higher.

"I just want to tell you that we didn't find anything unusual. No mushrooms."

"That's nice," I said, cocooning deeper into the chair.

"Trixie, did you hear what I said, darlin'?"

"Mush . . . rooms."

Why didn't he just stop talking and let me sleep?

"Uh . . . well . . . okay," he said. "Get some rest. I'm going now."

"Mmm . . . arrest. You're going to arrest."

It was dark when I woke up, and I couldn't figure out where I was. Oh yeah, blue plaid recliner in the living room of Aunt Stella and Uncle Porky's house. Uh . . . my new house.

I checked the anniversary clock on the mantel.

It was almost five p.m. eastern-dark-way-too-early-at-nighttime. I had to jump into the shower and hustle over to the diner to cover for Bob and relieve Juanita and Cindy.

I could barely stand. But I couldn't entirely blame the blue plaid recliner. I was out of shape.

Well, in all fairness to me, I had been on my feet nonstop for forever yesterday and early this morning. And I needed better shoes or sneakers or Crocs—another item to add to the list in my notebook.

It was a chore getting up the stairs, but a hot shower was the prize at the end of the trail. It had to be a short shower or I'd be late, and Juanita might quit yet again.

I wondered how Cindy Sherlock did on her first day as cook-in-training. I'd soon find out.

I didn't even take the time to dry my hair thoroughly, so by the time I trudged to the diner, it was frozen crispy.

Both Juanita and Cindy were glad to see me. The diner was packed and two shifts of waitresses were yelling out orders, so both Juanita and Cindy stayed overtime to help me. The word hadn't gotten out yet to the general public about the murder—the results of the autopsy would take some time—but my staff knew because they were all interviewed.

After a few bumps and crashes, and even some laughs, we managed to forget for a little while that the health inspector died in the kitchen.

Before Juanita left, I thanked her profusely for

not quitting (yet), and she told me that Cindy was a quick study.

That was great news.

I found Cindy putting her coat on by the back door. "Juanita tells me that you did a terrific job."

"This was much more fun than cashiering all day at the Dollar-O-Rama."

I smiled. "Now what are you up to?"

"Watching my brothers and sisters. My mother has to work tonight."

"Where does your mom work, Cindy?"

"The box company in Oswego."

I nodded. I knew exactly where the box company was located because I'd graduated from SUNY Oswego, the State University of New York, there. It was a grueling forty-five minutes from Sandy Harbor on country roads under the best of circumstances. In wintery weather with blowing and drifting snow, it would take twice as long—at least.

"Thanks for staying overtime. I'll make sure you are paid accordingly."

I probably should keep some kind of record, so I could make out paychecks. Where was my notebook? I had to write that down.

"Keep track of your hours, okay?" I said.

She nodded. Suddenly, a lot of laughing and noise came from the restaurant. We both turned in the direction of the pass-through window to check it out.

Ty Brisco. He must be off duty as he was in full cowboy regalia, and he looked fabulous. Not that I noticed. He sported a white cowboy hat, which, according to all the Westerns that I've seen, meant that he was one of the good guys.

All right, I noticed my heart rate accelerating just from looking at Ty, and I didn't like it one bit.

Cindy whistled softly. "He's hot."

I couldn't disagree.

He saw me staring at him and waved. Ugh. I didn't have time to put any makeup on. It'd melt off anyway with the heat from the kitchen. I raised my arm and gave a halfhearted wave back.

Did he have to eat all his meals here?

Cindy gave me a hug and walked out the door.

From the dining area, in walked Chelsea, the waitress with the tongue jewelry. She saw me on duty and grinned.

"In English, I know." She read from her pad. "An order of bacon and eggs, eggs over easy, a lightly toasted bagel with butter and cream cheese, and home fries with onions." Then she said, breathlessly, "It's for Ty."

Make that another woman enamored with the cowboy cop.

As I got his breakfast ready, I reminded myself that I had to do something to solve Mr. Cogswell the Third's poisoning, even though Ty said to butt out. But I was a suspect, and that made me crazy. I'd never had a ticket in my life, forget about the big stuff like murder.

All I needed was a free moment to myself.

One side of the swinging doors opened, and Ty Brisco stood in the doorway. He knocked on the frame. "Do you mind if I come in?"

"Don't you have carte blanche?"

"I'm not on duty right now, so I thought I'd ask."

I took a deep breath to release the tension building in my gut. "Sure. Come in. I'm making your order right now."

"I'll just make sure you don't spit on it." His blue eyes twinkled.

"You're too late."

He bent his head back and laughed. It was interesting how his cowboy hat didn't fall off when he did that.

As he walked over to the side of the steam table, the sound of his boots made a dull thumping sound on the cement floor. I liked the sound. Then I caught the scent of pine and spice. Yum.

In my craziness, I dropped an egg on the floor, just inches from his black cowboy boots. I picked up a towel and knelt down to clean up the mess from the floor. My hands shook.

"Relax, Trixie. If you're not guilty, you don't have anything to worry about."

"It's a little hard to relax, Deputy Brisco," I said with my face inches from a vat of ground beef. Oh yes, the evening special was spaghetti and meatballs. Then why was I making him breakfast? It was dinnertime.

How could I have forgotten? The diner had a full menu, twenty-four hours a day.

"Please go back to calling me Ty."

"That's equally hard to do when I'm a suspect." I shut the door of the fridge. "By the way, should you be fraternizing with me?"

He grinned. "I think that my reputation will survive."

"Good. I wouldn't want to tarnish your reputation."

"You know, I was teasing you this morning," he said.

"This morning?" I tried to remember. What was he talking about?

"After the search, you thought I was going to arrest you, and I didn't correct you."

My heart raced. "You were going to arrest me?" I pictured myself in a jail cell with a filthy sink, a filthier metal toilet, and a mega-filthy mattress. I'd have a wall full of hash marks for the days I'd spent there and would pass the time making lists in my ever-present notebook.

"No! No arrest. You were mumbling. I didn't think you'd remember. You were pretty sleepy."

"I don't remember, and thanks for bringing it to my attention—not!" I flipped his bacon over with a fork. I was frying about a half pound of bacon for him, don't ask me why.

"Even though I can't officially rule you out yet, you're one of the worst criminals on the planet."

"I'm guessing that's good?"

"Trixie, can you think of anyone who might want to set you up?"

"Set me up? I don't know anyone here, not really. I don't really know Juanita that well or even the two waitresses on duty yesterday. I have a passing acquaintance with Clyde and Max. Of course, I know Mr. Farnsworth at the bait shop from when I was a kid. And I just met the mayor when he gave me flowers early this morning. So, who would want to set me up, and why?"

"That's what I'm trying to figure out."

"I appreciate that, Ty." I really did. It made me feel a lot better that he was leaning toward being on my side. "I can help you. Please let me help. I'm going crazy."

"The mayor gave you flowers?" he asked, then grinned.

"As a welcome-to-Sandy-Harbor gift."

"Oh." He grinned. "By the way, Mr. Cogswell's girlfriend, Roberta Cummings, decided to have a little service at Happy Repose tomorrow morning at nine, then burial at the Sandy Harbor Cemetery. I'm going to go to the service. Would you like to join me?"

I was scheduled to finish my shift about eight. It would give me just enough time to hurry home and get ready.

"Okay."

He turned to go, but just then we both heard a noise outdoors by the back door. I really should have locked the darn thing, but Max and Clyde used that door to go in and out of the kitchen, and it was the most convenient way to the Dumpster. It got a lot of use.

Ty walked toward the back door.

"Stay here," he ordered. "It's probably nothing."

"It's probably Max or Clyde," I suggested. I followed him, even though he had told me to stay put.

The noise grew louder; then suddenly there was silence except for Ty's shallow breathing. I was holding my breath.

Then, I heard a whimper. That was me.

He pulled out his gun, reached for the doorknob with his free hand, and swung the door open.

Chapter 5

A happy bark greeted us. A dog. A big dog.

I let my breath out. The big blond ball of fur came bounding in, dropped to the floor, and rolled onto his . . . er . . . *her* back. Ty rubbed the dog's stomach, and she wiggled with joy.

"You're a sweetie. Yes, you are," he said to the dog in a falsetto voice.

"She doesn't have a collar," he said to me in his Texas twang. "I'll have to take her to the Humane Association. Maybe they can find a chip, and I can return her to his owner."

I didn't know much about dogs, but this one looked like a purebred golden retriever, and she wasn't very old. Most of her hair was matted and dirty, and she was soaking wet.

"Do you want to share my breakfast, girl?" Ty asked the dog.

"Please keep her by the storage area, Ty. I can't have her in my kitchen. I'll make her some hamburgers," I said. "She's probably hungry."

"Can you get her a bowl of water, too?"

"Sure."

I put four hamburger patties on to fry. I really didn't know how much a dog of this size would eat, because I had never had a pet in my life.

I got a couple of bowls, filled one with water, and set it down in front of her. She immediately started slurping the water. I cut up the cooked hamburger and put it in the freezer to cool.

I put that bowl down in front of her, and she quickly ate it. She was done in seconds and licking her mouth. She sat regally and stared at me, and I wondered if her owners were missing her.

I petted her head, then went to the sink and thoroughly washed my hands and the two bowls. I put the bowls under the sink, to be used just for the dog.

"Do you mind if I take her out front?" Ty asked. "I'll keep her out of your way until the Humane Association opens and they can see if she has a microchip or has been reported missing."

"I'd rather you didn't take her out front. There are customers out there."

"Just a couple of plow guys before duty."

"Still. It's against health laws," I pointed out.

"Mr. Cogswell was the only health inspector in this county. Until they hire someone to replace him"—Ty shrugged—"no one's going to be the wiser."

I was just about to point out that he was supposed to enforce the law, not break it, but I decided that it'd be better to get rid of him, and get him out of my kitchen.

I plated Ty's order and handed it to him. "Go and eat, and take the blonde with you."

My hair was blond, like the dog's, but she had a better haircut than I had.

"That's a great name," Ty said. "Blondie."

As if the dog knew her name already, she wagged her tail and licked Ty's hand.

I stood there waiting for them both to leave, but instead of following Ty out the front door, Blondie walked toward me. She nudged my hand, then nudged it again.

"Blondie wants you to pet her," Ty said.

"I'm cooking."

"Just do it, and she'll leave you alone."

I squatted down and petted her. I should have gotten a dog or cat, since I didn't have children with Doug. Maybe a pet would have made me feel less lonely.

I scratched her ears, and she closed her eyes. My heart melted when I held her cute little face in my hand.

"Okay, Blondie. Go with Ty. Don't tell the health department. And no barking out front. Hear?"

She gave a small yip, as if she understood what I was saying.

"Trixie, can you join us?" Ty asked.

I looked through the pass-through window. I should mention that we don't pass the food through the pass-window for some reason. The waitresses always pick up completed orders from the steam table's shelf, and the pass-through is just used as a window.

"I can't join you. More customers are coming in. Duty calls."

He walked out of the kitchen with Blondie walking at his side as if Ty had owned her forever.

They say that a dog can judge a person's character better than another human can. Judging by how Blondie warmed up to me, I was definitely a good person.

I hope Ty noted how Blondie licked my hand.

Then again, I'd fed her.

But still . . .

I decided to make another zillion dozen snowball cookies, as the supply was getting low. It was something I could do in between orders.

As the ingredients blended together in the industrial mixer, I sorted out things in my mind.

One good thing that came of my conversation with Ty was the news that he didn't really think I was guilty of poisoning Mr. Cogswell, even if only because he thought I was a terrible criminal.

"Amanitas," Ty said as I opened my front door the next morning. He was right on time to pick me up for Mr. Cogswell's service at the Happy Repose Funeral Home.

"Pardon?"

"Amanita mushrooms. They are a group of poisonous mushrooms. That's what killed Mr. Cogswell, according to the state police lab. They are trying to identify the exact type."

I shrugged. "Never heard of them." I motioned for him to come in. He stood on the rug by the door, and I was grateful for his good winter manners. He wasn't going to tramp through my house like the mayor had, tracking in snow and faux salt granules.

"I did an Internet check," he said. "They appear wild in the woods around here in the summer and fall, so the killer had to have picked them back then and saved them. Apparently, one cap of an amanita can kill a man."

I shook my head. "Wow." Then I remembered. "There were a lot of mushrooms on his plate. He didn't have a prayer."

"True," Ty said.

I remembered learning about wild mushrooms from my Girl Scout days. The lesson was to not ever touch, pick, or eat them. Duh.

"The killer had to have dried them, or maybe he, or she, precooked and froze them," I pointed out.

"The lab told me that after they're cooked, they look like regular mushrooms. Even if Mr. Cogswell knew about amanitas, he wouldn't have been able to pick them out."

I pulled my same red puffy coat out of the closet, and Ty took it from me and held it open for me to put on. I slipped my arms into the sleeves and smiled at the nice gesture. It was getting harder to keep up my semi-dislike of him.

"Where's Blondie?" I asked.

"At the Humane Association. I dropped her off first thing this morning. They are going to clean her up and look for her owner."

His blue eyes had lost some of their sparkle. He wanted to keep the dog.

"We'd better get going," he said.

The Happy Repose was only eight miles away,

past downtown Sandy Harbor, down country roads dotted with houses and farms and a couple of mom-and-pop businesses.

Men in dark black suits, coats, and hats were waiting in the parking lot. They greeted us and slotted us into a parking space. Ty took my arm and led me to the front door of the funeral parlor. I was grateful for the assistance over the hard-packed snow and ice.

I wiped my feet on the throw rug thoroughly so I wouldn't track anything into the room. Ty did the same.

There was no one in line to greet the lone woman who was standing on the side of the casket. She was tall and slender, with white-blond hair and gray eyes, a model-perfect snow queen. I assumed that she was Roberta Cummings, Mr. Cogswell's girlfriend.

Several other people sat in the chairs in the large room.

I signed the guest book, walked over to Roberta, and held out my hand.

"Miss Cummings, I'm Trixie Matkowski. I'm the new owner of the—"

"I know who you are," she said, looking at me with hate-filled eyes. "You are the one who poisoned my Marvin. What are you doing here?"

I dropped my hand as my whole body heated in embarrassment. "I'm paying my respects," I said quietly.

"You've paid them. Now you can go." Icicles dripped from each word.

I hadn't expected this reaction from her. Maybe it never dawned on me that she'd blame Mr. Cogswell's death on me.

Ty appeared at my side. "The investigation is still ongoing, Ms. Cummings. Don't jump to conclusions."

"This whole town knows that the Silver Bullet didn't pass Marvin's inspection," she said, her voice raised. It crossed my mind that she was playing to the audience of mourners. "Two weeks ago, it was in the *Sandy Harbor Lure*, for heaven's sake. She had it in for him."

She pointed her finger toward my boobs, and it took all my self-control not to squash her like a bug.

"And you are an editor at the *Lure*, are you not?" Ty asked.

"That doesn't have anything to do with this!" she said, stepping closer to me. I feared for my hair, thinking that she was going to grab it and start yanking. I would put up a good fight as I needed to keep every strand of it.

Ty stepped between us. "Ms. Cummings, Trixie is here to pay her respects. If she had something to hide, do you think she'd come here?"

She rolled her eyes and shrugged. "As soon as Marvin is buried, I'm going to make it my mission to see that no one eats in your diner ever again, Miss Matkowski."

She spit out my name as if each syllable burned her tongue.

I stepped back beyond her reach and said a

quick prayer in front of Mr. Cogswell's closed casket. On the casket was a grainy photo of him that looked like his high school yearbook picture. I figured that it had to be at least thirty years since he had graduated from high school. He wasn't bad-looking back then, but I wondered what he looked like now . . . er . . . before he'd died.

I was ready to scoot out the door when I saw Ty signal to me to take a seat. I whispered, "Are you nuts? I want to get out of here."

He jerked his head toward a folding chair. "Sit."

Taking a deep breath, I sat.

His hand hovered over mine. For a second, it looked like he was going to take my hand, but then he changed his mind and lowered it onto his thigh.

I didn't know what to make of that. He was either feeling sorry for me or wanted to make sure I wasn't going to bolt.

Why was I here, again? Oh yes, looking for some kind of clue with Ty—looking for something strange or out of the ordinary.

Roberta Cummings was strange, and the only thing out of the ordinary was me.

I sat perfectly still as she shot me scathing looks. Several more people appeared, including Mayor Tingsley, then left almost immediately. Soon, the only ones left in the room were Roberta, Ty, and I. And of course, Mr. Cogswell.

The funeral director/coroner, Hal Manning, came into the room and announced that we were going to say some prayers for the soul of Mr. Cogswell. Ty and I turned to page fourteen of the blue prayer book as instructed.

I guess it was the least I could do.

So I prayed for the happy repose of the soul of the health inspector at the Happy Repose Funeral Home.

Finally, the service was over, but Ty made no move to exit. Then I realized that he was waiting for our names to be called for the procession to the cemetery.

Oh no!

"Mr. Ty Brisco and Miss Beatrix Matkowski," announced Mr. Manning.

We were the only ones in the room now! He could have just waved us over. If that wasn't strange enough, we were driving the only ordinary car in the funeral procession. There was the hearse, a limo carrying Roberta Cummings and the black-coated guys, and then us in Ty's humongous black SUV.

An overwhelming wave of sadness for Mr. Cogswell washed over me. Here was a man whose life was unexpectedly cut short, and, besides his girlfriend, only a deputy sheriff and I were there at the cemetery. I was glad that I had attended the service after all.

After more prayers at the cemetery, where it seemed that Roberta was more interested in glaring at me than praying, we drove back into town.

"Did you pick up any clues, Ty?"

"Not really. I was just surprised that more people didn't attend. I mean, Marvin Cogswell inspected every food place in town; I would have thought that more people would have paid their respects."

"Maybe he wasn't liked," I suggested.

He shrugged. "I heard in the wind that he ate his way around the county, and some of the restaurant owners didn't like that—a free meal for every inspection."

"And maybe if the establishment didn't give him free food, they failed their inspection?" I made a mental note to check if the Silver Bullet cooks fed Marvin and to what end.

"Maybe they failed, maybe not. I'm going to check."

"But Marvin's mooching of meals is not reason enough to kill him," I said.

"I wouldn't think so." At a red light, he turned toward me. "How about breakfast? I'm thinking that you might like to check out the competition. How about Brown's Four Corners?"

"Great idea. I'm starving."

Brown's parking lot was snowy, slushy, and a major mess. My boots immediately started to leak. By the time we got inside, my feet were frozen stumps.

A blast of hot, greasy air hit me in the face as soon as I walked in. In the waiting area, there was a logjam of parkas and red plaid hunting jackets vying for seats.

As Ty hung up our coats, I shimmied my way

through the crowd toward what seemed to be a hostess stand. "Trixie Matkowski, a table for two, please."

A hush fell over the crowd. It started like a slow ripple, then picked up momentum, like a wave at a sporting event. Many pairs of eyes locked on me, and I wondered if all my buttons were fastened and all my zippers were zipped.

"Um, Ty, is the silence for you or for me?" I asked. "I know that you're a novelty around here, but it seems like I beat you out this time."

"Yeah, I think it's for you."

"Shall I wave, give a small speech, what?" I asked.

He shifted from cowboy boot to cowboy boot, and I felt his hand at the small of my back. Why on earth did my cheeks heat up?

"Let's just sit down," Ty said.

Springing into action, he winked at the hostess, complimented her "purty" dress, and said "darlin' " a couple of times. We were seated in a snap.

Just like magic, the noise level returned to normal.

"This place sure is hopping," I said as I slid into my seat.

"Since I've moved to Sandy Harbor, I've never seen it so busy. Not even close to this."

A harried waitress plopped two menus on the table in front of us and kept on walking. I could hear the incessant ringing of a bell coming from the kitchen. Annoying.

The sun peeked out from behind the clouds,

and light hit the grimy windows. I could see a smoke cloud hovering over us in the dining room. Something had burned, or was still burning.

This wasn't my idea of ambience, and the prices didn't seem to be all that low. The food must be extraordinary to draw so many customers.

I looked around to see what everyone was eating, and I checked the plates that the servers were delivering. Nothing struck me as extraordinary in the least.

Ty peered at me over his menu. "I've had their buffalo hot wings before, and they're pretty good."

"I have a rule: no hot wings before breakfast."

I noticed a woman in a floor-length muumuu covered with gardenias. She floated around the room, going from table to table and greeting patrons. Her purple turban, secured with a rhinestone image of the Eiffel Tower, slid forward when she nodded.

Lime green flip-flops peeked out beneath the hem of her flamboyant gown. I knew that because she was now standing at the side of our table.

"Well, hell-o, Deputy Brisco!" she said, offering Ty her hand. It seemed to me that she wanted him to kiss it, but he shook it instead.

"Howdy, Mrs. Brown," he said. "You're looking mighty purty today."

Wasn't he the Texas charmer?

She giggled. "Why thank you, Ty! And you're looking as handsome as ever!"

She then turned to me. "I'm Antoinette Chloe Brown, the proprietress of Brown's Four Corners

Restaurant," she said breathlessly, à la Marilyn Monroe. "And you are?"

"Trixie Matkowski. I'm the new owner of the Silver Bullet Diner and cottages."

"I thought you might be the new owner of the point." She tapped her index finger on her chin, and raised her voice two octaves higher. "Didn't Marvin Cogswell die after eating at your Silver Bullet Diner?"

There was that sudden drop in the noise level again.

My face flamed. "I—I . . . It didn't happen like that."

"Well, then how did it happen? I heard that it was your pork and scalloped potatoes that killed him."

She was playing to the crowd. Roberta Cummings and Antoinette Chloe Brown should be on Broadway.

Darn it. What was I doing sitting here? I needed to spend the time investigating what really had happened.

I stood, noticing with great satisfaction that many rhinestones were missing from the Eiffel Tower.

"Excuse me, Ty," I said, not moving my gaze from her eyes that were clumped with mascara and glittery blue eye shadow, "but I have lost my appetite."

I grabbed my coat and dove back into the crowd of people still waiting to get a seat. I didn't care if

Ty followed or not. I'd walk back home, leaky boots and all.

"Sheesh! Some people!" I heard Antoinette Chloe Brown say. "Some people are just jealous of others."

Jealous? Hey, I have my own muumuu collection from my poetry-writing days. And I don't do turbans.

Why would she think that I'd be jealous?

Of what?

I slid my way through their ice rink of a parking lot and walked onto the main highway. As I gave some unidentifiable roadkill a wide berth, I caught the edge of a major puddle, and more water seeped into my boots and soaked my stockings. My teeth started to chatter.

The next time I made a grand exit, I would be more prepared.

I heard a car drive up behind me and knew without looking that it was Ty Brisco's SUV. He pulled up alongside of me, rolled the window down, and waved me in.

"C'mon, Trixie. Get in. The roads are slippery and awfully sloppy."

No kidding!

I opened the door and climbed onto the front seat.

"What was that about?" he asked.

"How can you ask that, Ty? She was practically accusing me of killing poor Mr. Cogswell." I snapped my fingers as I remembered. "Come to think of it, you did the same thing."

He laughed. "It's my job."

"Well, it's not Antoinette Chloe Brown's job. And to broadcast it all over her restaurant—that was classless."

"I agree."

I simmered with resentment during the rest of the drive back home. When we turned down the road that led to my diner, I could see that there were only four cars in the parking lot of the Silver Bullet. Only four cars! From what I could remember, they belonged to my staff.

The parking lot was plowed to within an inch of its life. The walkways were clear and salted, unlike Brown's.

My heart sank when I walked into the diner. It was clean and sparkling and smelled of cinnamon buns and coffee.

Only two people were seated at the counter: Clyde and Max. And now Ty Brisco. There were no real customers.

I poured Ty a cup of coffee and leaned against the counter. It didn't take me long to realize that the word was out about Marvin Cogswell's last meal at my diner.

I needed customers to make a profit to pay Aunt Stella.

The mystery of the poor man's death had to be solved, and solved fast.

I was going to talk to Juanita about that day again. If I could keep her calm and rational, maybe there was something she remembered that would help me find out what had happened to the poor health inspector.

Pushing open the double doors, I saw Cindy Sherlock putting cinnamon rolls onto a flowered platter.

"How's everything going?" I asked.

"I love it here," she gushed. "I love to cook and bake, so it's not like a real job."

"Where's Juanita?"

"She went home."

"Home? She's supposed to be training you. She left you all alone?"

"We haven't had many customers, so Juanita said that there was no reason for you to pay two of us."

"I see." I wished that Juanita had stayed and continued Cindy's training.

A plan formulated in my mind. I was going to talk to Juanita, right now.

First, I had to give Deputy Brisco the slip—by sneaking out the back door.

Then I would see what I could find out from Juanita.

Chapter 6

I felt like a sneak as I watched Ty through the pass-through window and waited for him to position the *Sandy Harbor Lure* in front of his face again. He was probably rereading the story of Mr. Cogswell's death. Roberta Cummings had left nothing out and gave a new meaning to poetic license.

When Cindy turned to take another batch of cinnamon buns out of the oven, I slipped out the door.

Her beautiful cinnamon buns would go stale unless we had more customers.

A light rain was falling and fog had descended, making me feel like I was in the middle of a Sherlock Holmes novel.

I headed for my Focus that was parked in front of my house. I suddenly realized that it'd be easy for Ty just to turn around and look out the windows of the diner to see me.

I slid onto the stone-cold, faux leather seat and fired it up. With just a minor grunt, the engine started, and I backed out, trying not to breathe so I wouldn't fog up the windows.

I headed north onto Route 3 and enjoyed the ride without another car in sight, although I kept looking for Ty Brisco's black monolith SUV in my rearview mirror.

Ty had instructed me not to investigate on my own, but I couldn't entrust the future of my business only to him. A sudden burst of adrenaline shot through me as I realized that I'd succeeded in escaping his watchful eye and was going to ignore his "request."

This was the most fun I'd had in years, which goes to show you how unexciting my life had been.

I asked Clyde where Juanita lived, and he gave me step-by-step directions. It probably was an easy drive without the snow, but I was cautious and drove like a snail. I didn't want to slide and end up in a ditch, because no would find me until spring. I turned onto a side road that was labeled simply NUMBER 4.

Juanita's house sat on a little hill in the outskirts of Sandy Harbor known for its apple orchards. I knew the area well as I'd worked every weekend during the fall at Sonny's Apple Acres while I was in college.

I could see Sonny's huge barn from Juanita's driveway. The parking lot was buried under snow, but soon there would be buds on the apple trees and work would begin in the orchards. It took a great deal of work to ensure a successful harvest, one that would draw people from miles around to enjoy the bounty of the countryside and to pick apples.

I pulled over to the side of the road, took out my notebook, and jotted down my idea of doing a cross-promotion with Sonny's this fall. I could advertise his business at the diner, and he could advertise mine.

There was nothing like autumn in New York: the crisp air and even crisper apples, the brilliant colors of the changing leaves, the hint of wood fires in the air and the mouthwatering aroma of Apple Betty baking in the kitchen.

I could feature Apple Betty at the diner! I'd use local Honey Crisp apples. Yum. I could smell it baking now.

But unless I found out what happened to Mr. Cogswell, there would be no one at my diner this fall, no one to eat the piles of cinnamon buns that Cindy had made, and there would probably be no one staying at the cottages or shopping at my bait shop this season.

I cautiously walked up Juanita's steep driveway, hoping that I wouldn't slide or sink up to my knees in slush. I liked her house immediately—it was a cute, weathered Cape Cod that looked like it would be at home sitting in the middle of . . . well, Cape Cod.

A giant of a black dog started barking at me the second that I got out of my car. It probably thought that either my Focus or I was lunch.

I didn't move until I was satisfied that Cujo couldn't get to me.

"Poncho! Quiet!" Juanita yelled from her front door; then she noticed me. "Oh, Miss Trixie, come in. He won't hurt you. He's just a big baby."

Yeah, sure, I thought, looking at the bared teeth

and the drool suspended from the corners of his mouth.

I hurriedly sloshed up ice-caked cement steps to her front door.

"Sorry for the intrusion, Juanita, but I wanted to talk to you."

"Come in." She smiled. "I have a fresh pot of coffee perking and I just made a Wacky Cake."

A Wacky Cake! I hadn't had that in years. I started to drool, just like Cujo. Making a chocolate Wacky Cake was like a science experiment. All the ingredients are in one bowl, and when vinegar is added, it bubbles; then water is poured over the whole thing. Even the worst baker in the world can make a Wacky Cake.

"Juanita, I'll only bother you for a minute. I didn't want to talk to you at the diner."

Once inside, I breathed a little easier. Remembering my winter etiquette, I took off my useless boots and placed them on a rubber boot tray by the front door.

"Come into my kitchen. It's nice and toasty warm there."

I followed her and took note of all the pictures she had positioned on every flat surface and every square inch of wall—a massive shrine to the art of photography.

"They are my brothers and sisters, nieces and nephews, and their children," she answered without my even asking. "I have a big family, and that's good, because I don't have any children of my own. And when we all get together . . . oh my!" She laughed loudly, and her eyes focused on what looked like two shelves' worth of scrapbooks and/or photo albums.

Please don't pull them out; I don't have three weeks to spare.

I felt a pang of sadness for her.

"Where does everyone live?" I asked.

"Mostly in Mexico, Nogales. Some in Arizona, more in Texas. The closest are a nephew and his family in Rhode Island."

Juanita motioned for me to take a seat, and I pulled out a white chair from her white farmhouse table. She set out a small pitcher of milk, a bowl of sugar, and two white mugs. Even the silverware had white handles.

I noticed that in direct contrast to the living room, her kitchen was bare of any personal items. Everything was a stark white—walls, appliances. Even her china was without a petal or a leaf of decoration.

She poured coffee into the mugs, and for some reason the smell immediately brought back a memory of happier times with my ex-husband. We were newly married and living in a tiny apartment no bigger than Sonny's orchard shack, but we always had coffee and packaged doughnuts from the bakery outlet store for breakfast. It wasn't healthy, but it was cheap.

When Juanita put a slice of Wacky Cake in front of me, I took a look at the moist chocolate cake with the creamy white topping and prayed that it was cream cheese frosting.

I looked up at her. "Cream cheese?"

She nodded, smiling.

"Oh my!" I was going to faint from happiness on her white floor, but first I had to feast.

I took a bite. Pure heaven. It reminded me of every birthday celebration that I had until I got married. My mother would always ask what kind of cake my siblings and I wanted for our birthday. My sister and brother would spend weeks thinking about it and researching different cakes, but my answer was always the same: Wacky Cake with cream cheese frosting.

I wondered briefly why I hadn't made it in years. But not wanting to delve into my psyche, I went back to eating it like it was my last dessert on earth.

I enjoyed a second piece, then decided that Juanita had been patient enough, so I started the conversation I had come here for.

"Juanita, is there anything you might remember about the day Mr. Cogswell died?"

She thought for a while. "No, Miss Trixie. I told Deputy Ty everything that I know." Her eyes pooled with tears. "Deputy Ty thought that I had something against him, but I really didn't know him. I just fed him every time he came into the restaurant and I was on duty."

"Did you feed him the day that the Silver Bullet failed inspection?"

She shook her head. "Bob was the cook that day. Bob refuses to feed him. Those are the days that we fail inspection."

Steam came out of my ears. I couldn't believe that Porky and Stella had put up with that kind of nonsense from Mr. Cogswell.

"Juanita, did Porky or Stella, or you, or any of the cooks ever put mushrooms in the pork and scalloped potatoes?"

"No, Miss Trixie. Never. Porky and Stella didn't like mushrooms, so therefore . . ."

"No one else could like them," I finished.

"*Sí.*" She laughed. "And they said that was not the way their grandparents made it."

I nodded. "Purists."

"*No comprendo.*"

"Tradition."

"Ah."

"So Mr. Cogswell always ate in the kitchen?"

"*Sí.* At every inspection, he comes in the back door, pulls up a chair to the prep table, and waits for a meal. Then he eats. He eats at Brown's, the Crossroads, the Gas and Grab, the ice-cream place, every place he goes to. The other cooks at these places, they tell me so."

"And did he always use the back door of the Silver Bullet to enter the kitchen?"

"*Si.* The back door. That door should be locked."

"Maybe," I said, not liking the fact that Clyde and Max would use the double doors when they needed to get into the kitchen area to take out the trash or to load the walk-in cooler or freezer.

Juanita drummed her fingers on the table and stared at her floor. She seemed to be thinking.

"Tell me about Bob. What's he like?" I asked.

"He's a friend of Porky's. They were in the army together, and Porky gave him a job when he retired from his job. Bob keeps mostly to himself and is sick a lot, but I like him, and he's a good cook."

I leaned forward. "Could he be a murderer?"

"No. Absolutely not. He's as honest as the day is long, and he loves to help people. He was a social worker before he retired. He could no more poison Mr. Cogswell than me or you. Besides, he never fed him. Bob didn't believe in that, and Mr. Cogswell knew it."

Good point. I was leaning toward ruling Bob out as a suspect, but I really would like to meet him.

"Juanita, who else uses the back door?"

"I do. All the waitresses, mostly. And the delivery people. Lots of people. Too many. Sometimes I get scared when the door opens. It could be anyone."

Maybe a doorbell would be a better idea. Or an intercom system. I was just about to pull out my notebook and make a note about it, when it dawned on me.

There was a delivery from Sunshine Food Supply made on the day Cogswell was killed, and it was around that time! I remembered seeing the truck when I was sitting in my booth, trying to eat my Monte Cristo. That was after my lunch non-date with Ty Brisco.

Could someone from Sunshine Food Supply have a grudge against Mr. Cogswell? Someone who delivered food service products around town would know his schedule and habit of eating at every establishment he was inspecting.

And, more important, was this a clue?

It was probably something that Ty Brisco had already looked into, but I didn't know for sure. I could always place another order with Sunshine and ask for the same delivery person.

Yes, I could.

Juanita put a hand on my arm. "Trixie, maybe you want me to call some of the waitresses and tell them not to come in. Maybe for a while, that would be better. No sense paying them. Right?"

My stomach roiled. I hated the thought of having to tell anyone that their hours were being cut. Everyone depended on the income, or else why would they want to stand on their feet for hours at a time and serve?

I debated the pros and cons. It made good business sense to at least cut back. It probably made better business sense to close, but I'd have my own show on the Food Network before I did that with Aunt Stella's and Uncle Porky's legacy.

"Maybe not the full-time waitresses, just the subs and the part-timers," Juanita added. "And it's good that Bob is sick."

"Juanita, when did you serve the pork and scalloped potatoes to Mr. Cogswell?"

"When he walked through the door. I put it on the steam table. Mr. Cogswell, he always eats, same place."

I shook my head. Cogswell had some nerve to

note on my inspection that he found my employees eating in the kitchen when he did the same
thing.

"Then what?"

"Then he told me he was going to inspect the
men's room."

"Did you leave the kitchen around that time?"

"Deputy Brisco asked me the same thing. I did
leave, just for one *momento*, to pick up my cell
phone out front. I had lost it somewhere, and Roberta Cummings, she gave it to me. She said that
someone found it on the sidewalk in front of the
newspaper where she works. She traced it to me
through my contact list."

"But that was only for a moment?"

"Not very long. I just said *gracias* to Roberta,
and that was all."

My heart started beating wildly. The poisoned
mushrooms must have been slipped into Cogswell's meal while Juanita was out front and he
was "inspecting" the men's room. It had to have
been then.

Thanking Juanita for her hospitality and for
training Cindy, I pulled on my boots and accepted
a huge piece of Wacky Cake to go. I had a plastic
fork in the console of my car. That piece of cake
would be lucky to make it back home alive.

But when I saw Ty Brisco's black behemoth pull
in behind me on Juanita's driveway, I almost lost
my appetite for it.

Almost.

Chapter 7

Ty hustled out of his SUV as if his jeans were on fire.

"A little out of your way, isn't this, Trixie?"

"Just visiting a friend. The last time I checked, that wasn't illegal."

Beads of rain sparkled on his black cowboy hat. It was nice and waterproof, so his hair remained dry—totally unlike my own.

Cujo started barking and pacing in front of the chain-link fence. Ty eyed the dog, and I wondered if he was carrying pepper spray. Cujo would probably just gargle with it.

"It's only illegal if you're interfering with a police investigation," he said in a no-nonsense sheriff's voice.

"I'd never interfere with a police investigation," I said, and I meant it. "Just having coffee with Juanita. Coffee and cake. And I have proof." I held up the bag containing the piece of cake.

"Why did you sneak away from the diner?"

"Did I?"

"Knock it off, Trixie. You know you did."

A vein in his neck suddenly appeared. He was mad.

"And what did you two talk about? Anything

about the case?" He stood in front of me with his arms crossed. He might have been intimidating if I were shorter, but I wasn't.

"Just girl talk, you know." Juanita had said that she'd told Ty what she told me, so it wasn't as if I were keeping information from him.

"I don't know. Enlighten me. What did you girls talk about?"

"Girls?" I decided that the best defense was a good offense. "Aren't you being sexist? We aren't girls; we're women."

"You used the word first, Miz Matkowski. I never said you weren't women. You did."

"I said that we weren't women? I never said that!"

"I distinctly heard you say—"

"Deputy Brisco, really. You need sensitivity training." I got into my car, carefully placing the cake on the passenger's seat. I thought about buckling it in.

He knocked on my window, and I rolled it down. "Yes?"

"In all seriousness, is there anything I should know about, darlin'?"

A change of tactic. He asked this oh so sweetly, with his full-blown Texas twang that made me get all squishy inside. I'd bet he knew it, too.

Darn him!

I took a deep breath. "Juanita reminded me that we had a delivery from Sunshine Food Supply. It just dawned on me after talking to Juanita that Sunshine Food Supply might know Mr. Cogswell's schedule. Maybe someone there had something against him. They had access to the back door of the diner."

"So does half the world, Trixie. My investigation showed that that the back door never seems to be locked. What about Clyde and Max? What about one of your waitresses? What about Juanita herself? Then there's the Dumpster haulers, and the list goes on."

I waved a hand, dismissing his suspicions. "I can't believe that anyone I know is involved."

"You just moved here, Trixie. How well do you actually know anyone?"

Maybe he had a point.

"But still, can't I help you?" I asked. "Please? I have a lot at stake. The Silver Bullet and all . . . Well, I have a large payment to make to Aunt Stella. And I don't have any customers, and I need to get to the bottom of this in a hurry."

He leaned forward, and a river of water flowed from his hat brim onto the sleeve of my parka, soaking it.

"Oops. Sorry about that, Trixie." He stepped back. "Let's continue this conversation someplace dry."

"Does this mean you'll let me help?"

"I don't want to put you in danger. You're a civilian, not law enforcement. Leave this to the experts."

"Like you?"

"Yes, me." He took a deep breath. "Have you

ever thought that the pork and scalloped potatoes with the poisoned mushrooms might have been meant for someone else? What about Clyde or Max? What about Juanita? Or another customer? Or—" He paused. "What about you? What if Cogswell ate it by mistake?"

"You think it might have been meant for me?" My stomach turned. "You've got to be kidding."

He shrugged.

"Why would anyone want to kill me?" I shook my head. "My high cholesterol will get me first." I wondered if the people Aunt Stella mentioned who were interested in buying the point wanted it badly enough to kill to put me out of business, but that was a stretch. Wasn't it?

"Nah. You're fishing, Ty. Didn't you tell me that the mushrooms were only in Mr. Cogswell's meal? To me, that means he was the target."

"Maybe, maybe not. I just want to stress to you that you could be playing with fire."

"Understood. But I'll take that risk."

"It's my job to see that you don't take that risk," he said, "so stay out of it."

"I'll be at my house," I said, not wanting to continue this line of conversation. "I need some sleep."

He tweaked the brim of his hat. Did I mention how I loved that?

Deputy Ty Brisco was getting to me.

No. I couldn't let that happen. I had a lot to deal with right now, and I was still reeling from my divorce.

And I had so much to do.

But first, I had to eat my piece of Wacky Cake.

A shot of excitement ran through me every time I saw the Silver Bullet Diner sign in red neon. Today it blazed through the fog and guided my way home. I still couldn't believe that it was all mine—my diner, my home, and my twelve cottages.

Well, it would be mine when I paid off Aunt Stella.

When I noticed the empty parking lot, my excitement disappeared faster than a box of mint Girl Scout cookies with a cold glass of milk. The parking lot was completely empty, and it was noon.

Where was the lunch crowd?

They must all be at Brown's Four Corners or at the Crossroads Restaurant.

I could see Antoinette Chloe Brown now, with her flowered muumuu and turban, fluttering from table to table and thriving on the commotion and customers.

I remembered how Ty Brisco showed up at Juanita's house. I was hoping that he'd say that by working together, we'd get the murder solved in half the time.

But he'd never said those words.

I would check out Sunshine Food Supply and see if I could find anything suspicious. It could be a dead end, but since there had been a delivery from them just before Mr. Cogswell was poisoned, it was worth looking into.

Hurrying inside my house, I kicked off my boots and shed my coat. I went into Aunt Stella's office and fired up her laptop. I wanted to see if she kept track of what she ordered from Sunshine Food Supply.

Nothing.

From what I could tell, Aunt Stella used her laptop for buying clothes and for e-mail.

I checked a five-drawer oak filing cabinet. I opened the last one marked *S–Z*. There it was: a blue hanging file labeled *Sunshine Food Supply*.

All the invoices were there, with the exception of those from the last couple of months. I remembered that I had seen two envelopes from Sunshine Food Supply in the grocery bag that Nancy had given me.

I reached over and picked up the bag from the floor. Leafing through everything, I found just what I was looking for.

Of course, no mushrooms were listed. Not that I expected big, red letters that said "poison mushrooms, one can" along with the cost in the right-hand column; I just expected something— anything—to jump out at me.

I compared the two invoices. They were both basically a standing order for the same goods: to-mato sauce, produce, assorted boxes of cereal, eggs, bread, several cuts of meat, cold cuts—on and on it went.

The delivery person was listed as "M.C."

Funny, those were the same initials as the vic-tim, Marvin Cogswell the Third.

Was this just a coincidence? Would Marvin's father or son want him dead? And why?

Oh, wait! Roberta Cummings was his emergency contact, but did he have a next of kin? Was the obituary wrong? Was Ty wrong in not having discovered any relatives?

The doorbell rang, and I figured that it was Ty Brisco. He'd wanted to talk more, and I couldn't wait to show him what I'd found.

I practically skipped to the door, invoices in hand. It was Ty with a cardboard box containing two take-out cups of coffee and a waxed paper bag that looked like it contained doughnuts.

Bless his heart. I'd save my cake for another time.

I opened the door, and he stepped into the living room. He was just about to step out of his boots, when I noticed that at his side was Blondie. She was washed and fluffed, and two little pink bows were over her ears.

"No one seems to be looking for her. No microchip," Ty said, answering my unasked question. He petted the dog on her blond head. "So I'm going to foster her. When they put her up for adoption, I get first dibs." He shot me a charming grin. "I hope it's okay with my landlord if I have a dog in my apartment."

"As long as Blondie behaves herself, no one should mind."

Blondie seemed to know that she was accepted. She licked my hand, and I just melted. I bent over to pet her, and she rolled over onto her back.

"She wants you to rub her tummy," Ty explained.

"Oh, okay." I did so, and also petted her head and back for good measure. I just loved the feel of her soft fur. "I've never had a pet in my life."

Ty smiled. "We can share Blondie."

I liked that idea. "Blondie is more than welcome to come in. And Ty, forget about your boots," I said. Another couple layers of winter crud couldn't do much more harm.

As I spread out the two pieces of paper on the table in front of him, he set down the cardboard box. Blondie curled up in front of the furnace grate.

Smart dog.

"Look at these delivery slips," I said, pointing to the initials of the delivery person. " 'M.C.' was the delivery person on the last two occasions. Actually, I looked back even further. M.C. was the delivery person for all the deliveries in the last six months. Once a week, he came to the Silver Bullet."

"M.C.?" He raised a perfect black eyebrow.

"Yes. The same initials as our victim, Marvin P. Cogswell the Third. Could there be a Marvin the Fourth?"

Ty popped the lid on a take-out cup and handed me the other. "We couldn't find any living relatives when we went to look for the next of kin.

And this guy would be living in town, for heaven's sake, if he delivers for Sunshine. That means he would have been at the funeral, or at least the cemetery."

"Maybe not. Not if they were estranged."

"True. This is a good lead. Good work, Trixie."

I let myself bask in the glow of his compliment while I loaded cream and sugar into my coffee. "I'll ask Max or Clyde. They'd know if there were more Cogswells around. They seem to know everyone. Or Juanita certainly would know. She's lived in Sandy Harbor a long time."

"Then why wouldn't she have told me?" Ty asked.

My heart sank. I didn't want Juanita implicated. "Good point, but maybe she forgot. Or maybe she really doesn't know."

"Small town," Ty reminded me. "Everyone knows everyone."

A peek out the window told me that Max was sprinkling more ice-melting granules onto the sidewalk leading to the diner. "Let me call Max," I said, pulling out my cell. I punched in his number and could see him answer his phone.

"Hell-o. Max here."

"Max, this is Trixie. Do you know the name of the man from Sunshine Food Supply who usually delivers to the Silver Bullet?"

"Yup."

I raised my eyes to the heavens, praying for patience. "Would you like to tell me his name?"

"I wouldn't mind."

"Then tell me his name!"

"Mark Cummings."

"Mark Cummings," I repeated for Ty's sake, who then wrote it down on a small pad that he pulled from an inside pocket of his coat. "How long has he been delivering for Sunshine Food Supply?"

Max rubbed his chin. "For a long time. He delivers to all the restaurants in Sandy Harbor and round abouts."

"Anything else I should know about Mark Cummings?"

Max hesitated. "I don't think so. Other than his sister is Roberta. You know, the gal who was living with the health inspector who died in the kitchen."

"Oh! Of course I know her." I hung up the phone, and I repeated Max's statement word for word before I forgot. Then I sat down at the kitchen table as did Ty.

Ty grinned. "So the delivery person, who delivered for Sunshine Food Supply just before Marvin was poisoned, is Mark Cummings, the brother of Marvin's live-in girlfriend?"

"Bingo." I reached for the bag of doughnuts, suddenly famished, and pulled out a peanut doughnut.

"Don't get excited, Trixie. We have to find out if Mark had an ax to grind with Marvin."

"Maybe he didn't like something about Marvin. Maybe he didn't like how Marvin was treating Roberta."

Ty pushed his hat back with a thumb.

"I can tell you that Roberta called 911 three times on Marvin the Third. And he was charged with disorderly conduct. It's public knowledge because all arrests are published in the paper, so I am free to tell you. I hear that that their fights are legendary."

I swallowed. "And wouldn't a brother, like Mark, be upset if he knew that Marvin was using his sister as a punching bag?"

"Upset enough to poison him?"

I shrugged. "Maybe. Maybe not. It depends on what really happened. Maybe he really did assault Roberta, but she never said."

"It's worth checking into. I think I'll have a little talk with Mr. Cummings." He took another sip of his coffee and clamped the lid back on.

The beeping warning of a large motor vehicle backing up was loud enough to be heard in the next county. Blondie lifted her head, and her ears stuck up like radar. Then all three of us looked out the kitchen window at the diner.

Another bingo.

"You won't have far to travel, Ty. The Sunshine Food Supply truck is here, and unless I'm totally mistaken, Mark Cummings will be driving."

But why was he here? I wasn't expecting another delivery until next week. Besides, I was thinking of cutting back on the standing order since no one was patronizing the diner.

I followed Ty out the door, slipping into my parka and hopping into my sopping wet boots as

I walked. Then I sank into the slush that I'd grown to hate.

We crossed the parking lot in record time and walked around to the back of the diner where deliveries were made and the door was always unlocked.

Chapter 8

*W*hen Ty and I approached, the Sunshine Food Supply deliveryman was wheeling a dolly stacked with cardboard boxes down a ramp.

I could see Ty reading the colorful printing on the sides of the boxes. I did the same.

"Pies, doughnuts, crushed tomatoes, American cheese, lettuce . . . and what's that on the bottom?" I swallowed hard as I looked at the cartoon of smiling red toadstools dancing around the bottom of the box. "Sliced *mushrooms*?"

He pushed his cowboy hat back with a thumb. "You gotta be kidding!"

"I didn't order them! Why on earth would I?" I shrugged. "Remember, the diner is a mushroom-free zone—or at least it used to be."

Just as we were about to question the deliveryman, Ty's radio went off. I couldn't catch the garbled, static-filled message, but all cops seem to have some kind of radio ear.

He handed me Blondie's leash along with some kind of rope that I assumed was to keep her from running away. "I gotta go. The roof of the American Legion collapsed from the weight of the snow."

"Oh no! Were there people in it?"

"Yes." He shot the reply over his shoulder as he ran to his SUV.

I could already hear the sirens of emergency vehicles in the distance, and I said a quick prayer that everyone was okay.

I wanted to hop in my car and see if I could help, but first I had to check out this delivery and do something with Blondie.

"Uh, hello. Could you stop a minute?" I asked the deliveryman, as he wheeled another dolly full of boxes down a ramp from the back of the Sunshine Food Supply truck toward the back door of the diner. "I'm Trixie Matkowski, the new owner of the Silver Bullet. And you are?"

He froze in place, and I thought he looked like a scarecrow. He was as thin as a rail, and his royal blue jumpsuit was three sizes too big.

"I know who you are." He grunted. "You're the one who poisoned Marvin Cogswell. I saw you at his calling hours."

He must have been one of the few individuals sitting in the funeral parlor when I arrived with Ty. "You deserve a medal for offing him."

Looked like he wasn't a fan of Marvin. "No medal for me. I did not poison him," I said sharply. I was ready to throw him off my property, but then I decided that I'd get more answers out of him by being sweeter.

I offered my hand, and after the seconds ticked by, he shook it, not even taking off his grimy glove. Blondie sniffed him, and he took a step back.

"Is that a friendly dog?" he asked.

"I think so. I've only known her for a grand total of about fifteen minutes, but she hasn't bitten anyone yet."

He didn't crack a grin at my joke. As he looked down at Blondie, his lip curled on one side. Obviously, he wasn't a dog fan.

"And you are?" I asked again.

"Mark. Mark Cummings." He answered impatiently and pointed at the name embroidered on his jumpsuit.

Like I could see that through the folds of the material!

"You're Roberta's brother?"

He stared down his pointed nose at me.

"How did you know that?"

"Just a guess. Same last name. How's she doing today?" I was truly concerned. If she loved Marvin the Third, it'd be a difficult loss for her to handle.

"I don't know. Haven't seen her lately." He pushed the dolly a couple of feet, but I held up my hand like a traffic cop for him to stop.

"Mr. Cummings, I just had a delivery a couple of days ago. I don't need anything, and I never placed this order."

He shrugged. "It must be a standing order."

"Maybe, but not mushrooms. Never mushrooms. We don't use them at this diner. It's a . . . custom. Could you tell me who ordered these items, please?"

My heart pounded. Was this a cruel joke?

With a noisy sigh, he put his dolly upright, trudged to the front seat of the truck, and pulled out a clipboard. He scanned the paper on top with a bony finger. "It's a phone order."

"So, who phoned in the order?"

"It doesn't say. Just says phone order." He tossed the clipboard back onto the seat.

"Mr. Cummings, please call your office and ask who ordered it. Maybe someone remembers who phoned it in."

"Lady, I'm busy. You call the office. So, do you want this stuff or not?"

"Not."

He swore under his breath. Blondie growled next to me. She didn't seem to like Mark Cummings any more than I did. Mark Cummings and his sister were totally unfriendly.

He rolled the dolly back up the ramp, slammed everything that he could possibly slam, got in the cab, and finally pulled away. I walked through the silver metal doors to call Sunshine Food Supply.

I tied Blondie to a nice dry spot, retrieved her water bowl, and gave her fresh water. I had to remember to ask Ty if he had dog food for her. Maybe I'd head over to the Dollar-O-Rama and pick some up.

Blondie was going to be Ty's dog, but she was getting to know me, too. I petted her, and she licked my hand. I was falling in love with the blond-haired cutie.

Since there were no customers, Cindy and Nancy were out front having a cup of coffee. I gave them a wave through the pass-through window, and they waved back.

I pulled out my cell and phoned Juanita to ask her whether she'd placed a recent order with Sunshine.

"No, Trixie. *Nada.* We still have lots left. It's going to spoil if we don't get more customers."

My stomach sank to my knees. I already knew this, but I didn't want to think about it. I guess it was time to donate whatever couldn't be frozen.

Maybe the emergency personnel and rescuers at the American Legion could use some sustenance. It would give me people to cook for, and I loved doing that.

I'd talk to Nancy and Cindy and among the three of us, we could prepare food and desserts for everyone. But first I dialed Sunshine Food Supply. I had to get to the bottom of the mushroom delivery.

"Let the sun shine with Sunshine Food Supply. This is Candy, and I'm here to take your order."

"Candy, this is Trixie Matkowski over at the Silver Bullet Diner."

"Oh, hi! Welcome to Sandy Harbor, Trixie."

She was sweet, delightful, and perfectly named.

"Not even five minutes ago, Mark Cummings was here to deliver an order. Could you possibly tell me who placed that order?"

"Sure can." I heard the typing of keys. "It was a phone order."

"I know, but do you remember who placed it?"

"It was a woman. I thought it was you. I remember that she was in a hurry, and I was disappointed that I didn't get to welcome you to Sandy Harbor. So . . . welcome again!"

"Aww . . . thank you again." She really was adorable. "Did you recognize the voice? Anything?"

Candy hesitated. "Is something wrong?"

"Yes. Something is very wrong. I didn't place the order, and I don't know who did. I'm just trying to get to the bottom of this so it doesn't happen again."

"I don't remember anything else. . . . Oh, wait. . . ."

"Yes?" I held my breath, waiting for a clue to drop.

"She ordered a case of sliced mushrooms in water. The Silver Bullet never orders mushrooms, so I thought that was peculiar. Porky and Stella hated them. So I said, 'Mushrooms? Are you sure?'"

"Yeah, then what?"

"She said something like, 'They're a gift.'"

"A *gift*?" I asked.

"Isn't that funny?"

"Hilarious," I said, even though it was anything but. "Candy, from now on, take orders for the Silver Bullet only from me. We'll have a code phrase, like . . . uh . . . Sandy Harbor is a beautiful place."

"Okay! That'll be fun."

"Thanks for the information, Candy."

"And thank you for calling Sunshine Food Supply, in business since 1949."

I mulled things over. A woman ordered a case

of mushrooms to be delivered to the Silver Bullet. It certainly wasn't me. I doubted that the waitresses, Nancy and Chelsea, would have a reason to do that, and Juanita certainly wouldn't. But what did I know? I still hadn't met some of the other waitresses—the part-timers or the subs.

Had Juanita already phoned them and told them not to come in due to the lack of business? Would one of them hold a grudge, or think that such a practical joke would be funny?

No. That couldn't be it. I had just agreed to Juanita making the calls to them and cutting back their hours. No one would have had the chance to put together such a perfectly timed practical joke.

Would they?

Not to change the subject, but didn't I have to relieve Cindy sometime today or tonight? And when was Bob, the other cook, due to return?

And where was my notebook?

Nancy walked into the kitchen and found me staring stupefied at the large plastic container of snowball cookies that I'd made—when?—a day ago? A couple of mornings ago? I was losing all track of time.

Cindy's beautiful cinnamon buns were nicely arranged on a faux silver tray and covered in plastic wrap.

If only people were here to enjoy them.

"Trixie, are you okay?"

I shrugged. "Just thinking." I forced a smile.

"My sister just called me," Nancy said. "She lives near the Legion Hall."

"Is everyone okay?" I was so caught up in my own worries, I'd forgotten about the collapsed roof. How horrible of me.

"They don't know yet. They think that there were about a dozen people there. They were having some kind of meeting. I guess volunteers are digging through the debris—wood and shingles, ice and snow and water. It might take a while. My brother-in-law owns a construction company, so he's called in his crew and brought in some equipment."

My heart ached for those trapped inside and their families. I sprang into action.

"Nancy, grab Cindy. Let's pack up some coffee and treats for the volunteers and whoever else is there. We'll make sandwiches from whatever we can put together from the fridge."

I grabbed boxes and bins and a huge coffee urn. I started pots of coffee brewing and packed up sugar, stirrers, and creamers.

Then I phoned Clyde on the cell. "Would you and Max mind coming to the diner? And would you mind driving me up to the American Legion in your van? We are going to bring the workers some refreshments."

Nancy and Cindy were busy making sandwiches when I returned from the stockroom with a load of plastic utensils, paper plates, napkins, and a few bottles of salad dressing. I saw ham and cheese on rye, tuna subs with lettuce and tomatoes, and even peanut butter and jelly.

Max and Clyde took over the job of making coffee when they arrived. I wrapped the sandwiches and made a chef salad. I added cases of soda and bottled water, my snowball cookies, and the tray of cinnamon buns to the pile of food to be loaded in the van.

I had a nagging feeling that I'd forgotten something. I made a mental inventory, added more napkins and more cans of coffee, but the feeling wouldn't go away.

A movement in the corner of the kitchen caught my eye. Blondie!

"Cindy, would you cook Blondie up a couple of hamburgers?"

"Oh, good, a customer!" She quickly lowered her head when she looked at me. "I'm sorry, Trixie. I was just kidding."

I gave her a "don't worry" smile. "I know that."

Cindy said that she could both wait on tables and cook up any orders. Max would stand by in case she needed him. More than likely, they'd clean up the kitchen and read the *Sandy Harbor Lure*, futilely hoping that a paying customer would arrive.

Then Clyde and I headed for the Legion Hall.

The fog and rain from earlier had turned into a lightly falling snow when we turned onto Route 3. And by the time we turned onto Main Street, it was a raging blizzard.

Deputy Vern McCoy, who'd told me on the day of Marvin P. Cogswell the Third's unfortunate demise that he never missed a "Meat Loaf Tuesday," stopped us before Clyde got too close to the scene.

I could see the collapsed building, and I felt like

a piece of Sandy Harbor history had fallen. I had always thought that the Legion Hall looked like a transplanted Southern plantation, complete with fat, white pillars and a balcony.

"Oh my!" I said. Maybe we should just get out of the way.

Many people were already on the scene. They brandished shovels and axes.

Deputy McCoy furiously waved us along.

"Hey, Vern." Clyde stopped and rolled down the window. "Trixie brought coffee and sandwiches, cookies, pastries—my van is loaded."

I leaned forward to talk over Clyde. "I could set it all up somewhere and everyone can help themselves whenever they want."

"That's nice of you, Trixie. And certainly welcome. Looks like we might be here for a long time. I suggest you bring it all to the . . . um . . . uh . . . fire barn, across the street. I'll pass the word to everyone. But you have to move along now."

Each word came out in a puff of steam, and the poor man looked like a frozen block of ice. We'd try to run a cup of hot coffee out to him as soon as possible.

"One more thing, Deputy. Is everyone okay?" I needed to know.

"So far, so good. Some minor injuries. But more are still trapped inside. But you have to move along now."

"You got it," Clyde said, slowly pulling away through the maze of vehicles scattered along the street.

I scanned the area to see where Ty might be, but I didn't find him.

Clyde slid into the parking lot of the fire barn. While he parked the van by the door to unload it, I scooted in. I noticed that a couple of ladies had tables and chairs set up, and not much more. At least there was heat. They turned toward me and smiled. I smiled back.

"I'm Trixie Matkowski, the new owner of the Silver Bullet Diner and cottages. I have a van loaded with coffee and food for the workers. Deputy McCoy said that I could set it up here."

"How wonderful of you, Trixie! We've passed the word for donations, but it'll take a while for things to come in." She offered her hand. "I'm May Sandler, and this is my sister, June Burke."

May and June. I'd try to remember that.

They slipped into their jackets, and we all went to unload the van. Clyde met us at the door with the coffee urn and deposited it on one of the tables.

The three of us worked together, unpacking the sandwiches and putting them in a fairly empty refrigerator while Clyde ate snowballs like popcorn. We were soon ready for anyone who needed warmth and food.

Men and women came and went, getting equipment and using the restroom. They snatched cups of coffee and stuffed cookies and sandwiches into their pockets. "Thanks," they mumbled, hustling back out the door.

As I ate a tuna fish sandwich and washed it

down with coffee, I got to know May and June. I learned that they were both retired teachers from the Sandy Harbor Grammar School, and that they had heard that Marvin P. Cogswell had died in my kitchen.

It was then that I noticed that they hadn't eaten anything, not even one snowball. Nor had they drunk even a sip of coffee.

"Ladies, I didn't do it. I didn't know him. Please believe me." I took a deep breath. "At least have a cinnamon bun. I didn't make them. Cindy Sherlock made them. She's my new cook at the Silver Bullet."

"Oh, I taught little Cindy Sherlock in fourth grade. What a good student she was." June patted her tightly curled hair. Not a curl was out of place and it looked like a helmet, but she fussed like it was sliding off her head. Maybe it was a wig.

"Well, you don't seem like a killer, Trixie," May said.

"I agree." June nodded. "And I think I'll have a cup of coffee and a cinnamon bun. Sister?"

"I think I'll have the same."

More time passed and donations came in: a cake, a platter of crackers and cheese, another chef salad, four sheet pizzas from the Gas and Grab on the corner of Main and Route 3, and several cases of soda.

And then Roberta Cummings walked in carrying boxes of doughnuts.

She stopped in her tracks when she saw me, and her jaw dropped open. I held my breath. I wasn't in the mood to defend myself any more, and I was feeling like a pariah in my new town.

And I hadn't poisoned her boyfriend.

Her eyes narrowed into slits. This wasn't a good sign. "What are *you* doing here?" she bellowed, moving toward me.

"Now, Roberta," June said. "Trixie is here to help. She brought a lot of food and sweets. Let's all get along and play nice."

I felt like I was back in fourth grade, but I extended my hand. "I'd like to again express my condolences, Miss Cummings."

Roberta dropped the boxes of doughnuts on the table.

"I said that I was going to put you out of business, and I meant it," she said, hands on hips.

I wanted to say that she'd nearly succeeded in doing that, but I didn't want to give her the satisfaction.

"Miss Cummings, I doubt that we'll ever be friends," I began. "But let's just call a truce for the time being, considering the circumstances that brought us all here. Agreed?"

Gee, that was a terrific speech, but it didn't have much of an effect on Roberta.

"No one deserves to be poisoned in a sleazy, filthy, two-bit diner," she hissed.

"Miss Cummings, that's enough!" I spewed. "If you can't be civil, then just . . . shut up!"

Whew! That felt good.

Just then, a crowd filed through the doors, and the two sisters—who seemed a little shaken by my exchange with Roberta—and I manned the tables of food, refilling whatever was needed and making more coffee.

Just as Roberta stomped into the kitchen, Ty Brisco walked into the room. I watched him slip out of his bright yellow raincoat and hang it on a peg by the door. He was wearing a blue plaid flannel shirt, perfectly faded jeans, and black rubber rain boots that almost reached his knees.

I told myself that I was glad to see him just because he was a friendly face in the crowd. At least there was one person who thought that I didn't kill Cogswell.

He was surrounded by a group of men, but he managed to wave to me as he was pulling off big black gloves. I walked over and handed him a cup of coffee, black.

"You're a lifesaver," he said, inhaling the coffee's scent, then taking a couple of sips. His eyes closed as he let the hot liquid warm him.

"Ty, how about a ham and cheese on rye? Or pizza?" I turned to the men who arrived with him. They stood together and looked like they were involved in a serious discussion. "Take a seat at one of the tables, and I'll serve you," I said to Ty and the group. "You all must be bone tired."

They nodded their appreciation and sat down together at a rectangular table. They looked weary and half frozen.

Grabbing a box lid to serve as a tray, I poured six coffees, grabbed handfuls of sugar packets and creamer, and dashed back to them. They expressed their gratitude and helped themselves. When I returned with assorted sandwiches, slices of pizza, and cookies, they lavished more praise because I was waiting on them.

A warm feeling came over me because I was helping in my own way, doing what I did best. After the verbal brawl with Roberta Cummings, I needed to channel my energy into something positive, and this was it.

"How is everyone who was at the Legion, Ty?" I asked.

"Everyone's out of the rubble and being checked at the hospital," he said. "Luckily, they were having their meeting away from the area of the major collapse. There were only a couple of minor cuts and scrapes from when they tried to dig out by themselves, without waiting. Oh, and I heard that Lori Davendorf has a broken arm." He explained further. "She tripped and fell over some debris."

"Thank goodness it wasn't worse," I said.

I felt a tug on my shirtsleeve and reluctantly turned away. It was Clyde, with powdered sugar on his upper lip from eating snowballs. "Trixie, the two sisters wonder if there are any more sandwiches." He shrugged. "They're all gone."

"Oh!" I pulled out my cell. "I'll call Cindy and ask her and Nancy to start making up another bunch. I think there are still a lot more volunteers who haven't come in yet."

"That's correct." Ty nodded. "And there are a lot of workers still at the Legion who are trying to shore up the place and drape some tarps, to prevent more water damage. They'll probably come in later."

It was getting dark outside. Not much more could be done unless there was lighting equipment. But this was a resourceful town; it was probably already there.

"Trixie?" Ty looked around the room and shook his head. "Did you do all this?"

The men at his table and others within hearing distance all looked up with interest.

"She sure did," said May, who happened to be walking by. "Trixie was the first to arrive with a van full of . . . just about everything."

"Not the pizza. That was from the Gas and Grab," clarified June. "But most everything else is from Trixie."

Ty stood, holding up his cup of coffee. Someone gave a shrill whistle, and the room became silent.

"For those of you who don't know me, my name is Ty Brisco. I beat Trixie Matkowski to Sandy Harbor by only a couple of months, but I'd like to offer a toast to her."

People in the room held up bottles, cups, and an assortment of cans.

"Thanks for everything that you did today, Trixie," Ty said. "And welcome to Sandy Harbor. We are grateful to you and happy to have you as a resident and as the new owner of the point."

There was an appreciative flutter that went through the room and some "To Trixie" shouts. Although somewhat embarrassed, I glanced at Ty in gratitude, and waved away the attention. He smiled in that little half grin that I'd come to like and his sky blue eyes twinkled. I knew that he was trying to help me out by trying to help erase the stigma of being a suspect.

That was nice of him.

Maybe Ty's generous toast would help business at the Silver Bullet.

My eyes focused on Roberta Cummings noisily stomping out of the room and yelling, "I can't believe you people. She murdered my Marvin!" before slamming the door.

Hmm . . . Then again, maybe business would remain the same.

Chapter 9

*T*here was dead silence, pardon the expression, in the room, and I wished someone would say something, anything. Then the twittering started.

Ty came to my rescue again, bless his cowboy twang. He raised his hand, indicating that he had more to say.

Another man in a heavy green parka and a black ski cap stood up and moved next to him, hand also raised. It was Mr. Farnsworth, the bait shop/grape lollipop guy. He looked different without his usual attire of a flannel shirt and jeans.

Ty and Mr. Farnsworth both waited until the crowd became silent again.

"As lead investigator, I'd like to remind everyone that the investigation into Mr. Cogswell's death is ongoing," Ty said. "And if anyone has any information, see me or one of the other deputies immediately. Until this case is resolved, please don't jump to conclusions."

Mr. Farnsworth cleared his throat. "And I've known Trixie Matkowski since she was knee-high to a grasshopper. You all know her as Stella and Porky's niece. She's been vacationing here at the point for most every summer at the cottages, and she's a good girl."

I hoped that one of the firemen would toss some water on my flaming cheeks.

Mr. Farnsworth rubbed his chin. "Trixie was just divorced, you know, and she might have jumped into the frying pan by buying everything from Stella, but she's trying her best. And now no one is coming into the Silver Bullet, due to this poisoning nonsense. So she's in a real jam."

Okay. That was enough. Pretty soon he was going to tell everyone that I was addicted to grape lollipops.

I had to end this, so I raised my hand to speak, and Mr. Farnsworth nodded at me.

"I'd just like to say a few words to clear the air," I said. "I know everyone is tired and eager to get home, but I just want to say that I hope that the mystery of Mr. Cogswell's death is solved soon, so we can all move on. And, second, I am looking forward to getting to know all of you and becoming a part of this community."

There was light applause; then it became louder. At least I wasn't going to be run out of town on a snowmobile tonight.

But I had to get away from the spotlight for a while and regroup. The answer came when I spotted a big plastic trash can. I could clean.

May, June, and I cleared off the tables and got everything ready for the next wave of workers. More individual donations came in, but I was surprised not to see anything from Brown's or even the Corner Restaurant, the place that belonged to the mayor.

Maybe they were busy.

No, they couldn't be. Most of the town was at the American Legion or here at the fire barn.

Clyde finally returned from the Silver Bullet with tons of sandwiches and a big pot of chili. Nancy and Cindy had done a great job.

"More people are walking across the street," Clyde said to me. "And they look hungry and tired."

"We got it covered," I said, nodding at May and June. Three other ladies, whose names escaped me at the moment, hurried behind the tables and began arranging the sandwiches.

Just when I thought no more drama could happen, Antoinette Chloe Brown floated in, wearing a muumuu covered in large red bird of paradise flowers. It was a foot short of meeting her Maine hunting boots. She wore a bright lime green rain slicker, and her hair had a cluster of matching silk bird of paradise flowers gathered over her left ear.

She was holding an aluminum pan and stood in the doorway, scanning the room.

"I have Brown's world-famous chicken wings, mild, and our homemade blue cheese dip," she announced. "I hope we're not too late, but we were so very, very busy. We just couldn't make it here until now. Right, Sal?" She looked at the man at her side. He wore the black leather of a biker, and I couldn't tell where his hair stopped and his moustache and beard began. He was big and heavy, and he had kind brown eyes.

He looked down at his wife adoringly, and I

had to smile. Love. He took the pan from her and made his way to the buffet table.

I walked toward her. "You're certainly not late, Mrs. Brown. There are more volunteers who have yet to come in."

Her thinly plucked eyebrows came together. "Do I know you?" Then she snapped her fingers. "Oh yes, Trixie. The owner of the Silver Bullet." She raised her voice. "Have you had much business, dear?"

Interesting that she should ask that.

"I'm doing okay. Thanks for asking, Mrs. Brown."

She put a hand on my arm, and I noticed red glitter nail polish. "Please call me Antoinette Chloe." She fluttered her eyelashes. "I use both names."

"Okay. Antoinette Chloe it is."

I made my way far, far away from her, and continued to pick up trash.

Ty was slipping into his yellow raincoat as I cleaned off his table, dropping everything into the trash can.

"We could have done that ourselves," he said.

"No problem," I said. "You're going back out there?"

He nodded. "Vern, Lou, and I will be working in shifts. We have to keep everyone away from there. It's an accident waiting to happen. Some of the guys think that more of the roof is going to fall, so everyone has to be careful when shutting off the furnace, the electrical, and even the plumbing.

I don't know exactly what's involved, but we have some people on board who do."

I smiled. "Be careful out there."

He tweaked his hat brim.

Oh my. I wished he'd stop doing that.

"How long are you going to be here?" he asked.

I shrugged. "I don't know. As long as I'm needed, I guess."

He turned to go, then looked back at me. I thought he was going to say something more, but he just shook his head and left.

Huh?

May and June left at midnight. Only Clyde and I were left at the fire barn, with a handful of food and a huge urn of coffee.

I didn't think that there was anything else I could do until the morning. Coffee was probably what was needed most about now, and I had everything laid out for easy service.

I hesitated to leave everything unlocked, but Clyde assured me that this was the norm. "Besides, no criminals worth their weight in salt would be out in this weather."

On the ride home in the van, Clyde was very quiet. He was kind of the quiet type anyway. That was why it surprised me when he suddenly blurted, "Don't pay any attention to Roberta Cummings."

"I'm sure she's just upset. She lost her fiancé. That's hard to handle."

"She shouldn't take it out on you."

I watched as the wipers, caked with ice and snow, streaked designs across the windshield. The squeak/clunk of them was the only sound in the cavernous vehicle.

"Did you know Marvin Cogswell?" I asked.

"Knew him. Didn't like him."

"Why not?" I pushed, hoping that he didn't clam up.

"I didn't like how he mooched meals at every place he inspected. If you didn't feed him, he always found something that wouldn't pass inspection."

"Did the Silver Bullet always feed him?" I asked.

"Every time."

"Then why did the Silver Bullet fail inspection the last time?"

"Juanita and Cogswell got into a fight. He made a dumb joke about her not having a green card. Something like that. It set her right off, and she 'forgot' to feed him." Clyde chuckled. "Then Cogswell failed the Silver Bullet. It was the first time in the history of the place."

"Really?" I grinned. I could just imagine Juanita yelling at him. "But I can't believe that my aunt and uncle would bribe the health inspector with meals throughout the years so he'd give the Silver Bullet a favorable inspection."

"Porky and Stella fed everyone—the delivery people, the Dumpster guys. . . . They fed anyone who looked like they needed a good meal. And they were always the first to give to the soup kitchen."

I smiled. That sounded like Porky and Stella. I'd continue their practice, too.

"Do you know Mark Cummings, Roberta's brother?"

"Went to high school with him. Now there's a strange duck."

I laughed. "Tell me more."

Clyde shrugged. "He's a loner. Kinda on the mean side, but he always stuck up for his sister. Always. She was kinda . . . unpopular in school. She was a looker, but she looked down on everyone. Called us woodchucks."

"Woodchucks?" That was a new one on me.

"Country hicks," he clarified. "Bumpkins."

I could understand how Roberta Cummings wouldn't be liked in high school and that she might need a protector.

If Roberta Cummings was being physically abused by Marvin Cogswell, would her brother, Mark, go so far as to poison him?

Mark might know Marvin's schedule. They frequented the same places at work. He could have slipped the poisoned mushrooms into Mr. Cogswell's meal.

My heart beat wildly in my chest. I couldn't wait to find out more information.

"You and Max and my uncle Porky go way back, don't you?"

"Years ago, we all worked in the boiler plant

together on Main Street. Then Porky met Stella, and they started the Silver Bullet. I remember the day when the diner was delivered. It rolled right down Main Street."

He glanced over at me. "The town gathered like it was a parade. Anyway, me and Max went to work for Porky and Stella when the plant closed."

It must be wonderful to have good friends— friends with whom you shared a history. Deputy Doug had been my best friend, or so I thought, but his betrayal had knocked the breath right out of me.

I had hoped that when I made Sandy Harbor my permanent residence, I'd be able to make friends in the community, but that was going to be difficult when everyone thought that I was a murderer.

"So tell me about Max," I said.

Clyde grunted. "Fisherman. Married. Three grown kids. Six grandkids that he never stops talking about."

"Does Max know Roberta and Mark and Marvin?"

"Yup."

"And?" I prompted.

He shrugged, and I knew that I wasn't going to get any more information from him. I'd have to ask Max myself.

As we pulled into the empty parking lot of the Silver Bullet, I remembered that I'd promised Juanita that I'd speak to Clyde and Max about their practical jokes.

"Clyde, there's something I have to know. On the day you and Max scared Juanita half to death, was there really a mouse in the kitchen?"

The laughter bubbled up inside of him, and it made me laugh, too. I needed that.

"What do you think, Trixie?"

"I think that you and Max just like to tease Juanita."

He turned to me and winked, and I knew that the mouse was just a pit stop on the long line of practical jokes that Juanita had to endure.

"I can't afford to lose a cook," I reminded him. "Go easy on her."

"Of course," he said, a twinkle in his eye.

It was then I realized that Clyde had a school-boy crush on Juanita. "Why don't you just ask her out instead of playing games like that?"

Another shrug. Clyde was a man of few words.

"I'll take care of unloading the van, Trixie. You go and take care of business," he said.

I opened the back door so Clyde could have easy access to the kitchen, and I went out front. Cindy and Nancy were having coffee and reading magazines. Max was sprawled across the front booth, snoring.

"Any customers?" I asked hopefully.

"Just someone asking directions. He got a cup of coffee to go."

Total income of the day: one dollar.

Total expenses: I couldn't even think about it.

Speaking of which, didn't I have to do the payroll?

"When's payday around here?" I asked.

"Today," Nancy said quickly.

"I'm so sorry!" And I was. Darn it, I've never felt so scattered in my life, and I didn't like it. I was anal, compulsive, a list maker, and I was organized.

This wasn't like me.

"I will immediately write you all a check." I yawned. If only I could stay awake long enough to write them. Since there was no money coming in, I was going to write them from my personal checking account. It would have to do for now. "Just get your time cards and write how much I owe you on it. Gross pay. That's what I'll write you a check for this time. I'll figure out the rest later."

Everyone made their way to the back, and I sat there alone in my diner, really feeling like I was in over my head. I'd felt it before, but now it was overwhelming.

Deciding that I had to snap out of my funk, I gathered up all my change and headed for the jukebox. It was made to look like an antique, and I just loved the colorful bubbles that gurgled through the arcing tubes, complete with glitter.

I emptied my change and bills into the machine and punched in the Beach Boys, Frankie Valli, some Motown, Frank Sinatra, Elvis, and lots of fifties tunes.

Taking out my checkbook from my purse, I poured myself a cup of coffee and slipped into a booth.

My staff filed out and gathered around me. "We don't feel right taking your money like this," Nancy said.

"Yeah," Cindy added.

Clyde and Max shuffled and didn't want to make eye contact with me.

"You all deserve to be paid. You did the work, so now let me pay you," I said, taking Nancy's time card from her hand. I quickly wrote her a check as Elvis sang about a hound dog.

Dog!

Blondie!

"Where's Blondie?" I asked, looking around.

Just then, I heard a whimper, and Blondie walked across the floor from the corner of the diner. She stretched, yawned, and wagged her tail at me.

She put her chin on my leg, and my heart melted. What a sweet puppy. I petted her soft blond head with one hand and wrote checks with the other.

Blondie's barking woke me up out of a sound sleep. I grabbed the nearest thing to me, a Bic pen, and was ready to ink someone to death.

I tried to get my bearings, noting that I was in a booth at the Silver Bullet. In front of me, the pastries, all aglow, were rotating in their refrigerated showcase. Judging by the stiffness in my neck and back, I had fallen asleep.

The intruder was Ty. His hat was off, his chestnut hair, with a glint of red, was sticking up like a brush cut, and he looked sexy as all hell.

Not that I was looking. Not that I cared.

He shed his yellow raincoat and tossed it on one of the stools at the counter.

"Can I get you some coffee?" I asked.

"If I have another cup of coffee, I'll float out of here." He slid onto the seat across from me and stared. "You look like roadkill, Trixie."

I could barely keep my head up, but I wasn't going to let his remark go by without comment. I knew I'd looked better than this lately. My blond hair needed a good cut and some gray coverage. I needed to find and unpack some of my better clothes, which were still in my boxes and bins. Primarily, I needed a sleep schedule.

"Why, Deputy Brisco," I said in my best Texas accent. "Is that how you charmed all the women at the Houston honky-tonks? You must have had those buckle bunnies hovering around you like planes over O'Hare."

He grinned. "Good one, but your accent needs more work. Sounds more like . . . uh . . . Pennsylvania, or maybe Transylvania."

I stood up and got some ice water. I downed it in seconds, then poured another and took it over to the table. "I am totally pooped. I don't even know what day it is."

"Early Sunday morning, I think." His gaze followed Blondie. "I think she has to go out."

"I'll do it. I'm standing." Blondie followed me to the kitchen. I planned on letting her out the famous back door, the place where we'd found her. I looked back at Ty. He was slumped in the booth, his neck leaning on the back of the red vinyl of the bench seat. "Can I get you anything, Ty?"

"No, but thanks."

As I waited for Blondie to do her business, I stared at myself in the reflection of the glass. I did look like roadkill. My eyes were slits, my face was puffy, and my neck looked like a turkey's waddle.

Well, what did Deputy Cowboy expect? This had been a very long day.

Blondie barked at the door, and I let her back into the kitchen.

"What do you have there, Blondie?" I bent over to see what she had in her mouth. Whatever it was, she was proud of it. Please, not an animal!

Blondie pranced around the kitchen with it in her mouth. I followed at a safe distance, calling her name.

Finally, she stopped and came over to me. It was a piece of floral fabric. And I'd seen that kind of pattern before.

Blondie dropped the material at my feet. I picked it up, soggy and dirty. I pressed it flat. A white gardenia.

Antoinette Chloe Brown's muumuu!

But how did this piece of her dress get here?

I grabbed a flashlight and headed back outside. I ran the light over everything for several minutes, looking for more material. Then I found it. The corner of the Dumpster had a bolt-type thing sticking up. There were several threads sticking out from the bolt, with the same kind of white-green color.

This had to be another clue!

Antoinette Chloe Brown must have been in the back of my diner—maybe she was spying on Marvin P. Cogswell, waiting for the opportunity to poison him. She had to have been hiding by the Dumpster, looking into the window, and her muu-muu got snagged.

I should tell Ty!

Could he get into her house, check her muu-muu collection, and see if her gardenia dress was damaged?

If he didn't or couldn't, I would!

But first, I was going to cook Blondie up a steak for her excellent investigative work.

Chapter 10

"That sure smells good, Trixie," Ty said, walking into the kitchen. "Steak?"

I chuckled. "It's for Blondie, but I'd be happy to put one on for you."

"No, thanks. I'm too tired to chew." He leaned against the steam table. "What did Blondie do to deserve such an honor?"

I showed him the scrap of gardenia material. "What does this look like to you?"

He took the small uneven rectangle and shrugged. "Fabric?"

"Exactly!" I punched the air. "And who wears fabric like this?"

"I don't know, but I think you're going to tell me."

"Antoinette Chloe Brown!" I waited for his reaction, but I could have been waiting until the salmon ran before he responded.

"Ty, she wears those flowing muumuus with the tropical prints. She has a gardenia one, and a bird of paradise one, and probably more, too."

None of that seemed to hold any weight with him.

"And where did you find this?" he asked, staring at the fabric.

"Blondie found it. I think Antoinette Chloe was hiding by my Dumpster out back, waiting for an opportunity to poison Mr. Cogswell. I found threads caught on a bolt. That's probably where Blondie found this material."

"But you don't know for sure," Ty said.

"No, but—"

"And why would she be hiding by your Dumpster?"

"To wait for Juanita to be distracted," I said. "And she was. Remember? Roberta called her to the front of the diner to return Juanita's cell phone. So, when Juanita was out front, Antoinette Chloe Brown slipped the poison mushrooms into Mr. Cogswell's pork and scalloped potatoes."

He stared at me, expressionless.

Why wasn't he following this?

"Okay. Okay." He rubbed his eyes. "What's her motive for killing Mr. Cogswell?"

"Um . . . uh . . . I don't know. I haven't gotten that far yet."

"Okay." He handed the scrap of material back to me.

"Don't you want to test the threads hanging from the Dumpster to see if they match the material?" I asked.

"Remind me, and I'll bag it all up tomorrow and send it to the state police lab."

His enthusiasm was underwhelming. Maybe he was just too tired to appreciate the brilliance of my discovery.

I cut up Blondie's steak and put it onto an aluminum pie tin, then popped it into the freezer to cool for a few minutes. I then lowered the pan and watched her lap up the steak. At least Blondie was appreciative. It was gone in seconds.

"You know, Ty. I think that a lot of people have motives to get rid of Marvin Cogswell."

"Oh yeah? Tell me."

"I've also discovered that Mark Cummings is very protective of Roberta," I said to Ty, "and he probably didn't like it that Marvin physically abused her. I also found out that it was a woman who phoned in the mushroom order to Sunshine Food Supply. I think it was Antoinette Chloe Brown who called it in."

"Why her?"

"Because I think she likes being the Queen of Sandy Harbor with all the business at her restaurant, and because it would look like I was lying about the Silver Bullet never having mushrooms in the place."

"All good information," he said, "but I'm not quite ready to rope that steer."

"Nice cowboy rhetoric, but I'm going to need a translation."

"You're just guessing."

"So what do I do now, Ty?"

He shook his head. "You do nothing. I'm in charge of this investigation." He snapped his fingers for Blondie, and the dog walked to his side and waited.

Yeah, I knew that he didn't want me involved in his investigation, but I couldn't wait forever for this case to be solved. "Good night, Ty," I said, walking toward the double doors to go into the kitchen.

"Aren't you going home?" he asked.

"Can't," I said. "We're open twenty-four hours. You must have missed the red neon sign on the top of the diner." I grinned and pushed through the doors to the front. "Time to make another pot of coffee, strong."

"I can't leave you here," he said, following me.

"Yes, you can. Go home."

"Dammit, Trixie, there's a murderer on the loose. And it's two o'clock in the morning! Why don't you just close the place?"

"I can't, Ty. I just can't. The Silver Bullet has never closed, not since Porky and Stella bought it and had it towed here."

"So you're going to wait in a booth overnight, hoping for a customer?" He shook his head.

"I'm the owner now. It's what I'm going to do." I plopped my tired, ample butt into the front booth. I positioned my coffee to my right and my notebook in front of me. I had a lot of lists to write, and I also wanted to write some notes about what I'd discovered so far concerning Mr. Cogswell's death.

I slipped the piece of material into my notebook. That was my biggest clue, and Ty hadn't paid it much attention.

"What if I leave Blondie here to keep you company?"

"I'd like that."

"Stay with Trixie," he instructed the dog. "Stay." Blondie looked from Ty to me, and then collapsed in a half circle on the floor, her chin resting on her paws. Poor Blondie was tired, too.

"Call me if you need me." He took a deep breath and let it out. "I mean it, Trixie."

I was flattered, but I realized that his concern was just the law enforcement part of him. You know: to serve and protect. It was the protection part that was rearing up.

"Ty, I'm fine. Go already. Go!"

Finally, he left. I could picture him walking down the front stairs and crossing in front of the boat launch to the bait shop. Then he'd walk up the outside stairs and open the door to his room above the shop.

At least there was another person nearby.

I stared at the dessert carousel again. Everything was going to go stale if I didn't get more customers in here.

I thought about Uncle Porky. I could feel his jovial presence in the diner, talking to everyone, joking with his old pals. I could picture him grabbing Aunt Stella in a big bear hug and planting a noisy kiss on her lips. He was rarely seen without his white chef's apron and floppy white cap.

And darn, the man could cook.

I'd follow him around like a puppy every rainy day during the summer when I was a little kid, and whenever I'd ask to help him, he'd wrap a bright, white apron around me, find me a floppy hat, and we'd cook orders together for the diner.

Uncle Porky would give his last dollar to anyone who needed it. He was always throwing benefits for someone who was sick, or for the library, or for anything and everything for kids—probably because he never had any of his own.

A tear slid down my cheek. I felt like I was failing him, failing to keep his legacy. I had to solve this murder to save his legacy.

An hour went by and then lights flashed across the diner. For a second I thought it was Uncle Porky sending me a message. But it was a car pulling in. A customer!

I quickly cleaned up my booth and stuffed my notebook back into my purse. I tried to look nonchalant and less like a piranha waiting for prey.

Someone rolling in at two in the morning might want some serious food. Nah, probably not. Probably just coffee. Maybe a cinnamon bun.

I rearranged the buns to show them off.

The bells above the door jingled, and in walked . . . Mayor Tingsley.

"I didn't think you'd be open," he said, looking around at the empty diner.

"Twenty-four hours, seven days a week. We are open even on Christmas, in case someone needs a place to go. They are welcome at the Silver Bullet."

This was Uncle Porky's usual speech, and I knew that he never charged anyone for their meal on Christmas Day. I was planning on continuing that tradition.

I sure was channeling him tonight.

"What can I get you, Mayor?"

"I'd like to remind you about my offer for the Silver Bullet, the cottages, the boat launch, and the farmhouse. The whole point. Two million bucks. Cash."

I stepped back. He sure cut to the chase. "Can I get you a cup of coffee?"

"That depends."

"On what?"

"If you're going to jerk me around or not."

I poured him a cup of coffee anyway and slid it in front of him at the counter. "Mr. Mayor, it's been a long day. I'm dead tired. I don't even know my own name about now. It's not a good time."

"Just remember these words: two million bucks."

"I remember them from when you made an offer to me before." My head was pounding, and I was getting cranky. "What, no flowers this time?"

"Laura and I want this place, and we usually get what we want."

Isn't that special?

"The poisoning of the health inspector in your kitchen has turned this diner into a ghost town," he said.

I wished people would quit reminding me of that.

I remained silent, but I wanted to toss the pompous jerk into the nearest snowbank.

"I can either buy it from you now or when it goes up for auction." He sniffed. "Obviously, you're going to go under."

"I don't think it's all that obvious, at least not to me. The season hasn't even started yet."

"It's the diner that keeps this place afloat. Ask Stella."

He took a big gulp of coffee and grunted. I should have told him that it was flaming hot, but he seemed to know just about everything.

"Where is Stella anyway?"

I didn't want her involved in this. I was the owner. "She's incommunicado."

"Where's that?" he asked.

I bit back a grin. "Italy."

"Oh."

He slammed back the rest of his coffee and winced. "Terrible coffee." Reaching into his pocket, he pulled out a business card and tossed it on the counter in front of me. Then he was gone. He didn't even offer to pay for the coffee.

I would have charged him for it, too, just because he was an ass.

I read his card: RICK TINGSLEY, REAL ESTATE AND INVESTMENTS. MAYOR OF SANDY HARBOR, NEW YORK, SALMON CAPITAL OF THE WORLD.

Did Mayor Tingsley want the point so badly that he'd try to put me out of business? Would he go so far as to kill Mr. Cogswell? Maybe he had something against Mr. Cogswell.

I returned to my favorite booth, got out my notebook, wrote his name down, and circled it.

Mayor Tingsley had a motive. He wanted the Sandy Harbor Guest Cottages and the Silver Bullet Diner. He wanted my Victorian house.

He wanted my memories.

Well, he could just forget it.

I was here, and I wasn't moving. I'd just moved, and I had the unpacked boxes, bags, and plastic bins to prove it!

I stared at his business card. He probably wanted to develop the property. Condos and private boat slips? Something like that.

A lot of family resort places were selling out to developers. Given the choice, wouldn't a kid opt to hit a famous resort with thrill rides and high-tech whatnot rather than camp with his family in a sleepy cottage colony that didn't even have cable TV?

I must have fallen asleep, because the next thing I knew, Juanita was calling my name.

"Trixie? Trixie, wake up. Go home."

She nudged my shoulder, and I reluctantly tucked away my dream of a full diner and children making sand castles and mud pies on the beach.

I opened my eyes. Ick. Instant headache. I tried to stand, but every bone in my body was sore and stiff.

"You look like something that the dog dragged in," Juanita said.

The dog did drag in something last night. I scooped up my notebook with the gardenia material tucked inside. As soon as I saw Ty, I'd remind him to get the threads from the Dumpster and send everything to the state police lab.

How could I get into Antoinette Chloe Brown's

house to see if she had a piece missing from her gardenia muumuu?

It was just too early in the morning for my brain to be swirling like it was. I fished in my purse for some aspirin.

"Juanita, I'm going to go home, take a shower, and crash for a while. Can you take care of things here?"

"Of course," she said, looking at me like I had the impression of the spiral metal of my notebook tattooed on my face. Feeling my cheek, I realized that I did.

I gathered up all my things, stuffed myself into my coat, laced up my boots, and headed out the front door. Blondie followed me, taking care of her business on a snow-covered dip in the lawn. I made a mental note of the location. Not that I was going to clean it up—hell no!—but I'd tell Ty. He could pick it up.

It was seven-something in the morning, and a strange foreign object was beginning to light up the sky. Could that actually be the sun?

And then I stopped crunching on the snow to hear . . . what? Was that actually a bird chirping?

I didn't hear it again, and I decided that the noise must have been me, wheezing from exertion.

My shower felt heavenly. So did the big springy bed when I burrowed under the fluffy comforter, wet hair and all. Blondie curled up on the braided rug next to the bed.

My body was exhausted, but I couldn't get my brain to shut down.

I kept thinking of tropical flowers, dancing mushrooms, Roberta Cummings storming out of the fire hall, her scarecrow of a brother making deliveries to all the local restaurants, and the late health inspector, Mr. Cogswell the Third.

Who would want him killed? And why?

I thought of Mayor Tingsley's offer to buy everything, and how I'd never sell to him. Not even for millions.

And then it hit me. No, it wasn't a breakthrough on the case, or a clue that dropped from the sky— it was that I'd forgotten to eat the piece of Wacky Cake from Juanita.

That wasn't like me.

The cake was calling to me more than the mystery, so I finally gave in and went downstairs. I got the cake from the counter and sat down at the kitchen table, ready to indulge.

Blondie stretched across my bare feet, keeping them warm.

This was living!

Just as I looked lovingly at the moist cake, the doorbell rang.

Wacky Cakeus interruptus!

Blondie was on full alert, which meant her ears were up. If it was an intruder, she'd probably lick him to death.

But it was Ty Brisco, complete with a white cowboy hat, mirrored sunglasses (the foreign object was still bright in the sky), jeans faded to perfection, and his snake cowboy boots.

I had bare feet and wore a ratty chenille, snap-up bathrobe over a Mickey Mouse nightshirt. My reflection in the window of the door showed lumpy, still-damp hair, and puffy eyes.

What did I care? I wasn't trying to impress Ty Brisco or any man, but I didn't want to scare the stuffing out of anyone either.

I opened the door and motioned for him to come in.

"Are you okay?" he asked, raising an eyebrow or two at my hair.

"Just cranky because I'm dying to eat the cake I got from Juanita."

He grinned. "Don't let me stop you." He sniffed the air. "Is that coffee I smell?"

"You know darn well that I don't have coffee on, Wyatt Earp, but I can take a hint. Come in the kitchen. And don't worry about taking off your boots."

My floor was a mess anyway. I still hadn't cleaned up from the impromptu visit from Mayor Tingsley a few days ago.

I got the coffee started and took a seat across from Ty at the kitchen table. He was rubbing Blondie's tummy. She was lying on her back, legs spread apart. If a dog could actually smile, she was smiling.

Ty pointed at the cake. "Don't let me stop you."

"Oh, I won't." I finally, finally took a bite. Heavenly. "What brings you here?"

"You didn't get much sleep, did you?" he asked.

"I dozed in the booth."

"What did our esteemed mayor want?" he asked, his voice heavy with sarcasm.

"You saw?"

"I noticed his car pull in. It was pretty late for him to be paying a social call. I got dressed, started downstairs, but then I noticed that he was driving away."

"How come you decided to come to the diner?"

"Something just didn't sit right with me."

I liked the fact that Ty was looking out for me. It wasn't necessary, but I liked it anyway.

"So, what did Mayor Tingsley want?" he asked again.

"He offered me two million bucks for everything."

Ty whistled, long and low. "That's a lot of meat loaf specials."

"Sure is. I really didn't answer him, but I'll turn him down. He's not family. Aunt Stella wouldn't like it. She offered the place to me, Ty, and I believe that she turned the mayor down before. And probably the Browns, too, but I don't know for sure."

I took another bite of the cake, and then I decided that I was being impolite. "Can I make you something to eat? Eggs or something?"

Notice that I didn't offer him a piece of cake.

"I ate at the diner. Juanita can make a mean western omelet."

"Any other customers there?" I don't know

why I asked. I could just look out the window at the parking lot.

He shook his head.

"We have to solve this mystery, Ty. I'm going to go bankrupt."

He pulled a plastic bag out of his pocket and set it in front of me. "I took these fibers from a metallic protrusion located on the southwest corner of your trash receptacle."

Cop talk: the art of being verbose.

"I thought you blew off my 'Antoinette Chloe Brown hiding by the Dumpster waiting to poison Mr. Cogswell when Juanita turned her back' theory."

"After sleeping on it, I think your theory might be worth looking into."

"Good!" I cleaned up every crumb of the Wacky Cake and got up to pour him a cup of coffee.

"Where's that piece of material with the flower on it?"

"Hang on."

I set a mug of coffee in front of him, got my notebook, and handed him the fabric. "Gardenia."

"Whatever you say."

"Can you search Antoinette Chloe Brown's closet?" I asked.

He shook his head. "I don't know if I'd ever get a warrant. What would I tell the judge? That she wears muumuus?"

"Yes!"

"Probably more than half of the women in this county wear muumuus."

"Or caftans."

"What's the difference?" he asked.

"Not much." I don't know why I brought up the caftan vs. muumuu debate in the first place.

"I need more, Trixie. But in the meantime, I could get this to the lab and at least get a positive match."

"Good." And I was going to add Antoinette Chloe Brown to my list of suspects in my trusty notebook.

But the list was ever-growing. I think I had just about all the population of Sandy Harbor listed in it. It might have been easier just to use the phone book.

"Ty, what could Antoinette Chloe Brown's motivation be for killing Mr. Cogswell?" I asked, flipping my notebook open to a new page. "To put me out of business and increase hers?"

He sighed. "You're not going to quit investigating, are you?"

"No," I said, meeting the glare of his eyes. "Can't we just share information? Maybe I can help you. Heaven knows, I have time on my hands."

He still didn't agree to my helping him, but he said, "I'd have to do some checking for sure, but you're right. I've noticed that Brown's Four Corners Restaurant has been hopping since the poisoning."

I nodded. "So has the Crossroads Restaurant, Mayor Tingsley's place."

"And the mayor made you an offer. I wonder if

he made the same offer to Stella. If he bought you out, there'd be one less restaurant to compete with, or he could make more money with two."

"Aunt Stella was vague when we were talking about it. She just said that two people were interested, but they weren't family, so she wouldn't sell to them."

"Wish you could get in touch with her," Ty said. "But it's a good guess that the two are the Browns and the Tingsleys."

"I probably could if I tried, but I don't want to, Ty. Let her have fun. She needs it, especially after she lost Uncle Porky. I can handle this."

Yeah, sure I can. And I'm doing such a great job of it.

It was then I decided that I was going to get into Antoinette Chloe Brown's house and somehow see her muumuu collection.

And see if a chunk of material was missing from the gardenia one.

But first, I had to get rid of Wyatt Earp. He'd never agree to my searching her closets.

"Ty, I hate to give you and Blondie the bum's rush out of here, but I sure could use more sleep."

"I have to get going anyway." He drained his coffee. "I'm heading over to the American Legion, or what's left of it." He snapped his fingers. "Which is another reason why I'm here. Seems like the commander of the Legion, John Nunnamaker, and the Ladies Auxiliary have some meetings scheduled, and they can't use the Legion Hall. I suggested that they could meet in the Silver Bullet. Hope you don't mind."

"Ty, that'd be great!" Finally, people in the diner.

"There will be a lot of meetings because now they have to plan some fund-raisers for a new roof. I think they have a high deductible."

"I don't care how many times they need to meet. They can use the back corner with all the tables. It's more conducive to meetings than the booths." My mind was whirling already. I'd have a big pot of coffee ready for them, and maybe Cindy could make her cinnamon rolls, and . . .

"Good. I'll let John Nunnamaker know."

"Thanks for suggesting the Silver Bullet, Ty." A wet wool blanket of guilt settled over me. Ty was wonderful and considerate for steering business my way, and I was going to sneak behind his back and search Antoinette Chloe Brown's closet.

I walked him to the door. "Get some sleep," he said.

I pretended to stifle a yawn. Not my best performance.

He tweaked the brim of his hat and headed for his black SUV. I took a quick power nap on the couch, then zoomed up the stairs to get dressed to pay a visit to Antoinette Chloe Brown and her muumuu collection.

Chapter 11

A half hour later, I was in my car armed with several banana nut breads, courtesy of Juanita. Juanita was killing time baking. She didn't like Sunshine baked goods any more than I did, and we had a lot of produce to use before it spoiled.

I had to find the time to visit Mrs. Stolfus.

I dropped six banana breads off at the fire hall for today's volunteers and headed for Brown's Four Corners Restaurant with the seventh.

I didn't have a clue where the Browns lived, but I was going to find out.

I made my way through the throng of people waiting to get into the restaurant. There was still a cloud of smoke hanging in the air, the windows were still dirty, and the food being delivered was plentiful, but it looked like nothing special.

The Silver Bullet was so much better than this place.

I smiled at the young girl with the moussed crown of hair behind the scratched black podium.

"Is Mrs. Brown here today?" I asked. "I have a meeting with her, but I can't remember if we planned to meet here or at her house."

"She doesn't come in until dinner today."

"Then our meeting must be at her house." I looked confused. "Hers is the big white house on Pine Street?"

"No. The Browns live on Sycamore. Yellow house with lavender shutters."

"Of course. Thank you very much."

That was easy. I made my way back through the crowd, got into my car, and drove to Sycamore Street. It was a left turn by the small movie theater, the Bijou, which I remembered fondly.

I noticed that they were playing *Gone with the Wind*. Yup, that was what they were playing the last time I'd driven by here some ten years ago.

The bright yellow house with the lavender shutters was easy to find, but the lime green and fuchsia touches were a surprise. The whole house was as ostentatious as the owner herself, and it stuck out like a tie-dyed T-shirt in a neighborhood of pastel blouses.

A white van was in the driveway, with fancy red letters painted on that proclaimed BROWN'S FOUR CORNERS RESTAURANT. EAT IN, TAKE OUT, CATERING. YOU'LL LOVE OUR WINGS.

I pulled in behind the van and took a deep breath; then, armed with banana bread, I climbed the stairs and rang the bell.

Out of the corner of my eye, I saw the lace curtains of the side window move. After a few moments, Antoinette Chloe Brown herself opened the door.

She wore a muumuu covered in hibiscus flowers that billowed like a curtain in the early-morning breeze. I expected her to take off like a hot air balloon any second.

"Hello, Antoinette Chloe! I'm sorry to surprise you, but I was in the neighborhood and I wanted to drop by since we are both women in business." I thought that the latter was a good hook. "I hope I'm not bothering you, but I'd like to get to know you, since I'm new to the community and new to the restaurant business. Maybe you'd even let me pick your brain. Your restaurant is such a success."

She stood for a while, billowing, but then finally opened the door wider and motioned for me to come in.

Looking down her nose at me, she finally said, "And you are?"

She obviously had no short-term memory. "Trixie Matkowski. I bought the Silver Bullet from my aunt Stella and uncle Porky. And although I'm a new permanent resident in Sandy Harbor, I've been coming here most every summer since I was a kid."

"Oh yes. I remember you. I'll make some tea," she said.

She left me standing in the entranceway like one of her green plastic plants next to me. I looked up the dark wooden staircase and wondered how I'd get into her closet.

"What a beautiful, historic house. I just love houses like this!" I said loudly. "May I look around?"

"Suit yourself," was the answer from somewhere in the back of the house. She didn't seem glad to see me, but I did drop in unexpectedly. I slid off my boots and draped my coat over a chair by the door, since she hadn't asked to take it.

I just couldn't wander upstairs, could I? I settled for walking through her two parlors, all loaded to the gills with Madame Alexander dolls, glass, china, and swags of plastic and silk flowers. Everything was coated with two inches of dust. She had a fainting couch with a cabbage rose print and tassels, and furniture that matched. There were tassels hanging from the curtains, the lamps, and from doilies. There were more tassels in that room than at a strip bar.

Antoinette Chloe appeared at my side. "Would you be more comfortable in the kitchen?" She eyed the banana bread that I was holding like a football.

I handed it to her. "Banana bread. It's still warm."

"I'll slice it up."

That sounded a bit ominous. "Antoinette Chloe, do you mind if I look around upstairs? I just love your house."

She looked at me suspiciously.

"Old houses are really my thing. That's one of the reasons I love my aunt Stella's house. There are so many nooks and crannies in the old place. I haven't even begun to explore it. Would you mind me looking?"

I could tell that she was going to say no. But I had another brilliant idea.

"The Sandy Harbor Historical Society is in the

planning stages of a tour of the old houses in Sandy Harbor—you know, as a fund-raiser. And I think that your house would be the highlight of the tour, if you were willing to open your doors."

Her green eyes sparkled for a brief second, then narrowed. "I'm in the historical society, and this is the first time I've heard of such a tour."

Oops. "Well, it's totally in the planning stages. Very hush-hush." I lowered my voice. "You know how it is in a small town."

"Oh, I do." She put the banana bread on a dusty round table and raised her muumuu, showing me red flip-flops. She walked up two stairs and then turned to me. "You'll love the second floor. I even have a third floor."

"No!" I proclaimed.

She nodded, and I thought that the white turban on her head would fall off. She tugged it back into place.

When we got to the top of the stairs, she showed me three bedrooms, all equally gaudy and equally dusty. I sneezed into my sleeve.

Finally, we got to her bedroom, which had a queen-sized sleigh bed piled high with pillows and stuffed animals. There wasn't a square inch of wall that didn't have a hat hanging from it. Straw bonnets, felt hats, hats with netting, turbans— there was even a sombrero.

I didn't see a closet. It must be camouflaged by all the hats.

"There's never enough closet space in these old houses. Don't you agree, Antoinette Chloe?"

She headed for a black mantilla. Under it was a doorknob.

"Look, a walk-in closet," she announced. "I have a lot of closet space."

"The committee will be astonished."

She pulled a cord, and a bare lightbulb lit up her wardrobe, which I can only describe as a floral explosion. I quickly scanned the hangers for a gardenia muumuu.

She exited the closet. There was not enough time!

"Oh, Antoinette Chloe! Did I hear your teapot whistling?" I was brilliant. "Go ahead and tend to it. Don't worry, I'll shut your closet light off."

She took off, her muumuu floating around her. Nice exit.

And she'd left me in her closet. Alone.

I zipped through the rack like it was a sale at Walmart. But the muumuu wasn't there. Darn. Then something made me look at the floor. There it was, surrounded by flip-flops of all colors, the gardenia muumuu.

Picking it up, I quickly scanned it. Yes, it had a chunk missing, and it matched the piece of material that Blondie had found.

Now what was I supposed to do?

I wadded up the muumuu and tried to stuff it in my purse. No chance. Why didn't I bring a bigger purse?

I put it back where I'd found it. Maybe Ty could get a warrant after all.

I shut off the light and closed the door behind

me just as I saw Antoinette Chloe Brown standing in the doorway. Her arms were crossed in front of her, and she looked down her nose at me.

Had she seen me looking at the muumuu? Yikes!

I smiled, trying to appear casual, but my heart was thumping wildly and my face was on fire. I was sure I looked guilty, for heaven's sake.

"Let's talk about our restaurants." I took her arm, and we went downstairs.

"What about the tour of homes?" she asked eagerly.

"I am going to definitely recommend your home."

"You are?"

"Oh, absolutely."

Antoinette Chloe Brown was putty in my hands after that. Over tea and banana bread, she told me her life story and how she met her husband, Sal, in high school, and how she wanted to build a year-round ice-cream parlor onto Brown's.

Now, I like ice cream more than anyone, but I doubt that I'd make a special trip to an ice-cream parlor in the middle of winter.

She leaned over and whispered as if telling me a grand secret. "And the fact that the health inspector was poisoned in the Silver Bullet did a world of good for Brown's Four Corners Restaurant. We've never been so busy! It was heaven-sent for my restaurant."

Hell-o? Would she want the business enough to sabotage me?

She driveled on. "And Sal said that we are making oodles of money."

"Oodles is good." I nodded. I needed some oodles.

"And the Ladies of the Lake asked me to be the chairwoman of their annual lawn party and fundraiser for town beautification. They said I was the perfect choice for chairwoman, being such a successful businesswoman." She actually giggled. "I've been waiting for them to ask me for years. It's quite the honor, you know. Only the most prominent women in Sandy Harbor are asked."

I raised my flowered teacup in a toast to her. "Good for you, Antoinette Chloe." Dabbing at the corners of my mouth, I smiled at her. "And since we are both businesswomen, maybe we can help each other out—or at least you could help *me*. I'm pretty new to the diner business, and you have a lot of experience."

I wanted to leave the door open to talk to her at a later date. She nodded like a bobblehead, and her turban shifted over her left ear. Copper-colored hair with four-inch gray roots made an appearance. She truly needed a trip to the beauty parlor, as did I. Pushing the turban back to center, she tugged it over her ears.

"I'm noted for my Hawaiian muumuus," she said, lifting her chin and stretching out her arms as if posing for Muumuus "R" Us.

"Not to change the subject, Antoinette Chloe, but I haven't seen you at the Silver Bullet lately. When was the last time you paid a visit?" I wanted to place her at the scene, I thought, feeling like a faux investigator on TV.

Her mouth moved, but no words came out. She finally blurted, "I've been quite busy."

"Oh, but I thought you might have come to visit the diner, maybe welcome me to Sandy Harbor."

"Forgive me for not welcoming you. Like I said, I've been very busy. You should have come into *my* restaurant. I would have welcomed you with a free dinner!"

I waved away her apology. "I did visit your restaurant. Remember? But you were very busy, and then I left when you brought up the poisoning incident for all to hear. It was very upsetting."

She squirmed in her chair, and part of me was glad. Now it was time for me to exit.

I stood. "I'm so glad that we got to know each other. And thank you for your hospitality. I'll surely recommend that your house be on the tour."

"I just don't understand why I haven't heard of this tour. The historical society—"

I put my index finger over my lips. "Don't breathe a word! Things are strictly hush-hush at this time."

"Yes. Hush-hush." She copied my gesture, and I tried not to laugh. "My lips are sealed."

"See you soon, Antoinette Chloe."

I hurried down her lavender stairs and was soon on my way.

Since I was downtown, I should do something— anything. But what?

I headed to the fire barn. Maybe I could do something to help today.

As I drove, I thought about what I had discovered about Antoinette Chloe Brown. She'd been hanging around the Dumpster at the back of my diner. The chunk of material proved it. And she was obviously uncomfortable when I asked her if she'd been to the diner lately.

So what did it all mean?

My stomach took a dive. How would I confirm that Antoinette Chloe was peeking around my Dumpster, lying in wait for Marvin P. Cogswell on the day that he died?

I slapped my forehead. I had forgotten to look for poisoned mushrooms in her home! I was even in her kitchen, if that was where mushroom poisoners kept the tools of their trade.

What kind of detective was I?

A pathetic one.

For heaven's sake, I was a tourist information guide in Philly. What did I know about being a detective?

I thought about getting a *How to Be a Detective* book from the library. It might help me with my investigation. It certainly wouldn't hurt.

First, I decided to call Juanita at the Silver Bullet. She was full of news: Yes, she could handle things. Chelsea, the waitress, decided to go home because she had things to do and there wasn't any business. Juanita was baking for the American Legion volunteers again, and she was filling up the freezer with baked goods, just in case we had a big rush. Bob, the elusive other cook that I'd never met, was still sick and he was thinking of going to Atlantic City to see a specialist.

Hmm . . . office hours at the Borgata? Or maybe the Showboat?

I pulled into the library's parking lot and went in. I loved the old place with the big cement pillars out front and shiny marble floors. It was filled with thick, dark wooden tables and desks with green banker's lamps hovering over each one for extra light. It was a cavernous place, the kind of place where the smallest whisper echoed for an eternity.

The library was relatively busy. Many of the residents seemed to be gathered there, reading in kiosks or Queen Anne chairs or working on laptops at the desks. This was the only place I knew that had an old-fashioned, dog-eared, card catalog complete with ancient fonts on the majority of the cards.

I thumbed through the card catalog, looking for "*Mystery: How to Solve a—*" when I came to *Mushrooms of New York State, When to Eat Them and When to Run*.

Cute. And just what I was looking for. I found scrap paper and pencil stubs located in a basket on top of the dark oak cabinets and wrote down the Dewey decimal number.

I wandered through the stacks, and as luck would have it, I found the book. Skimming the index, I found amanita mushrooms.

Bingo. Page 231. I skimmed the chapter.

One kind of amanita mushroom, the Destroying Angel, is commonly found in North America in the spring and fall . . . in the woods . . . base of trees . . . One cap would kill a man.

Destroying Angel . . . What a creepy name.

There was more. Pictures of a pretty white mushroom with an umbrella cap. It looked harmless enough.

Just then, I was approached by May—or was it her sister, June?—my pal from the fire barn.

She looked at the book that I was reading, then stared at me, her eyes popping out of their sockets.

I held my hand up like Deputy Doug, the traffic cop. "No! No! I was just . . . doing research!"

That didn't help. She pointed to me, and not a sound came out of her mouth. She took two steps back.

"Please, no. It's not what you are thinking. Please don't scream." I snapped the book shut, put it on the nearest shelf, and led her over to a chair.

She took several deep breaths. "I'm so sorry, Trixie. I don't know what made me react so. Maybe it's because I was just talking to Mayor Tingsley, and the subject of Mr. Cogswell came up and how unfortunate it is that the Silver Bullet isn't doing well. It's been a landmark in Sandy Harbor for more than sixty years."

"Isn't that nice of Mayor Tingsley to be so concerned about my diner?" I asked sarcastically, but May (or June) didn't get it.

"The mayor was talking about his plans to buy

your property and develop it. I must say that he has the town in a buzz. He said that he'd be able to bring in many needed jobs to the area."

"Oh?" My stomach took a dive.

"Condos, boat slips, tennis courts, ice skating, a health spa—there's plenty more. He's calling it a residential resort. And it would cater to the rich and famous. Can you believe it? Maybe Harrison Ford would stay here! Or the Kardashians. Maybe even Brad Pitt!"

The mayor had big ideas to match his big mouth.

"But the Sandy Harbor Guest Cottages cater to *families*," I said in protest. "It's always been a place where families can boat, swim, and have fun together."

"Mayor Tingsley said, 'May, we have to keep up with the times. Those little cottages are too old-fashioned.'"

Tears stung my eyes. Was I too starry-eyed to think that families would want to vacation together on one of the best lakes in New York? Would the average family be content to watch the sunrise and sunset together or sit around a campfire toasting marshmallows?

According to May, it seemed like the whole town was thinking like Mayor Tingsley.

Speaking of Mayor Tingsley, he had a lot of nerve talking up a project that concerned *my* property.

Was this his way of putting pressure on me to sell to him?

What had May said? That it would bring many needed jobs into the area?

Talk about pressure!

I mumbled some lame excuse to May and hurried out of the library, my boots squeaking on the marble floor to a fast beat. Getting into my car, I drove to the nearest doughnut and coffee shop with a drive-through window and placed an order for a loaded coffee and a chocolate doughnut.

Pulling into a parking space, I popped the white plastic lid and let the scented steam fill up my little car.

I dove into the bag and pulled out the chocolate doughnut. It was soft and chewy, and I was in heaven.

Did I eat when stressed? Most definitely. And I was a pressure cooker these days. And I ate when happy, and when content, and when bored, and tired, and—well, you get the drift.

Then it hit me. The murder of Mr. Cogswell had to be premeditated! The murderer was waiting for the appropriate time to use the Destroying Angel.

And who would know enough about mushrooms to know that the Destroying Angel was grown locally and that it was poisonous?

A chill went right through me. Which one of the townspeople could be that evil?

I ticked them off one by one as I downed the last bite of doughnut and sipped coffee. Leading my pack of suspects were Antoinette Chloe Brown and Mayor Tingsley. With his grandiose development ideas, Mayor Tingsley seemed to have the most to gain.

Then there was Roberta Cummings's overprotective brother, the Sunshine delivery guy, Mark Cummings. I'd almost forgotten about him.

People I didn't know, but probably should get to know, were Mr. Brown and Mrs. Tingsley, spouses of my primary suspects.

I started up my car. I knew just where to find Mr. Brown. Since Antoinette Chloe was home, he'd be working at the restaurant.

It wasn't a long drive, just up the block. The parking lots for Brown's Four Corners and Tingsley's Crossroads, across the street, were jumping.

Well, it was lunchtime, and probably those who worked in town were grabbing lunch.

I waited in line at Brown's, choosing to sit at the counter. I could see two cooks behind a half wall. The bibs of their aprons looked like they'd worn them for a week. Their baseball hats were grimy, and if I were the owner, I'd require a hairnet on their chins, too.

They were both the same size and build, about five foot ten and just as wide. Were they brothers?

The waitress, a hard-looking woman with gobs of eye makeup, stood in front of me with her order book positioned on her ample boobs. "Do you know what you want?"

"Could I see a menu?" I asked.

She slid a paper place mat in front of me. "Lunch is on there."

"Oh." I read the place mat quickly as she breathed heavily. I just didn't want to eat here. "I'll have a piece of cherry pie and a cup of coffee."

"Okay." She used her boobs like a writing desk and scribbled on her pad. Then she speared the paper on a big nail sticking out of a block of wood.

She poured me a cup of coffee out of a filthy glass carafe and plopped it down in front of me.

I checked the rim of the cup for lipstick stains, always a turnoff. So far, so good.

She plopped down the cherry pie. It was straight from Sunshine Food Supply. Commercially made. Just like at my diner. Well, no more commercially made desserts for the Silver Bullet. Just as soon as we had more business, I'd get Mrs. Stolfus on board.

I asked the waitress to ask Mr. Brown if he could spare some time to talk to me.

"Yeah. Okay."

Over the rim of my coffee cup, I could see her walk over to the man with a Harley Davidson cap. I recognized him from the fire hall. The waitress pointed at me with her pen, and they both looked at me. He shrugged and went back to cooking.

I took my time drinking my coffee and eating the pie. Finally, Sal Brown stood in front of me. He had crumbs and some other kind of crud in his beard.

"Can I help you?" He had beautiful brown eyes that matched his name.

"I just wanted to introduce myself, Mr. Brown. I'm Trixie Matkowski of the Silver Bullet Diner."

He visibly relaxed. Maybe he thought I was from the IRS or was Mr. Cogswell's replacement from the health department.

"Glad to meet you. And call me Sal." He extended his hand, and his eyes twinkled. We shook and his grip was strong and warm. I liked him immediately.

"You have quite the business here. Is it always this crowded?" I asked.

"Only since the . . . uh . . . since Cogswell . . . well, since all that happened at your diner. With everyone passing up the Silver Bullet, we've gotten a lot of business."

"And so has Tingsley's Crossroads."

He nodded. "I've never seen anything like this. I've had to put on more help—my brother."

"I thought you looked alike." I smiled. "And I've met Antoinette Chloe on a couple of occasions. Matter of fact, we had tea just this morning."

Sal smiled and tips of perfect white teeth peeked out from the hair around his mouth. "That's good. She doesn't have enough gal pals. And she loves to entertain."

"She seems really thrilled at all the new business," I said.

"Antoinette Chloe has really blossomed lately."

And I'd bet he wasn't just referring to her muumuus.

He shook his head. "I'm sorry that our good fortune has been the result of your bad fortune. Obviously, someone was out to get Cogswell. He wasn't exactly well loved by anyone around town."

"But who hated him enough to poison him?"

He shrugged. "Beat's me. But, God help me, I don't miss him."

I took a deep breath. For some reason, I didn't think that Sal Brown was the type to poison anyone. He looked like a big teddy bear, and he seemed truly in love with his wife.

"I have to go, but as soon as I get a chance, I'll take a ride up to the Bullet. Do you still have the tuna noodle casserole special on Fridays?"

"For you, Sal, I'll have the tuna noodle special."

He slapped me on the back, and I had to catch my breath. He told the waitress that my order was on him. We shook hands again and went our separate ways. Sal went back to cooking, and I walked over to Tingsley's Crossroads.

The sun had turned the parking lot and the road into a biohazardous mix of salt, sand, and murky water. And, yes, my darn boots were leaking again. I should just buy a pair of waders from Mr. Farnsworth's bait shop and wear those until summer, for heaven's sake.

The Crossroads was a long, low structure that was made of logs painted a dark brown. Various neon signs promoting different brands of beer hung from each of several windows that faced the main street.

The entire rambling building seemed out of place for such a Victorian-style downtown, unless Davy Crockett once lived (or ate) there.

The battered wooden door was several inches thick, and it took two hands to open it. Once I was inside, it took a while for my eyes to adjust to the dim lighting. Davy Crockett must not have paid the electric bill.

The place was hopping, just like Brown's, but I didn't have to wait. "Just a cup of coffee," I told the hostess. "I'll sit at the counter."

But the counter was really a bar. The jukebox was playing a loud country tune, and a group of men were hunched together, trying to talk over the loud music. I took a bar stool at the end.

Yep, the music was way too loud. My head started to pound in time with the beat. I looked down at the counter, decorated with thousands of bright, shiny pennies under some kind of plastic varnish. Exquisite.

"What can I get you?" A cardboard coaster spun in front of me.

I looked up, right into the surprised face of Roberta Cummings.

"It's you!"

Isn't this my lucky day?

"I'll get someone else to wait on you." She looked around but didn't seem to find the person she was looking for.

"All I want is a cup of coffee," I said, and prayed that she wouldn't spit in it.

She hesitated, then poured coffee into a mug. She set it in front of me on the coaster.

"Cream or sugar?" she mumbled.

"Just black. Thanks." She was just turning around when I decided to make nice. "Roberta, can we talk?"

She took a deep breath. "I'm working."

"I see, but you don't seem that busy right now."

"There's nothing more you can say to me." She raised her voice, and the men stopped talking and looked up. "You poisoned my Marvin, Trixie Matkowski."

I raised my voice, too. "What can I do to convince you that I had nothing to do with Marvin's death?"

Tears flooded her eyes, and my heart went out to her. She must have really loved him.

I remembered what Ty had said, off the record, that the Sandy Harbor sheriff's department had been called to their residence for domestic violence on several occasions.

Maybe Roberta had tired of being Marvin's punching bag and reached her breaking point.

Could she have poisoned Marvin?

She of all people would have known Marvin's schedule.

Nope. According to Juanita, Roberta was in the front of the Silver Bullet returning Juanita's cell phone to her when Mr. Cogswell was poisoned.

So Roberta couldn't have poisoned her boyfriend.

Antoinette Chloe Brown, the new queen of Sandy Harbor with the damaged gardenia muumuu, was still on the top of my list.

Chapter 12

"How long have you worked here, Roberta?" I thought it was a simple-enough question, but she squinted her eyes, and took her sweet time answering, as if she suspected me of having an ulterior motive for asking her such a question—which I did. I wanted to know just how close she was to the Tingsleys.

"About six months. Laura needed the help, and I can work my schedule around the *Sandy Harbor Lure*."

I remembered reading the scathing article she'd written about the Silver Bullet and how Mr. Cogswell had died in its kitchen. Then the diner had become a ghost town.

Hmm . . . Maybe I could use the *Lure* to my advantage!

"Roberta, I've been meaning to take an ad out in the *Lure*. I want to advertise the daily specials at the Silver Bullet and maybe put in a 'two for one' coupon." I raised an eyebrow. "Who would I see there to help me with it?"

"Me." She relaxed somewhat. "I pretty much do everything. It's part of my job to design ads."

"That'd be terrific. When can we meet?"

She took a deep breath and smoothed down her

gray pants, which she wore with a gray satin blouse. The outfit didn't do anything for her pale coloring and fairer skin and blond-white hair. She looked . . . icy.

It was obvious that she didn't want to meet with me, but I was sure she wanted the advertising money.

"How about my office at the paper?" She pulled out her cell phone and punched in something. "Tuesday. Nine o'clock?"

"Sounds good to me."

A woman with dark hair, sunglasses, and a kerchief walked through the door of the Crossroads. If she was trying to look like Jackie Kennedy Onassis, she was pulling it off. Roberta raised a hand in greeting and smiled warmly.

"Hi, Laura!"

Laura slipped out of her coat, uncovering a light blue suit with a pink blouse and white pearls. I noticed that she wore white heels, an interesting choice in this slush and before Memorial Day no less! Some people would consider pastels and white heels in mid-March a horrible faux pas. I simply admired her bravery for going without boots.

"How are things?" Laura asked, patting her black hair into place, but not a hair had the courage to move. The ends flipped up around the back of her head in a perfect semicircle.

"Very busy," Roberta said.

Laura turned to me. "I don't believe we've met. I'm Laura Tingsley, the owner of the Crossroads and the mayor's wife."

I offered my hand. "Trixie Matkowski, the new owner of the Silver Bullet Diner and the point."

She took my hand and gave me a cold, limp handshake. "I've been meaning to call on you, but I've been terribly busy."

"Feel free to stop in anytime. I've already met your husband—twice."

"Oh yes. The mayor is always on top of things. He's just . . . wonderful. He's done so much for Sandy Harbor, and"—she winked—"there's so much more to come!"

She sounded like his campaign manager or a doting wife.

I smiled. "I understand that he runs a real estate company and an investment firm. And then he owns the Crossroads? Where does he find the time?"

"The Crossroads is in my name." Laura Tingsley lowered her voice. "Besides, it wouldn't reflect positively on the mayor to own a bar, especially if he has his sights set on the state senate."

"I see."

Roberta backed away from us, probably glad to be free of me. That was okay; I'd see her on Tuesday. Maybe I could get some more information from her then.

"Excuse me, please. I have to make sure that everything's running smoothly." Laura walked away, her shoes making a nice click-click on the hardwood floor.

In her perfect suit, pearls, and shoes, and what looked like a fresh manicure, I couldn't see her cooking or doing much work, other than greeting customers. In that way, Antoinette Chloe Brown and Laura Tingsley were alike.

I drained my coffee, nursing a sudden headache from the music, along with a caffeine buzz. I left money on the bar for my coffee and a big tip for Roberta.

After I pried open the heavy front door, the frigid, fresh air slapped me and almost brought me to my knees. So did going from the dimly lit restaurant into sunshine. My head felt like a throbbing drum on my neck.

I staggered in the direction of my car like a drunk. Where could I go for an aspirin?

There was a drugstore within walking distance, and I headed there. I'd get a bottle of aspirin and a bottled water to wash some down with.

I was just about to open the door when I heard a voice behind me.

"Thought you were going to get some sleep."

I couldn't mistake that slow, easy drawl— Deputy Ty Brisco. He had Blondie on a lime green leash, and she sported a fuchsia-colored bandanna around her neck. Cute.

"I—I couldn't sleep," I said, not quite meeting his eyes.

"So you visited Antoinette Chloe Brown at her home, Sal Brown at his restaurant, and now I see you coming out of the Crossroads, where you probably saw Roberta Cummings. You've had a busy morning."

"You knew that Roberta works at the Crossroads?"

"Of course."

He could have shared that with me. "Are you spying on me, Ty?"

"Yup." He nodded. "What are you up to?"

"Just visiting my neighbors."

"Uh-huh. Seems like I've heard that before." He didn't believe me at all, and I guess I didn't expect him to. "So, what did you find out?"

"I found out that Antoinette Chloe Brown—let's call her ACB to save time—has a chunk of material missing from her gardenia muumuu. It matches the size and shape of the swatch that Blondie found."

He raised a black eyebrow. "How did you find this out?"

"I said that I was going to include her house on the historical society tour, and I got into her closet. The muumuu was there, on the floor, bottom right."

"You did *what*?" He pushed his cowboy hat back with a thumb as if to see me better. He looked like a soufflé baking, all puffed up and ready to blow. "And?"

"She seems to be blooming with all the attention, according to her husband, Sal. And by the way, Sal looks like a big hairy biker, but he seems like a gentle soul. And he just adores ACB."

"And was Roberta working?"

"Yep."

"Go on."

For some reason, I didn't want to tell him that I had an appointment with Roberta on Tuesday.

"And then Laura Tingsley walked in. I haven't

figured her out yet, but she seems like the woman behind the man. I believe that she knows about the development that her husband has in mind for my property. Actually, the whole town knows about it and is giddy with excitement. It'll create jobs, you know, and this area needs jobs."

"Who said that?"

"May, the sister of June. I ran into May at the library this morning when I was researching Destroying Angels."

"Destroying Angels?"

"It's a variety of amanita mushrooms that grows around here. You know, you were the one who said that the autopsy showed amanitas. I figured out that it was the Destroying Angel amanita that killed Marvin the Third."

Ty smiled for the first time since we started talking. "You have been busy, and you've really scored on that garment of ACB's. I'll get a search warrant. But you have to be careful, Trixie. There's a murderer on the loose here, and you're shaking things up. I can't believe that you're still investigating when I specifically told you not to. So listen to me: I don't want you investigating on your own anymore because I don't have any more time to keep an eye on you. Hear me?"

"I can hear," I said.

"And you were supposed to be sleeping!" He lowered his voice. "You purposely didn't tell me that you were going to go off half-cocked and—"

"I didn't go off half-cocked. I was fully cocked. And I knew you'd never let me search her closet."

"Not in a million years."

He opened the door for an elderly customer going into the drugstore and tweaked his hat brim to her. The woman visibly blushed. "Thank you, Deputy Ty."

"You're welcome, darlin'. And you have a glorious day, hear?"

She giggled, and he winked.

Oh brother!

He waited until she was gone, then repeated his warning. "I mean it, Trixie. I thought you wanted to work together."

"Yeah, but you didn't. And you're not sharing things with me."

"You know I can't share everything, and—"

"Things are taking too long, Ty. I'm going broke."

He snapped his fingers. "By the way, have you called the diner lately?"

"Is something wrong?" My heart started to race, and he waved away my concern.

"There's an impromptu meeting of about thirty or so American Legion people at the Silver Bullet."

"Oh, that's wonderful!" Finally, people at the diner! And I had Ty to thank for it.

"I don't know if they're going to order lunch, but I suggested it."

"Oh, I have to help Juanita!"

"Don't worry about it. She called Cindy in *because she thought that you needed the sleep!*"

"Oops." Funny how Ty knew what was happening at the diner more than I did. But I'd scored big at ACB's house.

"I'd better go see the judge," Ty said. "Then I'm going to have a long talk with ACB."

"Can I come?"

"No, but you can take Blondie for me." He held up her leash. He must have just bought it for her. "And I have dog food in my car. I'll put it in yours."

I decided to forget about the aspirin. I felt a lot better. My head was clear, and Ty seemed to be happy with my ACB news.

Maybe ACB would confess, but what would be her motive? Putting me out of business so she could be Antoinette Chloe Socialite?

We walked to his sheriff's car where he pulled out a huge paper bag of dog food. And several plastic bags of treats and toys. He handed me the small bags, and hoisted the dog food to his shoulder. We walked to my car with Blondie between us. I grinned. It seemed so—I don't know—comfortable, maybe.

After we put everything into my car, he handed me an envelope from his pocket. It was a little metal dog bone, but upon further inspection, I realized it was Blondie's dog license.

"She's yours now, isn't she, Ty?" That was so nice of him to be so concerned over a stray dog. But if he hadn't adopted her, I would have.

"I thought we could share her, since you obviously like Blondie, too."

I smiled down at the beautiful golden retriever.

How could anyone dump a sweet, gorgeous dog like that?

Somehow she was meant to be mine . . . uh . . . ours.

Blondie climbed into the backseat of my car without a prompt and immediately curled up. I rubbed her head and scratched her chin, and she laid her head on the palm of my hand.

My heart just melted. I loved this dog!

I yawned. It was time to actually get some sleep.

"See you around, Ty. And congratulations on Blondie."

My heart skipped a beat as I was rewarded with his charming smile and the tweak of his hat. Telling myself that I was just overreacting due to lack of sleep, I headed home.

When I got within sight of the parking lot, I had to give a hoot. "Yee-haw! Customers! Look at that, Blondie!"

Parking in front of my house, I let Blondie out to do her business. Then I called her inside, got her settled in the living room, and hurried out the door to the diner.

I let myself in the back door. Juanita and Cindy were busy filling orders.

"Trixie! Isn't this great?" Juanita said. "They're all ordering lunch, too."

"Did you make a special, Juanita?"

"I made cream of tomato soup with basil and grilled cheese sandwiches for them."

"Excellent!" Thank goodness for Juanita.

"And they're loving it," Cindy added as she

dipped a ladle into a big soup pot and poured the contents into a white bowl.

"Do we have enough desserts?" I asked.

"We did a lot of baking this morning—pies, brownies, cakes—when we found out that they were going to meet here," Cindy said. "The pies in the carousel from Sunshine Food Supply were . . . uh . . . old. We got rid of them."

Thank goodness they did. I slipped into a clean white apron and plucked an order from the rack. "Cheeseburger, medium rare, and fries." That was easy. I plucked off a couple more orders and worked on all three. It was good to get back into the swing of cooking. An hour zoomed by, and it seemed like only five minutes.

"The crunch is just about over," Juanita said. "We're okay."

"Thanks so much, ladies. I really appreciate it."

Both Juanita and Cindy shooed me out the door. They both worked like crazy, and I vowed to give them both a raise. Someday. When the diner was back on its feet.

I walked into the diner and people were sitting everywhere. There were still a lot of empty seats— the diner seated about seventy-five, and only about forty people were present—but I wasn't complaining.

As I walked around with pots of decaf and regular coffee, grinning from ear to ear, I knew that I'd joined the ranks of ACB and Laura Tingsley.

But I needed a theme: "Hawaiian floral explosion" and "First Lady" were already taken.

I looked down at my dark denim jeans and navy blue polo shirt. It was slimming, and casual. Perfect diner attire.

I felt like I was walking on sunshine. Here I was in tiny Sandy Harbor, New York, with a coffeepot in each hand, in my own diner, on my property, and I had customers.

I had finished refilling everyone's coffee cups, so I fixed a large tray with the various desserts and began passing them out. No charge for dessert today, or even coffee. I'd let Chelsea and Nancy know that it was on the house. I felt like I was welcoming them into my house, and I wanted them to return.

I met lots of new people, and got reacquainted with others, many of whom remembered my family coming to Cottage Number Six every summer and when I worked at the apple orchard.

"Don't let that health inspector thing bother you, dearie," said my former communications professor from Oswego State, Mrs. Leddy. "That sexy cop from Texas will get to the bottom of it."

I wanted to believe her, but this was the same professor who still maintained that the Internet would never catch on.

I'd already decided to muddle through on my own, either with or without Ty's help. I'd done a pretty good job so far. I was the one who'd followed through on the muumuu clue.

Right about now, Ty should be getting a warrant to search ACB's house. I wondered if she would associate me with the sudden warrant.

If she could add two plus two, she would. I was the one inside her closet. I was the one with the fishy story about a tour of historical homes.

"Mrs. Leddy?"

"Yes, dearie?"

"Do you know who is the president of the Sandy Harbor Historical Society?"

"Why, I am, dearie."

My luck continued. I should buy a lottery ticket today. "Have you ever thought of a tour of homes, maybe as a fund-raiser?"

"We used to do it at Christmas, but we haven't done a tour in years. It was just so much work, and most of it centered around getting the houses clean and presentable." She tugged at my arm to get me to bend over, and whispered in my ear. "You can't believe some of the housekeepers in this town. Terrible!"

"Have you thought about trying it again?"

"We can't get a volunteer to coordinate it."

"I volunteer!" This job would be a good opportunity to make more friends in the community.

"That would be wonderful, dearie! I'll tell the board of directors of the historical society."

"Do you think they'll go for it?"

"Absolutely! It was our best fund-raiser."

"Well then, Mrs. Leddy, I'll get started immediately."

"Bless you, dearie."

I let her get back to her meeting about the American Legion's roof.

Just then I heard the president of the Legion ask

for suggestions as to where they could hold events like card tournaments and wine tastings and whatnot until the roof was replaced.

I raised my hand. "You could hold them right here, Mr. President. The Silver Bullet is at your disposal."

He didn't hesitate. "Thank you, Trixie. That's very generous of you."

There was a murmur of comments about Mr. Cogswell's poisoning that happened just inside those double doors, but it was Mrs. Leddy who saved the day.

"If any of you believe that Trixie Matkowski would poison anyone, you need a shrink. She's Porky and Stella's niece, for heaven's sake. She was the cutest little girl—always walking around with a grape lollipop. And, wow, could she swim! And the poor thing is divorced now. He was fooling around on her, you know."

Several pairs of eyes grew round, probably not because they just heard my life story in a couple of sentences, nor because they might have heard just about the same thing earlier from Mr. Farnsworth at the fire barn, but in amazement at how Mrs. Leddy could equate my innocence with grape lollipops, swimming, and being cheated on.

The president asked for a vote as to whether they should hold their indoor fund-raisers at the Silver Bullet. Most all the hands were raised. The "ayes" won.

Several people jumped up to shake my hand and to thank me. I felt accepted, and I loved the fact that the Silver Bullet would be busy, because people would still order food at their events. I'd have specials and discounts, and I would donate a share of my profits to the fund-raiser, but at least the diner would be busy.

Suddenly I felt like I'd slammed into a brick wall. I was dead tired, even zombielike. Time to get some sleep.

I gave everyone in the front of the diner a cheerful wave good-bye and ducked into the kitchen.

"You look like something that Blondie dragged in," Juanita said, reminding me again of how Blondie dragged in a piece of ACB's gardenia muumuu. Was Ty searching her house for the garment at this very moment?

"I'm going to get some sleep," I said. "Is everything okay here?"

"Go!" Both Juanita and Cindy waved me away. "And Chelsea and Nancy have the front covered."

"When do I have to come back to cook? Or is Bob back?"

"Bob is still out," Juanita said. "Come in after you get some sleep."

I was beginning to think that Bob didn't exist.

I plodded over to my house and was greeted by Blondie. She nudged my leg, wagging her tail. I patted her soft head and under her chin.

"Do you have to go out, Blondie?"

The dog got up, hustled down the front stairs, and walked to her favorite spot. When she was done, she hurried back inside the house, probably fearful that I would abandon her like her previous owner.

She walked at my side, up the stairs and to my bedroom. I was too exhausted to change into nightwear, so I plopped on top of the comforter.

It felt heavenly.

I didn't know how long I'd been sleeping when I felt something wet on my lips. Ty Brisco kissing me was the first thought that entered my mind. He had hung his cowboy hat on the bedpost, and he was snuggling in next to me. I felt the bed shift.

Hmm . . . another kiss. This time it was much wetter. More like a lick. Ty?

No. Blondie.

She was stretched out on the bed, next to me. Her head was on the other pillow, and she was staring at me.

"What?" I asked.

She looked at me and closed her eyes.

I glanced at the clock. Three in the afternoon. I got up, hit the bathroom, and when I came back, Blondie was stretched across two pillows.

I grinned. "Oh no, you don't. Move over, you bed hog." I gave her a gentle nudge, and she moved enough for me to slide in next to her.

I tried to get back to sleep, but a steady parade of suspects filed past me, with ACB as a drum majorette, leading the parade.

Then there was Mark Cummings, Roberta's brother, the surly deliveryman for Sunshine Food Supply. He was at the diner around the time of Marvin's demise.

And let's not forget the anonymous woman—perhaps ACB, also—who ordered a case of mushrooms to be delivered to the Silver Bullet, when no Matkowski had ever allowed a mushroom to enter its hallowed silver walls.

I figured that Mayor Rick Tingsley and probably ACB and Sal Brown made offers to Aunt Stella for her little corner of the Sandy Harbor, now my little corner. She'd turned them both down.

Would they have tried to close me down, thinking that I'd sell to them? If one of them had a grudge against Mr. Cogswell the Third, it would be like eliminating two birds with one stone.

Mr. Cogswell and I were the two birds!

I thought of Mr. Cogswell as a seagull, scavenging for meals. I preferred to think of myself as a . . . flamingo—a pretty fuchsia color with long skinny legs.

I liked Sal Brown. He was absolutely devoted to his wife. He had twinkly eyes and seemed to be a sweet guy. But I'd been wrong before, such as in my choice of a husband.

I didn't have an opinion on Laura Tingsley. She seemed okay, having the guts to go bootless and to wear white shoes before Memorial Day in Sandy Harbor, one step down from the North Pole.

Mayor Tingsley was another story. He was blunt, rude, and pushy. I didn't know yet what his mayoral skills were, but he was definitely absent the night of the American Legion roof collapse. He should have been there helping, or at least checking on the townsfolk.

And I totally didn't like the way he was pushing me to sell—shoveling the guilt on me like quick-setting concrete if I didn't let him bring jobs to the area.

I'd never be able to concentrate on my long to-do list for the diner if I kept hashing and re-hashing the same suspects. I had to solve this soon.

There was a knock on the door. I willed who-ever it was to go away. But Blondie hoisted herself up, jumped down from the bed, and headed down-stairs.

I quickly ran a brush through my hair and ran a cold washcloth over my face. I noticed that my eyes were brighter and less puffy, and I felt more alert.

I answered the door. It was Ty Brisco, dressed in full deputy sheriff regalia. I opened the door and stifled a yawn.

"Sorry to disturb you, but I thought you'd want to hear what's new in the Cogswell case."

He bent over to pet Blondie, and her tail wagged in sheer pleasure. I couldn't help but look at his lips, remembering my Blondie-induced dream.

Snap out of it!

I motioned for him to come in. "Did ACB con-fess? I hope so."

"No. In fact, there was no gardenia dress in her closet or anywhere else in her house."

My stomach dropped. "Come on, Ty. I saw it. I touched it. I picked it up from the bottom of her closet. It had a chunk of material missing that matched the piece that Blondie found."

"It's gone."

"Gone? What did she do with it?" I asked. "And that proves that she's guilty, doesn't it?"

"No. Not yet."

I needed coffee or perhaps something stronger like a giant milk chocolate candy bar with almonds—I'd heard that almonds are healthy.

"What can I get you, Ty?"

"Nothing. I'm fine."

I went to my fridge and pulled out a bottle of iced tea, twisted the cap, and took a long draw. Then I put fresh water into Blondie's bowl, and she slurped noisily. I smiled. Now there was a gal who enjoyed her drink.

I wanted to keep her. All the time. Forever.

Ty pulled out a chair at the kitchen table and stretched out his long legs.

"ACB said that she hasn't been to your diner since before Stella left, and if she wanted to visit, she'd use the front door, not hang around your Dumpster."

"I tipped off ACB, didn't I?" I asked, the guilt settling in. She must have hidden the evidence after my illicit visit.

"I don't think so."

He was just being nice. I knew that I had blown it.

"What about Sal the biker? Is he mad about the search?"

"Livid. ACB called him when we knocked on the door, and he arrived in less than a minute. She kept sobbing into his chest, wailing about how she could never hold her head up in Sandy Harbor again."

"Ick. Did you ask her about the muumuu?" I asked.

"She said that she never owned a gardenia muumuu."

"Liar, liar, pants on fire," I said, maturely. "What did Sal say?"

"He said that he doesn't know one flower from another."

"Someone must remember seeing her wearing the gardenia muumuu the day of Mr. Cogswell's funeral. That's when I saw her wearing it. At her restaurant."

"I don't need to ask anyone. Not yet. I know she's lying."

"And her motive?"

"I don't know yet."

He scratched Blondie's ears, but he seemed to be thinking.

"Ty, do you have other suspects?"

"I shouldn't discuss this with you, Trixie."

"Ty, you said that we'd work together; then you won't share anything."

"I agreed that we'd work together?" He rubbed his chin. "I think I remember only agreeing to work together relative to Sunshine Food Supply. Nothing else. But if I did, how do you explain going to ACB's house without telling me? Matter of fact, you lied and told me that you were going to get some sleep. Then you snuck out." He raised a black eyebrow. That was his "I gotcha" tell.

"It wasn't like that."

"Sure was, darlin'."

He sang his last sentence and reminded me of George Strait.

"But you aren't including me in anything! You won't tell me anything about the investigation, and it's my diner. It's my life! So, if there's anything you can tell me, anything at all, spill it, cowboy."

Chapter 13

*T*y shifted in his chair. "Trixie, like I said before, there are some things I can't tell you. I probably shouldn't have even told you about our search of the Browns' today."

I let out a deep breath. This was so frustrating.

"Have you searched around the Browns' house? You know, garbage cans, the woods behind their house, dug-up dirt?"

"This isn't my first rodeo, Trixie." He looked amused rather than angry.

"Okay. Rick Tingsley, our loudmouthed mayor, has made it public that he wants your property," Ty said.

"Yeah. I know. I was the one who told you that."

"But the interesting news is that he doesn't have the money to buy you out. There's not a lot of real estate moving on the market here, or anywhere for that matter. As for investments, he's made some bad decisions in a bad market. He's going under," Ty said.

"If he doesn't have any money, then why is he making it his mission to buy me out? He made me a cash offer. Two million."

"Bringing jobs into a depressed area makes for

a good political campaign. His party has nominated him for the senate, so it's a go."

"Laura is already starting to campaign for him."

"Speaking of Laura VanPlank Tingsley, her parents live in Palm Beach, and they're loaded. They gave her the best house in Sandy Harbor for her wedding, and they bought the Crossroads for her because she wanted something to do. They bought the building where the mayor's real estate and investment business is located." Ty shook his head and frowned like he couldn't imagine living off someone else's money. "Maybe they want Laura to be married to a senator. It certainly would be several rugs up the social ladder from being the mayor's wife in a small town in upstate New York. It's probably his in-laws' money that he's going to use to buy you out."

That made sense to me. "And since his campaign is depending on him creating new jobs, maybe he decided to bankrupt me to buy the land. Since paying cash didn't work."

"That's what I was thinking."

"But did Mr. Cogswell really have to die because Rick Tingsley wants to be a senator?"

Ty shrugged. "If he wanted to bankrupt you and force a quick sale, it would make sense."

My headache was returning.

"What other suspects do you have, Ty?"

He shook his head. "ACB and our mayor are about it, but all I have is suspicion so far, with nothing specific to go on."

"Ty, what about Mark Cummings, the Sunshine Food Supply deliveryman and Roberta's brother? He was at the diner prior to Mr. Cogswell's poisoning. He could have slipped poisoned mushrooms into his meal when Juanita wasn't looking."

"He has no prior criminal record, and I found him to be a weird duck when I questioned him. But he volunteered to take a lie detector test and passed," Ty said.

"Oh." I guessed that ruled out Mark Cummings. "I understand that Marvin abused Roberta. That's what's floating on the gossip grapevine anyway. What else have you found out about the victim?"

"There's nothing but three arrests for disorderly conduct. Cogswell has no convictions and no ties to anything criminal. Roberta reported domestic violence on Marvin's part, and the Sandy Harbor police were called for a couple of loud fights between him and Roberta. And it was well-known that he mooched meals from area restaurants."

"In exchange for favorable evaluations," I said.

"Yeah, but it's been going on for years. Why would anyone kill him now?"

"Maybe someone got sick of it. Or maybe he was going to fail someone, regardless of how well he was treated."

"His records show that that wasn't the case. He hasn't really failed a restaurant in more than four years. He just sends out 'fix this' warning letters."

"Yeah, I got one of those."

I realized that I really didn't know anything about Cogswell. I'd never even seen his face.

Twice I was near him in his deceased state. The first time, he was facedown on a plate full of pork and scalloped potatoes. The second time, I was at the Hal Manning's Happy Repose Funeral Home where he had a closed casket. The picture of him in his obit was from high school, and it was awfully grainy. The same picture was on his casket.

"Was Marvin Cogswell a handsome guy?" I asked.

He looked at me like I had snakes crawling out of my ears.

"Would you say that he was handsome?" I repeated.

He drummed his fingers on the table, thinking.

"Ty, from a purely non–*Brokeback Mountain* standpoint, would you say that Mr. Cogswell was a good-looking guy?"

He laughed. I just loved how he bent his head back and laughed from his gut—a deep, manly laugh. "What are you going for, Trixie?"

"I'm thinking of a love triangle. Maybe he was cheating on Roberta, and Roberta got jealous. Or maybe the other woman got jealous of Roberta. I was wondering if he was a hunk? A stud? A player?"

"I guess you could say that he looked a little like Bob, your night cook."

"I've never seen Bob, my night cook! Give me another kickoff point. Let's use you, Ty. Is he cuter than you?"

Just as the words spewed out of my mouth, I realized my mistake.

"How could anyone be cuter than I am?" he said.

"Forget it!" I said. "I'll go to the library and look up a clear yearbook picture of Mr. Cogswell. Or maybe his picture is on the Internet somewhere. Maybe Facebook."

"It's not. I searched all that. However, in his personal effects, I have his driver's license, which is almost four years old, and his twelve-year-old ID badge from the health department. I didn't look up his old yearbook picture."

"Can I see his driver's license picture?"

"His personal effects are locked up in the basement of the sheriff's department, and I don't know how his looks would point to a murderer." His tone of voice held a hint of impatience.

"Yeah, you're right. Forget it." Deputy Brisco just wasn't taking me seriously.

"If you really want to see his picture, I'll get it out of the evidence locker."

He was throwing me a bone. "No. Don't bother."

I was mad now. Ty had shot down my piece of material evidence that pointed to ACB being by my back door somewhere around the time that Cogswell died, and now he was shooting down my love-triangle theory.

Granted, a man didn't have to be handsome to have two women after him, but it certainly would help. Since I was a woman, albeit one with a libido that was paralyzed after my divorce, I could still tell if a man might be worth pursuing.

Even though I had no intention of running after a man, or even walking at a snail's pace toward one, I could still tell if they had that certain . . . uh . . . animal magnetism.

Ty had that magnetism, much to my chagrin.

Then I remembered that I had an appointment with Roberta Cummings on Tuesday—Meat Loaf Special Tuesday. She had to have pictures of Marvin Cogswell in her office, her wallet, or maybe on her phone.

I didn't need Ty to go to the trouble of getting me Marvin's old driver's license picture. On Tuesday, I was going to meet with Marvin Cogswell's girlfriend, and have a woman-to-woman conversation. She'd have a recent picture of him.

And Wyatt Earp didn't have to know about it.

In the next three days, I slept, worked, and played with Blondie. I worked on checking things off my notebook lists as I accomplished them. I made more lists. It made me feel better that I was making progress on finally getting things done.

I cut checks for the payroll, noticing that there was even a little money coming in from the American Legion people. There was more going out, but I still felt optimistic.

I even did some unpacking and cleaning, when not at the diner, still covering for the elusive Bob.

I made the meat loaf, the gravy, and the mashed potatoes for the Tuesday special. If I say so myself,

it looked fabulous, and I used Uncle Porky's recipe, but with one exception—I used mild salsa in
the burger. I found that it gave it a little something
extra.

Before getting ready for my meeting with Roberta Cummings, I'd made an apple pie and
packed up two meat loaf specials in a take-out
box. She could have it for lunch or dinner.

On the way, I stopped at the Gas and Grab and
picked up a bouquet of flowers. At the Dollar-O-
Rama, I bought a box of chamomile tea.

Perhaps I could charm her into talking to me
about Marvin.

The office of the *Sandy Harbor Lure* was on Main
Street next to the combination dry cleaner and
Laundromat. I pulled up right in front of the
newspaper office, fed the meter, and walked inside. An older woman—June!—greeted me.

"Hello, Trixie."

"Why, hello, June. How long have you worked
here?"

"Since I retired from teaching. It'll be five years
this August."

"And May works at the library."

She nodded. "And you're here to see Roberta.
She's expecting you." On the last sentence, she
rolled her eyes, as if Roberta didn't want to see me
at all.

No surprise there.

June reached for her phone and punched in a
number; I could hear a buzz.

"Trixie's here," she said into the phone. "I'll let her know." Putting down the receiver, she smiled at me and said, "She'll be right out."

"Thanks."

Roberta kept me waiting for ten minutes, but June filled in the time by talking to me about the Sandy Harbor Guest Cottages in "the old days when Porky and Stella used to own the point." There were tales of fish bakes and bonfires on the shore of the lake.

"Good, clean, family fun times," June said, remembering the past. "And dancing every Friday outside under the moonlight." She closed her eyes. "It was one of those Fridays when I met my Walter, God rest his soul."

I remembered their parties, too. There were fireworks and Uncle Porky would get out his harmonica and we'd sing around the campfire. Aunt Stella would play the accordion, believe it or not, and she could rock those polkas. And they'd always end up singing a few songs in Polish, joined by their relatives and friends.

I just loved to watch them sing. Their faces would light up, and they'd be grinning from ear to ear.

Hey, I could throw a fish bake this summer, along with dancing and a bonfire! It might not be the caliber of what Porky and Stella had hosted, but it might come close. I jotted down the idea in my notebook.

Finally, Roberta appeared, acting harried and

checking her watch. That was her nonverbal signal that this meeting was going to be held in record time.

"Please, come into my office," she said, holding the door open.

"Nice talking to you, June," I said as I walked past her desk.

June's phone rang and she reached for it, giving me a brief wave.

Roberta motioned for me to walk into her office. She followed. The first thing I noticed was that it was naked. There were no trinkets or other memorabilia gracing the faux-paneled walls or bookcases. I scanned her desk for something in a frame, anything. Finally, I noticed one plastic-type frame to the left of her computer.

"Let's get right to work," Roberta said. "What do you have in mind?"

I handed her the gas station flowers, a nice mix of daisies and yellow mums. "These are for you, Roberta." I felt sorry for her, losing someone that she loved. I knew how she felt.

Her mouth tried to form some kind of words, but nothing came out. She leaned back in her chair and took a deep breath.

"What are these for?" she asked, her ice-blue eyes narrowing.

"Just because I've been thinking about you, and Mr. Cogswell, and everything. It has to be tough on you."

She put the bouquet to her nose and took a deep breath. It seemed to relax her a bit.

"You have no idea," she said.

I remained silent, letting her enjoy the flowers.

"Well, let's get to work," she said. "When we've finished our business, I'll put these in water."

That was another indication that this meeting would be brief.

I pulled a couple of sheets of bond paper from my purse and spread them out in front of her. "I played on the computer, and this is what I came up with. One sheet lists the Silver Bullet's daily specials. The other is a 'buy one, get one free' coupon."

"I like it when a customer is organized," she said.

This was about the first positive thing that Roberta ever said to me. Maybe I'd softened her up. There was more to come.

"This is what I had in mind, but they need help. Some kind of picture or graphic." I handed her a copy of the Silver Bullet's menu with a line drawing of the diner. "I'd like to feature this picture in both items."

"Should be easy. I'll mock something up for you, using your content, and will get it to you for your approval."

This was going way too fast. I needed to look at that picture on her desk.

"Roberta, can I show you what I have in mind?"

I stood and walked around her desk to where she sat. I pointed to the paper with the coupon. "About here is where I'd like the sketch of the diner to appear."

"I understand." She rose to escort me out.

I pulled the other piece of paper in front of her, bending over to get a good look at the three-by-five photo. It was of Roberta with a very attractive man. They were both in casual clothes in front of an evergreen tree and smiling for the camera.

Picking up the picture, I asked, "Is this you and Marvin?"

She snatched it away from me and returned it to its place. "Yes."

"It's a fabulous picture. You two look so happy. It must be hard for you to have someone you love so much taken away so abruptly."

"Yes. It is."

"I brought us some chamomile tea, Roberta. And some comfort food—meat loaf and an apple pie. Can I make us some tea? I'd love to hear about Marvin. I mean it, truly."

Talking about someone you have lost is hard, but it's a good way to start healing. I thought about Uncle Porky and how he'd reminisce about his old army buddies and other friends he'd lost. He always got a little misty but ended up grinning.

I looked around for some hot water, anything, and found a water dispenser with a spout in both blue and red. I assumed the red was the hot water.

"I'll get the water for tea," Roberta said, getting up.

She returned with two steaming cups of hot water. I had the tea bags at the ready.

"Cream and sugar?" she asked.

"Plain for me."

I sliced us two pieces of pie. I'd brought paper plates, plastic forks, and napkins. Like a good Girl Scout, I was always prepared whenever food was concerned.

She seemed overwhelmed and, believe it or not, at a loss for words. This was a side of Roberta that I never thought I'd see.

"This is very nice of you, Trixie," she said as I handed her the piece of pie. "I've been hard on you."

I waved away her concern. "Don't worry about it."

She took a bite of pie and closed her eyes. "This is heavenly."

"Thanks."

"Did you make it?"

"Yes, but I'm a better cook than a baker. You'll have to tell me if you like the meat loaf."

"I'm sure it'll be delicious." She took the container and slipped it into a small refrigerator behind her desk. "Thank you again."

I smiled. "Did I hear that you and Mr. Cogswell were engaged?"

"We'd been living together for the past five years, but we were talking about marriage." She gave a half smile. "Marvin has . . . had . . . cold feet, but I thought that I was wearing him down."

Roberta laughed. It sounded rusty, like a car trying to turn over with a bad battery, but she was getting there.

I was trying to like Roberta, since we did have

something in common. A divorce is like a death—the death of a marriage.

"Can you think of anyone who'd want to kill Marvin?" I leaned forward, not wanting to miss a word.

"That hunk of a deputy asked me the same thing. I told him that I couldn't think of anyone. Marvin loved his job and the fact that he could eat at the places he inspected. I never had to cook for him, not that I can cook anyway."

"Would you like another piece of pie?" I thought I'd remind her of the delightful carbs that I'd brought. She could use some weight on her slight bones.

"I couldn't eat another bite. But it was delicious," she said. "Um . . . uh . . . I want to apologize to you for being so . . . horrible to you."

"It's okay," I said. She'd really ruined my business, but I was trying to get over it. I decided to ask the big question that had been on my mind.

"Did you ever suspect that Mr. Cogswell might have been cheating on you?"

She didn't speak, and it was so quiet that I could hear June in the outer office talking to her sister on the phone.

Roberta stared at the picture on her desk, her eyes half closed and unblinking.

"I'm sorry I asked." Actually, I had my answer.

After a moment, she spoke. "All the signs were there, but I didn't want to believe it: the sudden late-night hours and the out-of-town travel that he never had to do before, the smell of perfume on his clothes. The hush-hush phone calls."

"Do you know who the other woman is?"

She hesitated. "I called the number that kept appearing on his cell phone."

I found myself holding my breath. "And?"

"And the number belongs to Antoinette Chloe Brown."

I just sat in my car, stunned.

Antoinette Chloe Brown? There was that name again.

She seemed too flashy to have an affair with Marvin Cogswell, civil servant. And if she was having an affair, why would she poison him?

If she poisoned anyone, it would have been Roberta to get rid of the competition. Right?

But Roberta and Cogswell weren't married. He was actually free to leave her for Antoinette.

I headed for the library. I wanted to see if I could find anything about Cogswell. Since he was a local, I assumed he went to Sandy Harbor High. You could tell a lot from a yearbook—interests, sports, clubs. Who knew what I might find?

May was at the library, and—surprise, surprise, surprise—she knew that I'd had an appointment with Roberta and that it was going to be windy and rainy tomorrow.

I asked her where the yearbooks from Sandy Harbor High School were. She pointed to a low shelf near the travel section.

"There's at least thirty years' worth of year-books on the shelf, and some of the older ones are on microfiche," she said.

"Thanks, May."

I knew Mr. Cogswell's age from his obituary. I could guess when he graduated from SHHS.

Ty probably never thought of looking at year-books.

Maybe I was being too hard on Ty. He was investigating, researching, running record checks and the like, but I was just impatient that things were taking too long.

When God passed out patience, I jumped out of line because I couldn't stand waiting.

I pulled out five yearbooks, and I settled on the year right in the middle. No Marvin Cogswell was listed.

Then I looked through the following year. There he was. Under his picture was MARVIN "MARV" COGSWELL. "Voted class flirt."

That was interesting.

His interests included fishing, water skiing, and chasing women.

Oh, puh-leeze. I had to admit that he was quite handsome back then. He had smoldering black eyes, a square jaw, and a semi-spiked haircut. At least from the waist up, he looked fit and buff and wore his suit comfortably. He had on a conservatively striped tie with light blue hues.

I remembered the picture of Mr. Cogswell in Roberta's office. Over the years, he'd only gotten better-looking.

In my opinion, Marv was probably a player.

I leafed through the yearbook, specifically looking for Antoinette Chloe.

There she was. She was Antoinette Chloe Switzer back then. She was much thinner—who wasn't thinner in high school?—and quite beautiful. She wore flashy clothes even in high school and went heavy on the makeup. In her picture, she was wearing a gauzy peasant blouse with horizontal stripes of bright primary colors. She wore it off her shoulders with a chunky turquoise necklace. Behind her right ear was a red rose in full bloom.

That was an interesting look for a yearbook picture.

Under her name was "Voted the most interesting fashion maven of the senior class."

I could understand that. She probably had an interesting outfit every day to keep the class entertained.

Wondering by chance if her husband, Sal Brown, attended the same high school, I paged through the pictures. There he was, Salvatore Antonio Brownelli. "Most likely to lead Hells Angels." His interests included "My hog" and "botany."

I could see Sal as a biker, but botany? That seemed out of place for Sal. To me, he should have been more interested in mechanics or that kind of thing.

Botany was the study of plants, like mushrooms for instance.

Now, *that* was interesting!

Had Sal Brown kept up his interest in botany over the years?

Did he know about local poisonous mushrooms?

Stunned, I continued to leaf through the yearbooks. Then I came across a picture of Marvin Cogswell kissing Antoinette Chloe Switzer. The caption said, "There they go again! Get a room!"

Hmm . . . so Marvin Cogswell and Antoinette Chloe were a couple back then.

Wow.

Closing up all the yearbooks, I put them back in order on the shelf.

With a heavy heart, I knew I had to tell Ty about Sal Brown's interest in botany.

Chapter 14

*O*n the drive home, I realized that I hadn't done a very thorough job of checking the yearbooks. I felt like throwing something as a tribute to my lack of focus.

"Damn!"

I should have looked up the Tingsleys and even Roberta Cummings. They were all Sandy Harbor "townies." They were all about the same age, and this was a small town. They all had to have gone to Sandy Harbor High School or one of the region's private schools.

I didn't know what I'd find about the others in the yearbooks, but I thought I'd hit the jackpot.

In high school, ACB had a thing with Marv, and Sal had an interest in botany.

Maybe it wasn't a big deal, or maybe it was.

I stopped in at the sheriff's department building to see Ty, and he wasn't there, but Deputy Mc-Coy was. "He's off for the rest of the day. He said he was going home to get some sleep. Anything I can help you with?"

"No. I'm good. I just wanted to tell him something, but it's probably not important. Thanks, Vern."

"Don't thank me. I'm just glad that Meat Loaf Tuesday is back."

"Then I'll see you tonight at the Silver Bullet. You'll love my meat loaf. I added a special ingredient, just for you."

He put his hands over his heart and grinned. "You are the absolute best, Trixie."

"Aww . . . That's what all the men say."

He burst out laughing. I waved good-bye and left the building. I started for home and continued to think about everything that I'd learned today.

I needed to write it all down in my trusty notebook and get it out of my head.

I drove into the back parking lot of Brown's because it was the first place I saw where I could park and write in privacy. I pulled my notebook out of my purse.

As I began to write, I saw ACB in a muumuu covered in purple orchids and wearing a red turban. She was carrying a plastic grocery bag.

She looked right and left, and walked as fast as her flip-flops would carry her to the back of the Crossroad's Restaurant. I was more impressed with Antoinette Chloe plowing through the snow with red flip-flops on than I was with Laura Kingsley wearing white heels.

I sat, astonished, as I watched ACB toss the plastic bag over a wooden fence. I could see the tops of the green metal Dumpsters of the Crossroads Restaurant, and it appeared that ACB made a direct hit to the middle of the largest one.

She hurried back to her restaurant, head down.

Instinctively, I knew what was in that bag—her gardenia muumuu—and I knew what I had to do.

Dumpster dive.

Driving around to the rear of the Crossroads, I left my car running in the parking lot, in case I had to make a quick escape. Then I walked to the gated area, which contained the Dumpsters. The wooden gate was unlocked, so I pushed it open.

The Dumpster that I needed to search was tall and wide, and I hadn't a clue as to how to climb up onto it.

Looking around, I saw a bicycle covered in snow. It probably had been there since last summer. I didn't think whoever it belonged to would mind if I borrowed it.

I wheeled it into position on the side of the Dumpster and made several attempts to hoist myself up on the seat. Finally, I succeeded and stood shakily on top of garbage bags and whatnot. Ick!

I scanned the area for ACB's bag.

There it was—a bright yellow Dollar-O-Rama bag. I held on to the side of the Dumpster and reached over with my other hand and grabbed it. Peeking inside, I was happy to find the gardenia muumuu.

Holding the bag, I peered over the edge of the Dumpster, and I saw that the bike had fallen. There I was, standing in garbage without a way out.

Now what?

A black SUV drove into the parking lot and headed right toward me.

Don't let it be Ty Brisco!

Of course it was him. Just my luck.

He got out of his vehicle and leaned on it, arms crossed. "A little industrial spying on the competition, darlin'?"

"No. I was hungry and couldn't wait for a table," I said, sarcastically. "Now help me out of here."

"What have you got there?" he asked.

"A certain gardenia muumuu. I saw ACB toss it here."

He grinned. "Excellent work. Shoot the bag over to me."

"Not a chance. Help me out of here first."

"Why? Would you think I'd leave a lady stranded in a Dumpster?"

"This isn't my first rodeo."

Laughing, he sauntered over, and I do mean *sauntered*, as I stood, slowly sinking into some kind of goo like quicksand. I was going to throw out my boots anyway, which was a good thing, but I'd thought I'd toss them after winter, not now.

I kicked a pizza crust and some chicken wing bones from the toe of my boots.

"Lift your right leg up and over the side. Straddle it like you were riding a horse," Ty said. "I'll help you down."

I didn't see how that would help, but I did as I was told. "Yeow."

"Now lift your left leg over your right leg?"

"I'm not a gymnast, Ty."

"Make like it's a horse. And you're getting off."

"Darlin'," I drawled, just like he did, "I've never ridden a horse in my life."

"You city people . . . I just don't understand you. Never been on a horse. I learned to ride before I could walk."

"There aren't a lot of ranches in Philly, cowboy. It's not my fault."

"Just toss your left leg over your right."

Somehow, I did as he said. I got both legs over the edge of the Dumpster, and I was heading straight to the ground.

I took a deep breath, just as I felt strong arms catch me and move me away from the battered green steel. He set me down safely on the ground, but my knees wouldn't lock.

I swayed toward him, and, just like in the movies, I felt his arms around me, steadying me. I swear that I wasn't faking!

I looked up into his sky blue eyes, muttered, "Thank you," and moved away.

"Where's the bag?" he asked.

I pulled it out from under my coat and handed it to him. "Exhibit A."

"I'm not so sure about that," he said.

"What?" I wiped some corn kernels and wilted lettuce from my sleeve.

"ACB claims that she ripped it on *her* Dumpster while taking out the trash. She said that the wind of the last snowstorm caught her dress and it got hooked on a screw. She said Dumpsters are rotated at random by the garbage company, and that your Dumpster might have been hers at one time."

"Is that so?"

"Yeah, it is. I paid a visit to Dandy Dumpster.

And they don't keep a record as to which Dumpster is where, although they are numbered."

"If that's true, then why would ACB go through the trouble of tossing her dress into the Crossroads Dumpster?" I asked.

"That's what I'd like to know."

"Ick," I said, sniffing my parka. The wind shifted, and I caught a whiff of myself.

"Uh-huh." Ty had his hand positioned under his nose.

"I guess I need a shower," I said.

"No comment," he said. "And thanks for this." He held up the bag. "See you later, Trixie."

"See you."

I wondered what Ty was going to do with the rest of his day off. I knew what I was going to do: take a long, hot shower and get some more sleep.

I stunk so bad that I rolled down all the windows as I drove. Finally, turning off Route 3, I drove down the long road that led to the Silver Bullet. I was pleasantly surprised to see a good number of cars in the parking lot. It must be another meeting of the American Legion.

I called Juanita on the cell phone. "It's Trixie. Everything okay?"

"Everything's fine. I can handle it, and Cindy is going to cover for Bob. We don't need you."

"How's the meat loaf selling?"

"It's going like crazy. I'm so glad that you made a lot of it. It's a little different from Porky's meat loaf."

"Salsa," I said. "I put salsa in it. There're a lot of nice veggies in salsa, and it adds a little kick."

"Interesting. Well, the customers love it."

"I'm going to take a shower and catch some sleep. Call me if you need me. Oh, and I'll be over later with the paychecks."

"Great. I'll let everyone know."

I couldn't wait to see everyone's faces when I passed out the checks. I included a little bonus in them for everyone's hard work.

I wanted to visit Mr. Farnsworth, too, and see how the stocking of the bait shop was progressing. I hadn't seen him since his nice speech about me at the fire barn.

Blondie greeted me at the door, and after I played with her and rubbed her tummy, I let her outside. Instead of taking care of business, she zoomed away, chasing a squirrel. I yelled her name repeatedly, not wanting to lose her.

Running after Blondie, I kept calling her name. But soon she was out of sight.

Tears stung my eyes. How could I have been so stupid as to not put her on a leash? But she'd always stayed close to me before. I didn't want to lose her. It would break my heart and Ty's.

I tramped over the lawn, through icy snowdrifts and on crunchy patches of ground, following Blondie's tracks.

It started to sleet. Just what I needed. It was a snow-laden sleet, just enough to get my contacts wet and floating around in my eyes.

"Blondie!" I yelled, not sure if she really knew her name yet.

After a half hour of calling her name and tramping through the snow, I lost it and began to blubber like a little girl.

When my tears cleared, I noticed some pink fluorescent survey ribbons dripping in the sleet where I thought my property line ended. I didn't really know for sure since I'd never seen a survey map. I just knew that I owned "the point."

"Who would mark off my property like this?" I said out loud. Then I thought about it, and one name kept rolling around in my head: Rick Tingsley.

But the pink fluorescent tape didn't stop at my property. I saw more farther ahead. It seemed like either someone was buying or selling a parcel of land that abutted mine.

I made a mental note to take a trip to the assessor's office. Maybe they'd know if someone just bought this land.

If Mayor Tingsley bought the adjacent land, he'd own quite a chunk of Sandy Harbor. All the more reason for him to want my parcel, too.

I'd go to the assessor's office tomorrow. But right now, I needed to find Blondie. I trudged through the sleet, which turned to a wet snow, and followed Blondie's tracks until I lost them.

I kept calling her name. As I walked, I noticed a patch of dirt under an evergreen tree. The dirt had been disturbed. Then I noticed a small rusted trowel.

I squatted down, looking at the dirt. It wasn't as if I could read dirt like a tracker, but it seemed like the digging had been done before the snow fell—maybe in the fall.

It didn't seem like an animal had dug there either. Besides, the shovel was a dead giveaway.

And Sal Brown had an interest in botany.

Finally, I heard a bark, and Blondie appeared, her caramel-colored hair flying in the air as she ran toward me.

I stood up, and she jumped up on her hind legs with her front legs propped against my chest. She bent her head back for me to scratch under her chin, which I did. Then she started sniffing the air and ran off.

Even the dog couldn't stand my smell!

"C'mon, Blondie. Let's go home," I said.

Blondie waited for me; then she walked at my side. Finally, we walked up the slushy steps of my house, and I held the door open for her. She walked in and headed for her water bowl and food.

It was strange to think of the big Victorian as my home. There were still things that belonged to Aunt Stella that I didn't want to touch: clothes, knickknacks, pictures and other personal items. I did expect a phone call from her sooner or later, and I'd ask her then what her plans were for her possessions.

She did have some valuable antiques that I would've loved to have. Maybe she'd rather get new, lighter-colored furniture for her new digs in Florida, or maybe not.

Either way, I'd like to know so I could make the house my own.

I undressed in the laundry room, putting every article of clothing I had on into the washer, including my parka. I poured in laundry soap, a laundry soap booster, and set the dial for hot water and a large load.

"I know—I stink," I explained to Blondie, who was staring at me. I slipped into a robe that was hanging on a hook. Absolutely starving, I searched through the fridge for something healthy to snack on. I settled for peanut butter and jelly on a toasted English muffin. Oh well, the cold glass of milk that I added was relatively healthy, even though it wasn't low-fat.

Blondie followed me up the stairs to the shower. There, she stretched out on the tile floor.

After I scrubbed with every scented gel and soap in the shower and washed my hair with two types of shampoo and cream rinse, I declared that I'd banished the garbage smell from my person. Just in case, I sprayed on some tea rose perfume mist from a bottle on the shelf.

Just as soon as I could find the rest of my toiletries, I'd box up Aunt Stella's things and put mine on the shelves.

As I slipped into my Mickey Mouse nightshirt, I realized that I had bigger things to worry about than finding my toiletries.

I needed to find out about all those lovely pink survey markers on the border of my land. Wondering if Aunt Stella might have an old survey map, I walked down the stairs to check in her office.

The shiny wooden floor was cold under my bare feet. Actually, the whole house was cold. I shivered and tucked my wet hair behind my ears, but I kept looking through the old oak file cabinets that lined the wall.

When I was a kid, some of the land to the south of where the woods began was farmed. Cows grazed on thick green grass almost to the shore of Lake Ontario, but a fence kept them from walking onto the sand dunes and drinking from the lake. The fence didn't stop us from climbing in and petting the cows or trying to climb up onto their backs.

My sister, being more daring, tried to milk them from time to time, but nothing ever happened. It wasn't until the farmer had caught us one time and showed Susie how to milk the cow that we were welcomed through the gate. He was hard to understand, with a very thick accent and sun-darkened skin, but he had friendly brown eyes.

Oh! An old folder labeled *Our First Home*. The house was plotted out on a typical survey map, but there was no diner or cottages present yet. The land behind it was owned by—I turned the map around to read the faded printing—*Domenick V. Brownelli.*

He had to be related to Sal Brown. Maybe the farmer of my memory was Sal's father or grandfather.

I wondered if the land was still in the family, if

maybe Sal Brown now owned the property. If he did, it was logical that he might have made an offer to Aunt Stella. If she sold to him, then he'd be the one to have a nice stretch of fairly level land and more than a mile of prime sandy beach on Lake Ontario, not Mayor Tingsley and his campaign strategy to bring in jobs to the region.

Sal could do a lot of developing with that kind of beachfront, too. Then again, he could have developed his land long ago, but he'd kept it natural.

I wanted to find out if Sal Brown owned the property, or if he sold it.

And what about the digging of what could be mushrooms that I found in the woods?

It was unclear as to how this would help me figure out who killed Mr. Cogswell, but I assumed that if there was land development going on, as the new survey tags indicated, it might affect my business.

Or maybe the tags were from an old survey, but I didn't think so. They looked new, not faded.

Murder or not, I needed to check out the tags.

And what happened to the Sandy Harbor gossip hotline? I hadn't heard anything about a recent land purchase. News like that should have spread like wildfire. Why the secrecy?

Just as I was about to make the climb back upstairs, Blondie rushed to the front door and started barking.

Following her, I discovered that a black Amish carriage had pulled up alongside my car. The horse that had been pulling the wagon hung his great head, as if he were telling the driver that he didn't have the energy to deal with a noisy dog.

A woman climbed down from the carriage. She was dressed all in black, a long dress, a coat, and bonnet that covered all of her hair. She walked toward my front door, carrying a basket.

I suddenly realized that I was in my Mickey Mouse nightshirt with bare feet.

I reached into the closet on my left and pulled out a yellow rain slicker that had to be Uncle Porky's.

Shoes. I needed shoes!

There was no way that I was going to put my feet into my stinky boots that I should have thrown away. I checked the bottom of the closet and found matching yellow boots. I slid my bare feet into them. They covered my knees and were six sizes too big, but they'd have to do.

I told Blondie to lie down, and surprisingly she obeyed me. Whoever had owned the dog before— no matter how negatively I felt about him for dumping her—had done a great job of training her.

I opened the door before my visitor had a chance to knock.

"Hello," I said.

"Hello. I'm Mrs. Stolfus. Forgive me for intruding on you, Miss Matkowski, but Juanita said that I would be welcome."

"Of course you are! Come in."

She tried not to look at my strange attire, but I could see her eyes traveling up and down my Big Bird outfit.

"Did I come at an inconvenient time?" she asked.

"Absolutely not. You just caught me in my Mickey Mouse nightshirt, and I didn't think it was appropriate for greeting company." I laughed. "But this outfit is just perfect, correct?"

She chuckled, and I motioned for her to take a seat in the living room. My legs wouldn't bend at the knees because the boots were so high, so I had to step out of them before I sat down across from her.

"Sorry, Mrs. Stolfus. My slippers are upstairs."

"Don't worry, please."

"Can I offer you some tea? Coffee?" I didn't know what the Amish could drink. "Water?"

Dammit . . . oops . . . I mean *darn*. I didn't have anything sweet to offer her.

"I'm fine. Thank you, Miss Matkowski."

"Please, call me Trixie."

"I will. And my name is Sarah."

"Hello, Sarah."

She opened the lid of her basket. "I might as well come to the point of my visit. I bake, and I was wondering if you could use any of my baked goods in your restaurant." She pulled out a tray of samples and handed it to me. "You don't have to answer now," she said. "Please just think about it."

"I don't have to think about it, Sarah. I was going to contact you earlier, but then the diner . . . well, it wasn't doing much business, but things are picking up. We have some groups from the

American Legion who are meeting at the diner now, and they definitely like their sweets."

I saw what I thought was a hand pie: fruit filling in a flaky crust and crimped on the side. Mrs. Stolfus's had a sugar glaze, and I started drooling like one of Pavlov's dogs.

"Sarah, I'll take a dozen of everything every three days. Can you handle more if there are more meetings? Of course, I'll give you as much notice as I can. How would I get ahold of you?"

"Would you like to know my prices?"

"No. I trust you to be fair."

"I shall be fair," Mrs. Stolfus said solemnly. "Send a note with Sandra, your waitress. She lives nearby. And thank you, Trixie."

"Thank you, Sarah. Your baked goods will be a most welcome addition to the Silver Bullet. Oh, and I hear that you have just moved to Sandy Harbor. I'm new, too. Well, I'm sorta new."

She smiled. "Several families came here from Lancaster. We heard that there was good farmland and people who would welcome us."

"I came from Philadelphia. We were almost neighbors! And yes, there are good people here."

Except whoever murdered Marvin Cogswell.

"Sarah, have any of your people bought the land west of mine? Along the water?"

"My husband looked into that land. It was much too expensive, being on the water, and there was no house or barn or silo. We try to buy farms that are already . . . established."

"By any chance would you remember who was selling the land?"

"An Italian gentleman, by the name of—"

"Salvatore Brownelli?" I asked, my heart beating rapidly.

"Yes! That was his name."

"I wonder who bought it," I said.

"I'm afraid I don't know."

"That's okay. I was just wondering, since I'm going to get a new neighbor." Plus, it would have saved me a trip to downtown Sandy Harbor.

As I munched on Sarah's tray of goodies, we made small talk, and I found myself enjoying her company very much.

As she was leaving, she invited me to her farm to meet her husband, Levi, and their four little Stolfuses, two girls and two boys. It was then I noticed glints of metal on her dress, and realized that her outfit was held together with straight pins.

Fascinating.

I couldn't wait to chuck the rain slicker. I was sweating like a racehorse in the rubberized coat. Slipping it off, I felt that I could breathe.

I should go to bed. That was what I should do, but no. Not me. I had to go to the assessor's office and find out who owned the land, or I'd never be able to sleep.

I pulled myself up the stairs, slipped into jeans, and a T-shirt. I slipped on a pair of pink socks and went back downstairs to dig in my boxes to find another pair of sneakers. I'd left my other pair at the diner. And I needed a coat of some sort. I scored on both, finding a navy blue peacoat in another box.

I went into the laundry room, transferred everything into the dryer, and turned the machine on.

Then I threw my winter boots away. Maybe I'd stop at the Dollar-O-Rama and see whether they had any boots. I fed Blondie, gave her a pat on the head, and headed for my car, hoping that Wyatt Earp wasn't watching the parking lot.

I was the only one in the assessor's office. Finally, a pink-faced gentleman, his white hair standing up like a dandelion puffball, walked to the counter.

"What can I do for you today?"

"I'm Trixie Matkowski and I own the point, or I will after I buy it from my aunt Stella."

He stuck out his hand. "I'm George Shea. I remember you from Stella and Porky's parties. How you loved to dance!"

We shook hands, and I immediately liked George Shea. He was warm and had twinkling green eyes.

"Mr. Shea, I'd like to know who owns the land to the west of mine. I saw survey markers on the property line, and it seems like someone is getting ready to buy, sell, or build."

I thought he'd lift one of the heavy bound books lined up around the room, or maybe type something onto the huge computer sitting on a desk, but he didn't.

"That'd be Mayor Tingsley's in-laws. They bought

the land just last week from Salvatore Brownelli, or Sal Brown, as he goes by."

"I remember that there were cows on the property once."

"Sal didn't want to farm way back when. That flashy wife of his wouldn't stand for being on a farm."

"So they built a restaurant instead."

"Yeah." Mr. Shea shook his head. "And it's just too bad. That parcel of land has been in the Brownelli family for generations. Sal's had many offers throughout the years, but he always turned them down. He said he wanted to leave the land wild—for the birds, the native plants, and to protect the sand dunes. A lot of people forgot that he owned it. It was just there."

"Then why did Sal sell it now?"

"I asked him, and he just shrugged."

"And Mayor Tingsley's father-in-law bought it," I stated, wanting another confirmation from Mr. Shea.

"Yep. But the man's in Florida. I'm wondering what he wants with it."

I rubbed my chin, thinking. "I'm wondering, too, but I hear that Tingsley is talking of developing it. He must be partnering with his in-laws."

"It's a big parcel, but it's not big enough for what he wants to do."

"And what does he want to do?"

"He wants to put up a five-star resort. Attract the big spenders. Hollywood people. And he wants to put up condos, a marina, a fancy restaurant."

"That's what I heard, too. But you say that there's not enough land."

Mr. Shea shook his head. "Not by a long shot." He lowered his voice. "You know, he asked me about the value of your land."

"No!" I feigned righteous indignation.

"Yes."

"Did you tell him?"

"I told the lazy slug to look it up on the Internet. We have a Web site, you know. All the assessments are public information."

I chuckled.

But what did it all mean? I still had a nagging suspicion that someone wanted to put me out of business so that he could buy the point.

Tingsley had the most to gain by putting me out of business.

Why would Sal Brown sell? Why now? What had happened to his dream of birds, dunes, and native plants?

Plants?

I'd bet the diner that Sal Brown knew there were Destroying Angels growing on that piece of land. Someone dug them up under that tree in the woods.

But I had no reason to suspect Sal Brown. If he sold his land, he wouldn't have any reason to lust after mine. And how did his wife fit in with her ripped muumuu?

Rick Tingsley just zoomed past ACB on my list of suspects.

But I was going by my "land lust" theory. What about my love-triangle theory?

Was Mr. Cogswell cheating on Roberta? She had an alibi; she was in the front of the diner at the time of the victim's death.

I sighed. I was going in circles like the dough hook in the big mixer.

Chapter 15

*A*s I was coming out of the assessor's office, Ty held the door open for me.

"What are you, my bodyguard?"

He chuckled. "You might need rescuing from another Dumpster. I'm your man." He raised an eyebrow. "I thought—again—that you were going to get some sleep."

"I couldn't sleep. I had to know who owned the land by me."

"Tingsley's in-laws. They live in Florida. They bought it a week ago from Sal Brown," he said.

"How on earth did you know?"

He grinned. "My laptop. It's amazing what you can find without even leaving your home."

"Sure, I could have done that, but then I wouldn't have met Mr. Shea, and I wouldn't have heard about Sal's reluctance to sell for years. Then suddenly he does. To our mayor's in-laws."

We walked toward my car. "I think we can conclude that Tingsley's in-laws bought it for Tingsley and his lofty dreams."

"Yes. But why did Sal sell now? Did Tingsley have something against Sal? Did he blackmail him into selling?"

"I thought of that, too. I'm going to take a ride

to Brown's Restaurant and have a talk with ACB."

"Sounds like a plan. Can I come?"

"Of course not. This is official police business."

"I really need to hear what ACB has to say. C'mon, Ty. Maybe I can help. I've kind of bonded with her."

He sighed. "Okay, but don't interfere with my investigation."

"I promise." Maybe we'd have a breakthrough on the case. Even if we didn't, I'd get to see Ty in action.

He opened the door to his vehicle, and I got in. He drove the short distance to Brown's, and we stood in line to be seated. ACB was the hostess, and she smiled when she saw us.

"I'll be with you in a moment."

She was wearing a muumuu with large green palm trees on it complete with coconuts. I had to admit that it was pretty mild for her. However, on her toes was red glitter nail polish, and she wore lime green flip-flops with sequins. She was missing her usual turban, but a big orange velvet bow was perched on the top of her head. Her hair, freshly dyed a bright red with purple streaks around her face, was cut in a choppy pageboy.

Bangle bracelets of all shapes and sizes circled her wrists, and her earrings were balls of purple rhinestones that swayed when she moved.

The place was still packed, but the Silver Bullet was picking up. Thankfully, I'd be able to make my first installment payment to Aunt Stella without dipping too much into the "get lost" money from Deputy Doug and his trophy wife, and that made me feel happy and independent. The next installment would be all profit, I hoped.

ACB picked up two menus from a holder on the side of the podium. "Welcome to Brown's Restaurant. I can seat you now."

Ty tweaked his hat brim. "Mrs. Brown, we are not going to eat. Is there somewhere we can talk in private?"

"Why, uh . . . As you can see, I'm very busy here." She waved at a front table, but no one waved back. "See?" she asked. "Very busy."

"Can you get someone else to take over for you?" Ty asked.

She just pulled out a sign that read SIT ANY-WHERE and tacked it to the podium.

Without saying a word, she led us to a roped-off area in the back of the restaurant. The faux marble floor was dirty and sticky, and the tables weren't much better.

We each took a seat on the wobbly wooden chairs.

ACB's lips were clamped together, or maybe they were stuck together with her pasty orange lipstick.

"Mrs. Brown, do you mind if I ask you a couple of questions?"

"Why certainly not, Deputy Ty."

Suddenly, she was going to cooperate.

Ty leaned back in his chair. "You should know that the dress you threw away was recovered from the Dumpster belonging to the Crossroads Restaurant. I have a witness who saw you dispose of it."

Her lips stayed shut, but her eyes opened wide. She finally said, "So? The dress was damaged."

"I want to ask you again. Do you know how it got damaged?" Ty asked.

"I told you that I snagged it on my Dumpster when I was taking out a bag of trash. I was going to shorten it, but then I didn't want to bother, so I threw it away."

She continued. "Why are you questioning me about my dress again? I just don't understand why ... I just don't understand what this all means."

"It means that I believe that you were at the Silver Bullet the day Mr. Cogswell was poisoned," Ty said.

Her eyes grew as wide as saucers; then she turned toward the kitchen. Did she want her husband here, or did she want him to call her a lawyer?

"Deputy, please believe me . . . I haven't been to the Silver Bullet since Porky died and Stella had open house. And I didn't wear the gardenia dress. I wore my black dahlia dress. I always wear the black dahlia for the departed."

She took a deep breath, slipped her hand into the vee of her dress, and adjusted her bra straps.

Ty shook his head. It was obvious that he didn't believe her.

I took a deep breath. "Antoinette Chloe, I was the one who saw you throw it away over at the

Crossroads," I said. "How come you didn't use your own Dumpster? You have two of them."

"They were full."

"You didn't want anyone to find the dress, did you?"

"No."

"Why's that?"

She looked toward the kitchen. "No particular reason. I just wanted a quick walk in the fresh air. And I didn't kill Mr. Cogswell, if that's what you think." Tears flooded her eyes and dropped onto her powdered cheeks. "I can't talk about it."

"Antoinette Chloe, can I ask you a personal question?" I asked.

"I suppose so."

"I know that you and Mr. Cogswell had a relationship in high school. Did you still . . . uh . . . have a relationship with him?"

Tears flooded her eyes and black mascara dripped down her cheeks in small streams.

"I'm a married woman, Miss Matkowski." She dabbed at her eyes with a tissue that I handed her.

Suddenly, I felt sorry for ACB. It would be awful to have loved someone since high school and decades later still be in love with him, but be married to someone else.

If she was in love with Marvin Cogswell, why did she marry Salvatore Brownelli?

I didn't have a chance to ask that. Ty's cell phone started ringing.

"But I'm in the middle of something, Lou," I heard him say. "Okay, I'll be right there."

He looked at me. "I have to go."

"Go right ahead," I said. "I can walk to my car."

"Why don't you let me drive you?"

"I'm fine, Ty. I'm going to talk to Antoinette Chloe some more. Girl talk. You go and take care of business."

He glared at me, straightened his hat on his head, and hurried out of the restaurant, without so much as a good-bye.

ACB's eyes darted to the kitchen again.

I spoke up. "Antoinette Chloe, I understand that all three of you went to high school together: you, Sal, and Marvin Cogswell."

"And Laura VanPlank Tingsley and Rick Tingsley. Roberta Cummings was a year behind us. Most of the town went to SHHS."

"But you and Marvin Cogswell were a couple," I said, "And you never stopped loving him, did you?" I put my hand over hers.

She nodded, tears dripping down her face. "I loved Marv in high school," she finally said. "I've always considered him a good friend, but I love Sal now. And, Trixie, I don't know how a piece of my dress came to be at your diner. I'd never kill Marvin. Never!"

"Why did you marry Sal just out of high school if you loved Marv?" I asked, gently.

"I—I was pregnant, and Marvin . . . well, he wasn't the marrying type."

"Was it Marv's baby?" I asked gently.

She nodded, sobbing harder. "Sal married me so I could save face, but then . . . but then I lost the baby, but I stayed with Sal. He's a good man, and I owe him for marrying me. It was a different time back then."

She looked down, as if embarrassed. "I really need to get back to work."

I decided to change the subject, but I pushed on. "Antoinette Chloe, you really never said why you tossed your muumuu over the fence to the Crossroads Dumpster. It seemed like you were hiding it."

If looks could kill, I'd be the next thing she tossed in the Dumpster.

"I said that ours were full."

I didn't believe her. "But there certainly would have been enough room for a little bag."

"I just wanted to go for a little walk, to get some fresh air. The sun was shining, and I didn't think that Laura Tingsley would mind me using her Dumpster, for heaven's sake."

She dabbed at her eyes and raised her head. I could tell that our conversation was over.

"I know you were lying about wanting my house to be on the historical society's tour, you know."

"I most certainly was not lying. I'm the chairperson of the tour. Just ask Mrs. Leddy."

"Oh! Oh, that's wonderful! Have you made a decision on my home yet?"

She'd been sitting at the table with a deputy sheriff and had been questioned about a murder, but she was still concerned about being included on a house tour. Go figure.

ACB was either very naïve or very innocent. Maybe both. Or maybe she was just a good actress.

"I haven't made a decision yet, Antoinette Chloe, but as soon as possible, I'll let you know." I stood to go, but then decided we still had some unfinished business.

"I hear that congratulations are in order. I understand that Sal finally sold his property on the lake."

If possible, ACB went white under her heavy makeup. *"He did what?"*

I ignored her shock. "Are you and Sal going to do something special with the money? Maybe take a European cruise? Add that ice-cream stand onto the restaurant?"

For a moment, I thought she was going to faint.

"I just came from the assessor's office," I said. "Sal sold the land."

"We were going to build our retirement home on the waterfront," she mumbled to herself. She looked down at her glittery fingernails, and then gripped the edge of the table with her hands until her knuckles turned white.

"I'm sorry to break the news to you. Obviously, you didn't know." I truly was sorry. ACB seemed totally shocked.

"I—I have to get back to work." Fresh tears trailed down her cheeks, washing away more makeup.

"I'm so sorry to spring the news on you like that, but I'd like to talk to Sal. I'm curious to know who my new neighbor will be," I lied. "Would you ask him if he could join me for a moment?"

She dabbed at her eyes, then nodded.

ACB seemed to age twenty years in the twenty minutes Ty and I had been talking to her. She got up from the table and wobbled on her flip-flops to the kitchen door. She paused a moment before she pushed the doors open, then disappeared inside.

I waited at least ten minutes for Sal Brown to appear or for ACB to return and give me a reason why he wasn't coming.

He's probably finishing up an order, I thought, my patience wearing thin.

I waited another ten minutes, then decided that I was going to slip into the kitchen and talk to him while he cooked.

When I entered the kitchen, only Sal's brother was present. He was dropping a handful of potato chips into the middle of a plate containing a turkey club.

"They fought over her gardenia dress," the burly man explained as if he could read my mind. "She accused him of cutting it up and framing her. Then there was something about their retirement home on the lake. Seemed like a stupid fight."

"So where's Sal?" I asked.

"He hustled out of here like his hairy ass was on fire."

"Where's Antoinette Chloe?" I asked.

"He insisted that she go with him."

Chapter 16

"Do you mind if I use your side door?" I asked Sal's brother. "It'll be a shorter walk to my car."

He shrugged a shoulder.

"Thanks."

As I left Brown's, I ran through what Sal's brother had said: ACB accused Sal of cutting up her gardenia dress, and they had fought.

Why on earth would Sal do that?

My cell phone rang, and I immediately thought of Juanita and the diner, but it was Ty.

"I got the test results back on ACB's dress and the material that Blondie found."

"That was fast," I said.

"The lab tech owed me a favor," he said.

"I can imagine." I rolled my eyes. "And I won't ask why."

He laughed.

"So tell me about the lab results already!"

"A perfect match, but—"

"Yeah?"

"The results showed that a couple edges of the material were cut, not ripped."

"Cut? As in cut out of the muumuu with scissors?"

"Uh-huh."

"That's strange, isn't it? I would have bet the Silver Bullet that ACB caught her muumuu on my Dumpster when she was waiting for an opportunity to poison Mr. Cogswell."

"It's strange all right. It must have been planted."

"You mean that someone tried to frame ACB for the murder?"

"That's my guess."

I couldn't believe what I was hearing. This was huge. This was beyond huge.

"Who would want to frame Antoinette Chloe?" I asked.

"If we knew that, we'd have our murderer."

"Ty, do you think that Sal Brown could have discovered that ACB and Marvin were having an affair? An affair that has lasted since high school? Remember, they were a couple, according to the yearbook. And ACB told me that she was pregnant with Marvin's baby in high school. Marv wouldn't marry her, but Sal Brown did. I'm only assuming that their affair had continued, but it makes sense, doesn't it?"

"Hot damn. A love triangle, just like you suggested. Where are you now, Trixie?"

"Walking to my car."

"Good. Go home. I'll catch up with you."

"One more thing, Ty. I found out that ACB and Sal just had an argument about the gardenia dress and him selling the land. She was very upset. She didn't know he'd sold it. She said that they were going to retire there and build a home on the lake."

"This is huge. Let me handle it from here, Trixie. You did a great job; now go home. Promise?"

"Yeah. I promise. I'm exhausted."

My brain whirled as I walked to my car, cutting through the parking lots of the various businesses in the tiny downtown area of Sandy Harbor.

I wasn't paying much attention to where I was walking or what I was doing, but I found myself in another back parking lot. I almost bumped into Brown's white van.

A banging noise was coming from within the van, almost like someone was kicking the side of the van from inside.

With one hand, I reached for my cell phone to call 911, while with the other I opened the van doors. Someone might be hurt.

My eyes adjusted to the dark interior. There was Antoinette Chloe Brown, bound and gagged, lying on the van floor. She shook her head violently, and lashed out with her flip-flops on the side of the van. I guessed that she wanted me to untie her, but I wasn't going into that van. I needed to call for help.

But before I had a chance to dial, the phone was yanked out of my hand. I whirled around, ready with my knee to launch a swift jab.

Roberta Cummings jumped back before I could connect.

"Roberta, call the police!" I shouted. "Antoinette Chloe is in the back of Sal's van, and she's tied up and gagged."

"Why would I call the police? I'm the one who put her there."

Roberta Cummings walked toward me, a black metal gun in her alabaster hand. I don't know my guns or my calibers, but it looked B-I-G, and it was pointed right at me. Then she handed it to Sal Brown.

"What's going on here?" I asked Roberta. Her cheeks were almost flushed, she had a slight smile, and she looked . . . excited.

Sal and Roberta were in this together!

Of course! It was Roberta who called Juanita out to the front of the diner so Sal could plant the poison mushrooms in the pork and scalloped potatoes.

I moved a few steps toward Roberta. "It's not too late for you to get out of this. Roberta, call the police."

Instead she picked up a travel bag and hoisted it over her shoulder. I noticed more suitcases behind her.

"Now what are we going to do, Sal?" she asked.

"We have to dispose of both of them. My unfaithful wife and Trixie. It's too bad, Trixie. I liked you."

My heart was going to fly right out of my chest, I was so scared. "I liked you, too, Sal. But tell me, did you get the Destroying Angels to poison Mr. Cogswell from your land?"

Even with all his facial hair, I could still see his mouth curled up in a smile. "It's a good name for a mushroom, isn't it? Destroying Angel. That's just how I felt when I . . . when we . . ." He looked at Roberta, and she smiled at him.

"Premeditated murder," I said, digging my own grave. "And it looks like you are skipping town. Did you get lots of money from the sale of your lakefront property, Sal?"

"You've been busy, haven't you?" He clicked his tongue against his teeth. "Too bad."

"Your major felony made the Silver Bullet a ghost town." I said, trying to stall. Maybe ACB would attract more attention. I'd left the back doors of the van open, and she was still pounding.

"But the demise of the Silver Bullet made my Antoinette Chloe a happy person. And God knows that I've tried to make her happy over the years, but nothing I did ever satisfied her. She never loved me, so finally I gave up."

I swallowed hard. "But Sal, you tried to frame her, and now you're going to kill her! And me, too!"

"I'd had enough of hearing about Marvin Cogswell!" he yelled, then sobered. "He's all she talked about. 'Marv gave me flowers, this perfume.' 'Marv would never do what you did.' 'Marv dresses better than you.' 'Marv gave me this necklace. . . .' Marv, Marv, Marv!"

He was snapping right before my eyes. He professed to love his wife, but he'd tied her up in the back of the van to kill her. His big brown eyes were swimming in tears, and for a nanosecond I felt sorry for him.

Then he straightened his spine, wiped the tears

from his eyes with the hem of his tee, and took a couple of deep breaths. "Roberta and I are going to spend all the money that I got for my lakefront property. I knew it would come in handy someday. Now, enough chitchat, Trixie. Walk to the van, and don't make a sound."

"Where are we going?" I asked.

"You're so curious about my land. I know of a nice old well on the property. No one will find you and Antoinette Chloe for decades."

"Don't be too sure of that, Sal. Deputy Sheriff Ty Brisco is on your trail." At least I hoped he was.

"He's on a nice wild-goose chase," Roberta said. "All three of the deputies are. I called and reported that a little girl fell into the far end of Sandy Harbor where it meets Lake Ontario. The three stooges are gone."

"Aren't you the smart one?" I said sarcastically.

I wished I knew the moves to knock the gun out of Roberta's hand and get her in a headlock, but what did a Philly tour guide know? In all my years with Deputy Doug, he hadn't taught me one defensive tactic, and I'd never asked to learn.

I took a deep breath. "The Sandy Harbor sheriffs are not stooges. And they'll be coming to get the two of you."

"Walk!" he said, and I could feel his gun in my back.

"Roberta, dammit, call the police!" I yelled.

"Not a prayer, Trixie. Marv wouldn't marry me. I wasted years on him. Just like Sal wasted years on Antoinette Chloe."

"But Roberta, I thought that Marvin abused you. Why would you want to marry him?"

She waved a hand in dismissal. "Our fights were legendary. And I was the one who hit him." She grinned.

"So Marvin got a wrong rap?" I shook my head.

She shrugged. "All part of my plan."

I looked at both of them, partners in crime, and my stomach roiled.

"Walk or I'll shoot you right here," Sal said.

"Whatever you say, Sal," I said. I was mad now. I wasn't going to go quietly into an old well. I shuddered, thinking of snakes and spiders and spending that much time with ACB.

I wasn't worried that Sal was going to pull that trigger. He was a sneaky killer who used poison. He didn't want to see blood.

We walked to the van with Sal toting one of Roberta's suitcases and with his gun in my back. Roberta carried another suitcase and still pointed her gun. Where was everyone?

"I hope you're going someplace warm," I said, still fishing for information.

"We're going someplace without an extradition treaty." Sal laughed and, as he did, the gun jiggled up and down in his hand.

When Antoinette Chloe saw Sal, she began to thrash and tried to kick him. If that gag ever came off, there'd be a string of obscenities so loud that the people in Watertown would hear her.

"Roberta, do you have anything I could gag Trixie with?"

"I have a couple of silk scarves, but I don't want to—"

"Just give them to me!" Sal spit the words, and I felt the spray.

He stuffed a scarf into my mouth. It tasted like old Estee Lauder perfume. He tied the other around my head to keep the gag in place. Then he tied my hands with rope and pushed me down onto the hard metal floor of the van.

ACB looked at me, tears pooling in her brown eyes. Her cheeks were striped from dripping mascara. I blinked back my own tears. I wouldn't give Sal or Roberta the satisfaction of seeing me cry.

They both slipped into the front seats, and we started to roll.

Looking around for something to cut the rope binding me, I couldn't find anything. I turned on my side to ACB, hoping that she might have some fingers available to untie my hands.

She had to turn her back to me because her hands were tied behind her back, but I did feel her trying to untie my hands.

Luckily, Roberta and Sal were chatting away and didn't notice what we were doing in the back of the van.

I finally felt the rope loosen around my hands, just as my shoulder was growing numb. ACB did it!

Then I helped her, being careful not to give us away. I put my index finger over my gag as a sign for her not to talk.

We both loosened the ropes that were tying our ankles, just enough so Sal wouldn't notice.

We drove over smooth roads, and then a crazy bumpy road. We had to be on Sal's land, which was not far from my property. If only I could make it to the Silver Bullet! I didn't know the woods at all, but I could try to make it to the lake. Then I could find my way on the beach.

I glanced at my fellow captive. Could she and her flip-flops keep up with me?

Who was I kidding? Did wearing sneakers suddenly turn me into an athlete? I hadn't run three feet in my entire life.

But then again, I'd never had to run for my life.

I tried to signal to ACB that as soon as the doors to the van opened, we should kick with all our might.

She seemed to understand me. We took off our gags—thank God—and slid closer to the back door of the van, our knees almost touching it. Just as Sal opened the double doors, we kicked him with all our might.

ACB landed the best kick, right in Sal's jewels.

As Sal squirmed on the muddy ground, Roberta appeared with Sal's gun in her hand.

I kicked out at her, but she was too far back.

"Get out!" she screamed. "And put your hands in the air." She looked at Sal, holding his privates. "Get up, Sal. I don't know where the damn well is."

"Over there," he said, pointing. "Just go straight. I can't . . . walk."

"Don't do this, Roberta. Don't do it!" I pleaded.

"You can have Sal. Take him." ACB sniffed. "But leave us alone."

"I don't want him." Roberta looked down her nose at ACB. "I just want my share of the money he promised me for luring Juanita away from the kitchen."

"Were you the one who phoned in an order to Sunshine Food Supply for a box of mushrooms?" I had to know; it had been bothering me.

She laughed. "I thought it would cast more suspicion on you," Roberta said, pushing me forward.

"We were going to build our retirement home here." ACB started to wail.

Roberta raised her arm up to the sky and shot the gun. "Shut up! Both of you, just shut up."

The crack of the shot echoed in my brain. My scream echoed across New York State. Before Roberta could point the gun back at us, I reached for her skinny wrist and twisted it. Then I threw all my weight at her like a crazed wrestler, and we both fell into a pile of snow. For good measure, I heaped some snow on her face.

"Get the gun, Antoinette Chloe."

"I don't want to touch it," she said.

"Oh, for heaven's sake." I sighed. "Then take my place on top of Roberta."

"Okay."

She obliged, hiked up her palm-tree-and-coconut-covered muumuu, and sat on a probably very cold, very sore, Roberta Cummings.

I picked up the gun from the ground and looked over at Sal Brown. He was still curled up like a boiled shrimp in a foot of snow.

"Antoinette Chloe, by any chance do you have a cell phone?" I asked, wondering why I hadn't asked her that while our hands were semi-free in the van.

She grunted. I took that to mean yes.

I searched the pockets of her coat and found it. Before I could dial, I could hear police sirens getting louder and louder.

Soon, they found us.

Ty knelt down and handcuffed Sal Brown. He turned him over to Vern McCoy to be searched.

Then Ty ran toward us. "Are you okay?" he asked me, gently taking the gun from my hand.

He looked at me from head to toe.

"I'm fine. Really."

"And how about you, Antoinette Chloe?" he asked.

She made a face. "Considering that my husband is a killer and he was going to frame me and run off with this skinny skank, I guess I'm okay."

Ty stifled a laugh, and so did I.

"Get this elephant off me!" Roberta gasped for air.

Ty helped ACB off Roberta and helped a wet Roberta to stand up. He then cuffed her and patted her down.

"Let's all go back to the office and sort this out," Ty said.

"And, boy, do I have a lot to tell you!" ACB said, glaring over to where Sal stood with his arms cuffed behind his back, being guarded by Vern McCoy.

Her feet had to be freezing in those flip-flops, but that didn't stop her from stomping over to her husband, throwing back her arm, and slapping Sal's face.

"That's for poisoning Marv Cogswell. There was never anything between us, you stupid idiot. I just tried to make you jealous because . . . because . . . I wanted to keep you on your toes."

His mouth dropped open. "Oh, Annie! Dammit, Annie! Now you tell me?"

"Oh, Sal, you supreme idiot. How could you ever think I'd love Marv? He wouldn't marry me when I was pregnant, but you did, Sal. You did." She blinked back tears. "But I can't understand how you could fool around with the snow queen." She curled her top lip and sneered at Roberta.

"How did you and Roberta get together?" I asked Sal. I knew from Deputy Doug that once a suspect was handcuffed, he couldn't be questioned by law enforcement without his Miranda rights being read. However, that requirement didn't pertain to a certain diner owner who almost spent the rest of her days in a well and chit-chatting with ACB.

"Yeah, Sal, explain that," ACB ordered.

"One day, I went over to the Crossroads for a beer and to unwind. Roberta and I got to talking. We decided for our own reasons to take care of Marv."

"What was your reason, Roberta?" I turned to her, but she stared down at the ground. It was dawning on me that Sal was definitely not the mastermind criminal type. Roberta must have orchestrated the entire murder, but still I didn't understand why. "Roberta?"

"I had a boring, dead-end job and no savings. I needed cash to get away from here and start over. So when Sal told me he thought Marv and that floral explosion of a woman over there were having an affair, I decided to manipulate Sal into killing Marvin and running away with me. Believe me, I'd have spent all his money before he knew it."

"It's my money, too!" ACB burst into tears. "Oh! This is all my fault. I shouldn't have brought up Marvin all the time. He was no prize. Matter of fact, he was a no-good coward, a moocher, and a—"

"Let's go," Ty said, moving Sal in the direction of his cruiser.

Antoinette wiped her tears on the sleeve of her coat. "I can't believe this, Sal. How could you? And you were going to take off with our retirement money? I worked just as hard as you."

"It's in the green suitcase in the van. It's yours, Annie." His eyes lowered. He couldn't even look at her.

"Is that supposed to make me feel better?"

"It should," Sal said. "I love you, honey, and I always will. There's no other gal for me."

ACB rolled her eyes. "Men!"

I choked back a laugh. *Stay tuned for another episode of* Love and Murder in Sandy Harbor.

"Okay," Ty said, a bewildered look on his face. "Let's roll."

Everyone was loaded into the sheriff's department cars and taken downtown. Two were booked; the rest of us weren't. We gave long, boring statements to the three deputies, who could only type with two fingers, if that.

Finally, it was all over, and things could get back to normal, whatever normal was.

Ty drove me home, back to the old Victorian. I'd pick up my car later.

"Think you can get some sleep now?"

"Absolutely." I was crashing, and I couldn't stop my head from drifting left, onto his shoulder. "I'm always so tired. I really need my own shift. Maybe Bob is due back soon."

I took a couple of breaths to wake up. I could smell soap and leather and some kind of spicy aftershave, and if I looked up, I could see the brim of his white cowboy hat.

Good guys always wore white hats.

"Now that this is all over, do you think you could put pork and scalloped potatoes back on the menu?" he asked. "My mother used to make it for us all the time."

"Of course, I'll put it back on the menu."

"Poor Mr. Cogswell the Third," I said, yawning. "It was all just a big misunderstanding—one big, stupid, murder, mushrooms, misunderstanding, mistake."

Ty laughed. "That's right, darlin'."

"I'm glad you came along when you did," I mumbled, stifling another yawn.

"You seemed to have had things under control when we arrived."

Ty chuckled, and I loved the sound—throaty, deep, and masculine. "You were holding a gun and Antoinette Chloe was straddling Roberta. And Roberta had a ton of snow on her face."

"I made a hole in it for her to breathe," I clarified.

"Trixie, the next time, do you think you could let me handle things?"

"The next time? Cowboy, there isn't going to be a next time!"

Epilogue

Four Months Later

Hi, Aunt Stella! Isn't e-mail wonderful? I know you still like long, juicy, handwritten letters, but when traveling, like you always are with your friends, it's so easy to read your mail anywhere.

Well, the snow has melted and the ice has finally thawed, and the fishermen are returning. As you know, we are two weeks into trout season, and the diner is hopping. You don't know what a relief it is to have the diner filled to the brim. I love the hustle and bustle of the waitresses, the smell of fresh coffee being brewed, and the clink of silverware against china. The din of people talking and laughing adds to the fun. So does the bleep of the computer cash register!

Not too long ago, no one was coming to the diner, except me. I remember sitting in one of the booths on the graveyard shift, wondering if I'd be ever to make a payment to you for the diner and the cottages. I know you said that our payment schedule wasn't written in stone (just on a Silver Bullet Diner paper place mat!), but I took it seriously. Therefore, I'm happy to

report that I've deposited my payment into
your bank account.

"Trixie, Juanita wants to know if you could
help her out in the kitchen for a while." Bettylou,
the new waitress I just hired, leaned over the
counter and refreshed my cup of coffee. "I just
took a huge take-out order from a bunch of fishermen fishing at the bridge on Route 3. She said
that she'll do the big order if you can do the regular diner orders."
"Sure. I'll be right there."

Oops. Hang on a while, Aunt Stella. I'm being
summoned to the kitchen.

I closed my laptop and debated whether to take
it with me. Then I decided against it. Although all
the booths and tables were taken at the Silver Bullet, there were several stools available at the counter, so my laptop wasn't monopolizing a seat.
Besides, there was hardly any crime in Sandy Harbor.

No crime? What was I thinking? I'd just almost,
sort of, more or less, very nearly, basically, somewhat solved a murder on my own. Okay, maybe I
had help.

I clicked on my screen saver, left my laptop on
the counter, and hurried into my kitchen. It was
still hard to think of the gleaming chrome and aluminum 1950s diner as mine, but as long as I kept
making payments, it would be.

Pushing open the double doors to the kitchen, I caught a major whiff of garlic, oregano, and tomatoes. Yum! Tonight's special was spaghetti with sausage or meatballs, garlic bread sticks, and a small chef salad or vegetable soup. Our customers loved Spaghetti Saturday, especially the younger crowd and the kids.

I slipped into a clean apron and smiled at my second-shift cook and friend, Juanita Holgado. I pulled an order off the clip rack, read it, and started pulling various dishes off the stacks. I headed for the refrigerator to get what I needed.

"Big order from the fishermen, huh, Juanita?" I asked. "We are getting more and more take-out orders from all over the river and lake."

"Thirteen spaghetti dinners to go and four other assorted orders. The fishermen probably don't want to leave their spots to eat."

"I wouldn't either if I was catching fish."

"I guess," Juanita said. "And they all want dessert, too. And drinks."

"The waitresses can help pack the desserts and the drinks when they aren't busy."

"Nancy said that she'd get going on it."

"Great!" I just loved how everyone worked together when needed. I didn't have any complaints at all with my staff. Actually, most of them were hired by Aunt Stella prior to my taking over the diner. Well, maybe Clyde and Max should stop playing practical jokes on Juanita as much as they do, but Juanita puts them in their place quite nicely. Just in case they don't get the gist of her mixed Spanish and English hysterics, I make it clear to them that they should quit being so juvenile.

Then Juanita always tells me in confidence that she secretly likes their jokes, but she'd never tell them that. Neither will I. So the good-natured jokes continue and so does Juanita's yelling.

I quickly made the order. I was quite good at multitasking and might prepare two or three orders at once, but this one was for a party of ten.

I rang the bell twice to let Bettylou know that the first part of her order was ready—six small chef salads and four vegetable soups. Immediately, she hurried into the kitchen. "The rest will be ready in a few minutes, Bettylou."

It was important to give the guests time to finish their first course before I sent the main meal out. When I went out to eat, one of my pet peeves was having my main dish set in front of me while I was still working on a salad or soup. That was bad planning on the kitchen's part.

Checking the other four orders hanging on the rack, I sent out their first courses, too.

One ring for Nancy. Two for Bettylou. Three for Connie.

"Don't forget the bread sticks," I reminded the waitresses. They were in charge of serving those from the front.

I went back to the first order and picked out what would take the longest to prepare: the two Delmonico steaks—one rare, one well done. Getting those going, I got the spaghetti ready. The spaghetti was prepared during the day by Cindy Sherlock, rolled into individual servings, and then refrigerated in a big metal pan. I put the individual orders into a couple of metal "strainers" with big holes, and then dunked them into pans of boiling water. When the spaghetti was heated thoroughly, I strained it, put it on a heated plate, and scooped our special sauce over it from the steam table. I added meatballs to six orders, sausage to two. The steaks came out perfect, and I added mashed potatoes to them with gravy. I put all the finished plates on large trays under heat lamps and rang the bell twice for Bettylou.

She came in while I was checking the order. "Six lead pipes with rounded cows. Two lead pipes with zeppelins. One bossy that's walkin' and one bossy that's sunburned." I slipped the order under a plate. "It's all here, Bettylou."

Bettylou, the new hire, laughed.

"It's Dinerese. You'll get the hang of it, Bettylou. I did!" I said as she picked up the tray and headed for the double doors.

Juanita grunted. "But it took you a while. And most of the time you make up your own words."

"Just like you!" I shot back. We carried on a cheerful conversation while we worked.

Just as Juanita finished the take-out order, two of the fishermen came to pick it up. I helped the waitresses carry the boxes of foam containers to the front counter. Nancy checked them out. Max and Clyde, who just walked into the diner, helped load everything into their car.

I finished up my last order and rang once for Nancy.

"A cowboy on a raft, two lead pipes with zeppelins, and one bowwow with bullets." I just loved Dinerese!

Nancy smiled as she checked her order. "A western omelet on toast, two spaghettis with sausage, and one hot dog with beans. That's correct, Trixie."

"Good," I said to her, then turned to Juanita. "That's all I have."

Juanita waved a long stirring spoon at me. "I can take over now. Why don't you relax until your shift?"

I checked the clock on the wall. My shift didn't start until midnight. It was only seven o'clock. "By the way, have you heard from the elusive Bob, the alleged morning cook?"

Juanita shrugged. "The last I knew, he was in Las Vegas."

"The last I heard, he was in Atlantic City."

I have never met Bob, who apparently worked as a cook in the army with Uncle Porky. He was supposed to be the morning cook, but I had to hire Cindy Sherlock to take his place. Cindy was working out great, so I guess I really didn't need Bob, but I sure could use him as a sub.

"Hmm . . ." I didn't know what to say about Bob anymore.

I kept my apron on, and went back out front. I visited my customers, greeting everyone that I knew and introducing myself to anyone that I didn't know.

Laurie Cleary was there with her husband and daughter. She grabbed my hand as if she were drowning and I were a lifeguard. "I was hoping you'd be here, Trixie."

I grinned. "It seems like I'm always here, Laurie, but don't you usually come in earlier than seven o'clock at night?"

"A lot of us went to the grand reopening of the Bijou. They showed the latest James Bond, and it just let out."

"I heard it was fabulous," I said, remembering the Bijou from my summers at the cottages.

"What's fabulous? The Bijou or James Bond?" Laurie asked.

"Both."

"Yes. *They* were both fabulous, but I need to ask you something."

"Fire away, Laurie."

"Since Roberta Cummings is serving a life term at Bedford Hills, you may have heard that I'm the new editor of the *Sandy Harbor Lure*."

"No, I haven't heard, but I'm sure that you'll do a great job." I was afraid to guess what her question was.

"Would you let me do a story on you? How you investigated. How you caught the murderers. How you got away when you were tied up in Salvatore Brown's van. You know, the whole enchilada."

"Enchiladas are Juanita's lunch special on Thursday." I made a feeble attempt to change the subject. "Juanita feels that the menu should be more diverse, and who can make better Mexican food than Juanita?"

"So, you're not needed here around lunch on Thursday?" Laurie whipped out a black appointment book and made a note. "I'll be here at noon to interview you."

"Laurie, I don't think that I want to rehash the whole thing again."

"This is going to be a great story!"

I shrugged. What more was there to say? I'd told the story several times to Deputy Ty Brisco as he laboriously typed out my affidavit of the incident. I told the whole thing again at Roberta's trial and yet again at Sal Brown's trial.

I wanted to put it all behind me and concentrate on my diner and cottages. The cottages were due to open in a month, and they needed to be ready.

"I'll see you on Thursday, Trixie," Laurie reiterated.

"Okay," I said with my heart not into it.

The counter was still fairly empty, so I returned to my stool and to my laptop.

I'm back, Aunt Stella. The fishermen are ordering a lot of takeout, and this order was particularly big. Today is Spaghetti Saturday, and we must have sold a ton of it!

The customers probably think that things are not the same at the Silver Bullet without you and Uncle Porky. I could never replace the two of you, but I've been trying to make the place my own. Maybe they'll get used to me.

I'm making some changes, though. Mrs. Sarah Stolfus, a new friend of mine, is doing the fancy baking. In the revolving case and in another glass showcase, I feature her pies, cakes, and other desserts, all of which are for sale. Sarah has decided that the Silver Bullet will be the only place her goods will be available, so people come from all over the area to purchase them.

Sarah thanks me every day because she doesn't have to sit in parking lots with her horse and buggy in all kinds of weather!

I have also cut down on ordering various produce from Sunshine Food Supply. I've opted for more locally grown produce for the menu as much as possible, particularly in the summer and fall. I know that it's easier to just order from Sunshine all year long, but I want to support the local growers.

And then there's Deputy Ty Brisco. . . .

Speaking of Ty, he just pushed the front door open and was walking into the diner. It's strange that I can sense when he's near. His presence is like a force of nature. He walked down the aisle, his boots making a hollow sound on the tile floor as he walked like they always did. Ty smiled and tipped his black cowboy hat to the ladies and nodded to the men. He was greeted by friendly waves and handshakes.

Everyone liked him, and everyone respected him even more since he arrested Roberta Cummings and Salvatore Brown.

He wore a black bomber jacket and dark jeans with a crease down the front. The crease must be a Texas thing—no one creases their jeans here in the north. He was born to wear jeans—they accentuated his long legs and tight butt—but I wasn't looking.

Ty spotted me sitting at the counter and shot me a knee-weakening grin that made me glad that I was sitting. He sat on the stool beside me.

Aunt Stella would have to wait again. I hit the Screen Saver button and turned to Ty. "How are you?"

"Doin' great. Mostly, we're getting calls from campgrounds and hotels about drunk fishermen, being loud and causing a ruckus. I can't tell you how many drinks I've been offered along with trout. Too bad I'm on duty."

"The special is spaghetti."

"I know. That's why I'm here. I'd never miss Spaghetti Saturday. How are you doing?"

I shrugged. "My divorce lawyer called me. Among other things, she told me that my ex-husband and his new wife had twin girls: Tiffany and Brittany."

His deep blue eyes studied my face. "Are you okay?"

I'd never told him that I couldn't get pregnant in spite of many years of marriage with Deputy Doug, but obviously he'd had no problem getting

Wendy pregnant, so the fertility problem was with me. And they had twins, no less.

I had many years of angst, wanting children and doing everything but standing on my head to get pregnant. Whenever I thought about it, like now, it felt like an arrow was stuck in my heart.

"Yeah, I'm okay," I finally said, not wanting to confide something so personal to Ty. I didn't know why I even brought it up. Maybe it was because he was my first friend in Sandy Harbor. He sent business to the Silver Bullet, which kept it afloat in the aftermath of Mr. Cogswell's death in the kitchen, and I'd always be grateful to him for that.

Nancy appeared in front of him. "Can I get you something, Ty?" She batted her eyes like she had a nervous tic, and I could swear that she popped another button on her black uniform dress. Even though Nancy had only worked here for ten days or so, she already was hunting Ty. Correction: She was one of many who were hunting Ty.

He grinned, showing perfect rows of brilliant white teeth. "Howdy, darlin'. I'll have a cup of coffee and the spaghetti special with meatballs. Thousand Island dressing on my salad."

Nancy scribbled on her order pad, and immediately poured him a cup of coffee. "I know you take it black, Ty."

"That's absolutely correct. And strong enough so a horseshoe can float on top."

Nancy giggled—yes, giggled—like it was the best joke she'd ever heard.

Not talking her eyes off Ty, she backed away

from the counter and backed through the double doors that led to the kitchen. She was enthralled with Ty. He knew it, too, but he wasn't leading her on or playing with her emotions; that's just how he was—friendly.

Sandy Harbor was loaded with fishermen and farmers, so a cowboy from Texas was a novelty.

I wasn't immune to Ty either, but I wasn't looking for a relationship. I had to concentrate on my diner and the cottages.

He took a draw of coffee. "What else is new, Trixie?"

"Max and Clyde are getting the cottages ready for renters. They need to be painted, some calking, and some need new windows, funds permitting. I'm hoping that as soon as college and high school lets out, Aunt Stella's summer help will return. I need maids."

I shuddered at the thought of cleaning twelve cottages myself and cooking at the diner at the same time. Even though they were housekeeping cottages and rented by the week or month, there was still a lot to clean when each party left.

"Oh, I have some news. You'll be interested to hear this," Ty said.

"Spill. Don't keep me in suspense."

"It seems that Antoinette Chloe Brown is divorcing Sal. Sal's brother has moved in with her, and they went to Hawaii together, and they were seen making out at the Bijou and not watching the James Bond movie."

"Get out!"

"It's true. I worked the traffic detail, and they walked out with their lips glued together and their hands on each other's butt. It must be serious because ACB was wearing jeans under her muu-muu."

I laughed. "And she wore flip-flops?"

"Nope. She had on boots."

"No way!" I said, remembering the two feet of snow where we tackled Roberta Cummings. "ACB wears flip-flops in any kind of weather. What else can you tell me?"

"She did have bright red hair with a yellow flower behind each ear and huge feather earrings that dangled down her coat."

"It's good to know that ACB is still ACB." I picked up my coffee cup, only to find that it was empty. "I bonded with her during our recent kidnapping and almost death."

"I almost lost you." He mumbled this, but I still heard him.

My heart started to beat wildly in my chest. Too much coffee, I thought. I should quit the stuff.

He turned my stool so I would be facing him. "You know, Trixie, you never promised me that you'll let me handle things from now on."

"Things?"

"Murders." He whispered the word, and it sounded creepy.

I shivered. "I hope there are no more murders in little Sandy Harbor."

"Me, too, but if there are, stay away."

Nancy walked behind the counter and delivered Ty's chef salad with a swoop of her hand. She refilled both of our coffee cups, then backed away.

"You got it," I said when Nancy left.

"Good!"

Hmm. I didn't promise, but Ty didn't seem to notice. If something happened, and it concerned my point, I definitely would get involved.

We made small talk through Ty's spaghetti and meatballs, dessert, and several more cups of coffee.

"I'm going to call it a night," he said, standing and stretching. Several female diners paused with their forks in the air and just watched him.

"See you tomorrow, Ty."

"G'night."

In the mirror behind the counter, I watched him leave; then I turned back to my laptop.

Aunt Stella, I'm back. Speaking of Ty Brisco, he just left the diner. As you know, he's one of the regulars here, and everyone likes him. He's a very thorough and professional deputy sheriff, too. I should know, as I'm sure you've heard about the murder of Marvin Cogswell.

But I don't want to talk about that. I'm going to post some links to the local news and some articles on another e-mail if you want to read about it more.

I hope you are having a wonderful time with your BFFs bopping all around the world. You've worked hard your whole life and deserve to enjoy every second!

It's getting late, and it's almost time for my shift.

I want you to know that I just love owning the diner and cottages and meeting new people, and that I'm doing my best to keep your dream—and Uncle Porky's dream—alive.

Now it's my dream, too!

All my love,

Trixie

Family Recipes from the
Silver Bullet Diner
Sandy Harbor, New York

Aunt Irene Gladysz's Wacky Cake

2⅔ cups flour
2 cups sugar
⅔ cup cocoa
1 tsp. salt
2 tsp. baking soda
2 tsp. vanilla
⅔ cup vegetable oil
2 tsp. vinegar
2 cups water

Put the mixed flour, sugar, cocoa, salt, and baking
    soda into a 9" x 13" ungreased cake pan.
Make three wells in the above dry ingredients.
Into the first well put 2 tsp. vanilla.
Into the second well put ⅔ cup vegetable oil.
Into the third well put 2 tsp. vinegar.
Pour two cups of water over everything and mix
    it up with a fork.
Bake at 350 degrees F for 40 minutes.

Trixie's Delicious Cream Cheese Frosting

1 8-oz. pkg. cream cheese
1 Tbsp. milk
1 tsp. vanilla
5½ cups sifted confectioners' (powdered) sugar

Combine softened cream cheese, milk, and vanilla, mixing until well blended.

Gradually add the powdered sugar, mixing well after each addition.

Fills and frosts two 8" or 9" cake layers.

Trixie's Notes:

- You can substitute other kinds of extracts. I like almond extract!
- You could stir in ¼ cup chopped maraschino cherries and a few drops of red food coloring.
- Or how about stirring in ¼ cup crushed peppermint candy and using peppermint extract? Yum!
- This frosting is divine on banana cake!
- Don't forget to use this frosting on Cindy's Cinnamon Buns!

Grandma Rose Matyjasik's Snowball Cookies

(Good at any time of the year,
but especially at Christmas!)

2 cups flour
¾ cup butter
½ tsp. salt
2 tsp. almond extract (or your preferred extract)
1 egg
1 cup chopped nuts
1 cup chocolate chips
Approx. 1 cup confectioners' (powdered) sugar

Sift together 2 cups flour and ½ tsp. salt.

In a separate bowl, blend together ¾ cup butter and ½ cup sugar.

Add 2 tsp. almond extract (or vanilla or peppermint) and one egg to the wet ingredients.

Mix the dry ingredients into the wet ingredients.

Add 1 cup chopped nuts, 1 cup chocolate chips (chocolate mint chips are really good, too, or even peanut butter chips), and stir with a heavy spoon.

Shape into 1" balls.

Place on cookie sheet.

Bake at 350 degrees F for 15 to 20 minutes.

Cool slightly and roll in confectioners' sugar (or gently shake in a plastic bag).

This recipe works well when doubled.

Cindy Sherlock's Easy Cinnamon Buns

5 cups all-purpose flour
1 (18.25 ounce) package yellow cake mix
2 (.25 ounce) packages quick-rise yeast
2½ cups warm water (120 to 130 degrees)
¼ cup butter, melted
½ cup sugar
2 tsp. ground cinnamon

In a mixing bowl, combine 4 cups flour, dry cake mix, yeast, and warm water until smooth. Add enough remaining flour to form a soft dough. Turn onto a lightly floured surface; knead until smooth and elastic, about 5 minutes. Place in a greased bowl, turning once to grease top. Cover and let rise until doubled, about 45 minutes.

Punch dough down. Turn onto a lightly floured surface; divide in half. Roll each portion into a 14" x 10" rectangle.

Brush with butter; sprinkle with sugar and cinnamon.

Roll up jelly-roll style, starting with a long side. Cut each roll into 12 slices; place cut side down in two greased 13" x 9" x 2" baking pans.

Cover and let rise until almost doubled, about 20 minutes.

Bake at 400 degrees F for 10 to 15 minutes or until golden brown. Cool for 20 minutes. Frost.

Frost with Trixie's Cream Cheese Frosting!

Grandma Matyjasik's
Pork and Scalloped Potatoes

(Grandma never measures anything, and it was very difficult documenting her recipe! She says just to "play with this to suit yourself.")

Broil, grill, or bake several pork shoulder steaks.
Drain off grease and debone when cool.
Wash and peel (or leave the peel on!) several large potatoes.
Slice the potatoes (not too thick, not too thin).
Wash and slice three or so large onions.
Put some of the pork in a large, deep rectangular pan—3" x 15" would be good; deeper would be better—like a lasagna pan.
Put the onions and potatoes over the pork.
Then more pork.
Then more potatoes and onions.
Season with salt and pepper or your favorite herbs.
Pour milk or half-and-half over everything until all covered.
Cook uncovered at 350 degrees F until the potatoes are done. It might take an hour or an hour and a half, depending on the pan you use.

Trixie's Notes:

I divert from just the plain milk/half-and-half. I whisk together milk and (forgive me) a can or two of mushroom soup. If you aren't a mushroom fan, use cream of celery. Then pour this mixture over everything.

Aunt Helen's Pot Roast

3 to 5 lbs. chuck roast
1½ tsp. salt
¾ tsp. ground ginger
3 bay leaves
1 cup red wine
1 onion, cut into chunks
1 minced garlic clove
2 Tbsp. oil
¼ tsp. pepper
4 whole cloves
1 cup apple juice
3 apples, cored and quartered
zest and juice of 1 lemon or lime (optional)

Brown roast in oil. Add all remaining ingredients, except apples and onions.

Bring to boiling, reduce heat, cover and simmer about 2 hours.

Add onions and apples. Simmer an additional 1½ hours or until meat is tender.

Remove meat from pan.

Serve over egg noodles or boiled parsleyed potatoes.

Mrs. Stolfus's Delicious Chocolate Pecan Pie

1 (9") unbaked pie crust
3 eggs
⅔ cup white sugar
½ tsp. salt
⅓ cup butter, melted
1 cup light corn syrup
1½ cups pecan halves, or a little more
1½ cups semisweet chocolate chips

Preheat oven to 375 degrees F.

Beat eggs, sugar, salt, margarine, and syrup with
a hand beater.

Stir in pecans and chocolate chips. Pour mixture
into pie shell.

Bake until set, 40 to 50 minutes. Cool.

*M*y diner was hopping and so was I!

I'd just dropped the larger-than-a-manhole-cover cast-iron frying pan on my foot. It had bounced off my big toe and landed on the floor with a thud. Thank goodness there hadn't been anything in it yet.

I took a couple of deep breaths and willed myself to calm down. I had a big breakfast (served twenty-four hours a day) order to get ready, with a variety of eggs and an even greater variety of toast.

Wiping the sweat from my forehead with a towel that I kept draped over my shoulder, I took the pan over to the sink and grabbed another that was equally big and heavy and emptied a couple dozen patties of breakfast sausage—handmade by yours truly—into it, along with half a pound of bacon, and set it on the stove.

Then I readied another order and rang the little brass ship's bell that I bought because it was nautical and sounded better than the school bell that reminded me of Sister Mary's constant attempts to get our attention in fourth grade.

Chelsea, one of my waitresses, appeared and looked more

than exhausted. It had been an extraordinarily busy graveyard shift at the Silver Bullet Diner.

"You rang, Trixie?" Chelsea yawned, walking slowly toward the prep table.

"Hang in there, sweetie. We're almost done."

I handed her the plates over the steam table. "One cowboy on a raft, one hound on an island, a large Cobb with Thousand Island, three meat loaf specials with the works, and two kiddie specials."

I had become very fluent in Dinerese, the special language that diner staff uses to communicate orders. It had taken me a while to get the hang of Dinerese, but I kind of enjoyed it now. Truth be told, I even made up my own Dinerese as I went along, which sometimes stymied my waitresses or got us all laughing.

"Don't forget the free udder juice that goes with the kiddie specials, Chelsea."

"The wha—?" She wrinkled her face. "If you're referring to milk, that's pretty lame, Trix."

"I know!"

Chelsea set the western omelet with toast and the franks and beans and everything else on a large serving tray. "I've never seen the diner so packed at two o'clock in the morning."

I eyed the pile of orders wrapped with a rubber band that the day cooks, Juanita Holgado and Cindy Sherlock, had filled on the morning shift. Later, I'd enter the orders on a spreadsheet, somehow looking for a pattern as to what customers liked and what supplies I needed to order.

"It's been like this all shift." I plucked a couple of orders from the wheel and studied them. There were a lot of orders for the daily specials—cream of chicken soup, my salsa-infused meat loaf with mashed potatoes and gravy, and for those looking forward to a summer picnic, I offered the Silver Bullet Summer Clambake: a dozen steamed Cherrystones, an ear of corn, broiled or fried haddock, and salt potatoes. I could do both of those orders at the same time. "I love it when we are busy, though. Time goes by so fast."

And with the extra business, I can make the next balloon payment to Aunt Stella! I'd bought the diner on an installment plan from my aunt. It had been in our family for years now, and I hadn't been about to let it go under when Aunt Stella decided to retire.

I'd grown up inside the diner, learning how to cook from Uncle Porky and Aunt Stella. My aunt and uncle didn't have any children and had always wished to keep the property in the family, so when Aunt Stella wanted to sell, and Deputy Doug wanted me out of our Colonial and out of Philly, I jumped at the chance to buy.

"By the way, Trix, I love your new outfit," Chelsea said, balancing the tray on the palm of her hand and hoisting it to shoulder level.

I looked down and grinned at my new red jacket and my matching baggy pants covered with a never-ending tomato print. I'd ordered both items online on a chef's Web site.

"Thanks. I've decided that since I'm a chef, I ought to look the part." I brushed some panko crumbs from my embroidered pocket: *Trixie Matkowski, owner, Silver Bullet Diner, Sandy Harbor, New York.*

I'd ordered the embroidery in black script. Classy.

Chelsea scooted off with her tray, and I pulled an assortment of plates from the shelf for the next order.

Smiling, I thought about how the diner would soon get even busier since it was almost the official start of the tourist season in Sandy Harbor: Memorial Day. The fishermen arrived even before all the ice melted on Lake Ontario. Soon the sun worshippers would arrive at the state beaches, and so would the recreational boaters and those who had camps.

My heart raced when I realized that in addition to the Silver Bullet Dinner, circa 1952, I was ready to open the doors to my twelve cottages, which dotted the Point, a type of peninsula that jutted out into the lake.

I'd be doubly busy when the cottages opened!

Thank goodness my handymen, Clyde and Max, had

slapped a fresh coat of white paint on the cottages and freshened up their shutters and trim in forest green.

They did the same to my Victorian farmhouse, which I called the Big House, not that it looked like a prison in the least, but because it was way too big for one person.

The Big House was next to the diner. Now everything matched. I chuckled, thinking that it looked like the big Victorian gave birth to a litter of little cottages.

I remembered giving Aunt Stella, whose interest in the diner plummeted after Uncle Porky died, a down payment after we'd worked out the numbers on a Silver Bullet place mat. Aunt Stella had handed me a fistful of keys, given me a quick kiss, and headed for a long cruise to Alaska. Then she slid right into retirement in Boca with a gaggle of her friends.

I had always loved cooking, but to own and manage the Silver Bullet and twelve cottages seemed overwhelming at times. However, keeping busy took my mind off my divorce from Deputy Doug and his very fertile trophy bride.

I wondered why I was thinking about ancient history. I liked to believe that I had moved on from Doug. I took back my maiden name and was making a new life for myself in Sandy Harbor, so what was my problem?

I rang the ship's bell, placing the breakfast orders under the heat lamps. Chelsea needed to hurry, or the eggs would keep cooking. "Order up."

Wipe off hands on towel; fling towel over shoulder; fill another order. Ring bell. Repeat.

I helped Chelsea stack the plates onto two more trays and met her at the kitchen door to relay the orders to her.

Back at the prep table, as I made four large antipastos, six small house salads, and two Cobbs for what looked like a party of twelve, I mentally ran through a checklist of all the things I had to do to prepare for our busy summer season.

Then it dawned on me that I probably needed to hire more maids, er—housekeeping attendants—to clean the cottages. All of the cottages were designated as "bring your own stuff," but some customers opted for daily service.

I pulled my ever-faithful notebook from the pocket of my tomato-printed pants and scribbled "Hire more housekeepers. Put an ad in the *Sandy Harbor Lure.*"

Most of the cottages were rented for the entire season and beyond, with the same families returning year after year. That was just what my family had done. Cottage Number Six had been the Matkowski family's standard rental.

Where's Chelsea? I wondered, looking at all the antipasti and salads languishing on the shelf. I rang the ship's bell again.

Then I looked over at the pass-through window. I never used it to pass orders through, but it gave me a look into the dining area.

Chelsea was leaning over the counter, along with my two handymen and a dozen or so regulars. They were all reading what seemed to be the morning edition of the *Sandy Harbor Lure.*

Deputy Ty Brisco, my studly neighbor, who lived above the bait shop next door, was holding court and gulping down coffee. He was with the two other cops who made up the entire Sandy Harbor sheriff's department.

"It's been a long time," said Mrs. Leddy, the president of the Sandy Harbor Historical Society. "I've always wondered what happened to her."

Who were they talking about?

"'Several local children had been exploring Rocky Bluffs and stumbled upon a cavelike place,'" read Clyde. He turned toward those who were gathered, waving his hands. "And there she was. It probably scared the pants off them."

Who was in a cavelike place?

I looked over to where the party of twelve should be sitting and waiting for their salads. Half of them were missing, probably part of the crowd around the deputies and their staff.

"Chelsea, your order is up," I said, louder than usual.

She gave a nod in my direction and reluctantly tore herself away from the group, who were now all talking at once.

I could catch only pieces of the conversation, but I was dying to find out what the hot topic was. Ty Brisco suddenly looked up and smiled.

My face heated up as if I'd just opened the big pizza oven. Why did the former Houston cop have to be such eye candy? And why did he have to be a deputy like my ex?

Not that I was interested in the least. No. Not interested.

I gave a half wave to Ty and returned to my spot behind a big aluminum table just as Chelsea walked in. Time to get the big order started.

Time to cross-examine Chelsea.

"Chels, what's going on?"

"Some kids were climbing the rocks by the bluff, and somehow they discovered a cave. Inside the cave was a body." Chelsea's eyes grew as big as saucers. "The newspaper said that according to Hal Manning, the Sandy Harbor coroner, it's the body of a woman. Hal identified her, but I forgot her name. He checked the remains against dental records." She shuddered. "Everyone knows her. Oh, I forget her name. . . . Um . . . uh . . ."

"Claire Jacobson." I could barely breathe. I remembered Claire from when I was about eight years old. Claire was the prettiest and coolest high schooler I'd ever met, and she was so nice to me.

"That's the name." Chelsea hoisted the trayful of salads. "She disappeared from here a zillion years ago, from Cottage Eight, the one that everyone thinks is haunted."

After Claire's disappearance, I always thought Cottage Eight was haunted, too. Aunt Stella said that it was always the last cottage to be rented, and not to old customers, but to new customers who hadn't heard the story yet.

The back door of the diner opened and I knew it was Juanita Holgado, one of the day cooks. She seemed to appear right out of the fog and darkness. Or maybe I was just feeling overdramatic because of the news about Claire.

"*Hola*, Trixie!" She walked around the steam table and gave me a hug. Juanita was definitely a morning person. She always arrived happy and cheerful. "Look at you! Nice tomatoes!" She eyed my baggy chef's pants, grinning.

Juanita had been working as a housekeeping attendant at the cottages during the summer Claire Jacobson went missing. Juanita had helped search for her.

The recent news about Claire could wait.

"Hey, Juanita. Good morning. I have a surprise for you."

I handed her a gift bag and enjoyed watching my friend's face as she opened it.

Juanita pulled out a red chef's coat that matched mine, but her chef's pants were covered in red and green peppers. Juanita loved her peppers—the hotter the better.

"I love it. I just love it!" Juanita grabbed me in a big bear hug. "And my name is embroidered on it. We are really chefs now. We can have our own show on TV."

Juanita hurried to the storage room, probably to change. I had another gift bag for Cindy Sherlock, another member of my kitchen staff. It was a red coat and pants covered with colorful slices of pizza. Cindy was known for making the best pizza at the Silver Bullet.

Then there was Bob, the missing fourth chef, who was supposed to be helping me on the graveyard shift. I hadn't yet met or even talked to the elusive Bob in my several months as owner. He was always on sick leave and his doctors were suspiciously in either Vegas or Atlantic City.

I didn't buy him anything. As a matter of fact, if he ever showed up, I would probably fire him.

I went back to preparing the order for the party of twelve. Sometimes it felt like I was dancing in the diner, doing the quickstep. I twirled to the fridge and grabbed a steak. I tangoed to the freezer and scooped up an order of fried clams. I pirouetted to the toaster and loaded buns and bread onto the Ferris wheel.

Three tens from the judges.

I rang the bell, and Chelsea took it all away without any more news from the group still gathered around Deputy Brisco.

I cut up more lettuce and tomatoes and restocked freshly baked rolls and loaves of bread that Juanita had set to raise, and I had baked when I'd started my shift. The diner patrons just loved the smell of baking bread. Who didn't?

Soon Juanita appeared, twirling around the kitchen. "I just love the peppers!"

"I knew you would." I hated to spoil Juanita's good mood, but I had to tell her about Claire. "Juanita, they found Claire Jacobson."

"Madre de Dios." Juanita reached out and steadied herself on the cast-iron dough mixer. "I remember her. What a sweet girl. Where?"

"Rocky Bluff."

Juanita shook her head. "But everyone searched that area. I remember. I helped."

"The waves, the ice, the flooding, storms . . . The rocks must have shifted."

Juanita nodded. *"Si."*

"If you're ready to take over, I think I'll grab a cup of coffee and talk to Ty and the other deputies to see what I can find out."

"Go ahead. Then you can tell me. And thank you again for the peppers, Trixie Matkowski. You are a good friend and a good boss."

"Boss?" I chuckled as I headed for the double doors that led to the dining room. "Nah. We're all a team—team Silver Bullet Diner and Sandy Harbor Cottages. Yeah, salmon! Go, trout! Come, tourists!"

Juanita pumped an arm into the air. "Go, team!"

Walking behind the counter, I poured myself a sorely needed cup of coffee and then decided that I had to have an apple hand pie made by Mrs. Stolfus, my Amish friend and an extraordinary baker. I put it on a dish and set it on the counter in front of a vacant stool next to Ty Brisco.

It became vacant only when I raised a blond, nonplucked eyebrow to my handyman Clyde. Clyde cleared his throat and headed out the front door to either work or to find a place to sleep. I hoped it was the former.

I sat down on the stool and swiveled toward my coffee and hand pie. The crowd had broken up, the other two deputies had left, and I had Ty to myself. I sure could break up a crowd.

"Catch me up, Ty. I remember Claire Jacobson. I remember how we used to sit on the beach and talk, and she taught me how to float on my back. I thought she was the greatest. She reminded me of Olivia Newton-John in *Grease*."

Ty showed me the headline of the *Sandy Harbor Lure*: BODY OF MISSING TEEN FOUND AFTER 28 YEARS. I skimmed the article. I decided I would rather hear the news from Ty, spoken with his delicious cowboy twang, than read the long tome.

"Is it really Claire?"

He nodded. "Her dental records happened to still be here from the initial search. Hal Manning, our resident coroner and funeral director, who has the biggest mouth in North *and* South America, said that the remains are Claire's. We're going to verify his findings with the state police lab. Hal should know better, but I guess he's dating the new editor of the *Sandy Harbor Lure* and she was with him when everything hit the fan."

"Wow. Claire Jacobson, after twenty-eight years . . . and she was only about a mile down the beach, entombed on the bluff, in the rocks."

Ty nodded.

"I've always wondered what happened to her. I'd hoped that she'd run away to Europe with her Prince Charming and was ruling some country." I took a bite of my apple hand pie and a sip of coffee. Delicious. "Can you tell me anything more, Ty?"

"Not much." He sighed. "There was a kind of a cave where she was found, and we believe that some of the rocks that were placed in front of the cave's opening got dislodged throughout the years. Then the kids who were climbing on the rocks dislodged more, making the cave visible."

I sat for a while, thinking. I took a sip of coffee, and then it dawned on me. "Ty, someone had to have known that there was a cave on the bluff. Seems to me that only a local or a regular summer vacationer would know to hide her body there! Don't you see? Maybe a local person even killed her."

Ty nodded slowly. "I was thinking the same thing."

"Is there any chance that it was an accident?"

"No chance."

"Why do you say that, Ty?"

"I can't tell you. Confidential information."

"I understand," I said, but I really didn't mean it. I wanted to know . . . everything. Claire was special to me. She had made time to pay attention to a little girl who wanted to be grown up and beautiful like she was.

"The killer could be someone we know," I added, looking at the customers in the diner. Some were strangers, but most of them I knew from the community or because they frequented the diner.

Could I know Claire's killer? Could I have talked to him or her? Maybe we were even friends.

A shiver went up my spine, then turned into a nagging headache that I couldn't shake for several hours.